CALVINIA WAS NAKED
AS A JAYBIRD...

She moved closer and he took her in his arms as she asked, "Are you still angry with little me, you big growly bear?"

He was, but she sure felt good in his arms, and he didn't want her yelling her fool head off with coppers in the neighborhood. She snuggled closer and rubbed her naked body against him like an indecent kitten, and asked, "You are going to spend the night with me, aren't you, dear?"

Longarm scooped her up and headed for the nearest sofa...

*Also in the LONGARM series
from Jove*

TABOR EVANS

LONGARM

ON THE
BARBARY COAST

A JOVE BOOK

LONGARM ON THE BARBARY COAST

First Jove edition published February 1982

First printing

Printed in the United States of America

Jove books are published by Jove Publications, Inc.,
200 Madison Avenue, New York, NY 10016

Chapter 1

It was one of those hateful Monday mornings when the thin air of Denver tasted like soda water and the sun just popped up like a cork into a cloudless cobalt sky without a word of warning. An infernal bird felt so good about it that it hopped on Longarm's windowsill and commenced to sing its fool head off.

In his rumpled bed, the tall deputy rolled over and tried to ignore the ghastly sounds. He reached absently for the gal sharing the sheets with him. Then he remembered, wistfully, that he'd struck out the night before with Miss Morgana Floyd, head matron of the Arvada Orphan Asylum, and professional virgin. He grimaced and propped himself up on one elbow to contemplate aviacide. The bird cocked its head to regard Longarm with a beady eye as it experimented with a wary trill. Longarm's derringer was handy, but there was a Denver ordinance against fowling within the city limits. Longarm figured he had a fifty-fifty chance of hitting the fool bird with a thrown boot, but that would mean having to explain to the landlady as he searched for his boot in her garden, when and if he ever got up.

"Bird," he said, "there must be folks all over this fair city

1

who'd find your cheerful words more fitting to their present condition. But I ain't a milkman, and as you see, I am alone in this damned bed, and I don't have to be at work for hours. So just flutter off and we'll say no more about it."

The bird hopped to the other end of the sill, wagged its little tail, and spun around to cock its other eye at Longarm as it gave a quiet cheep. Longarm rubbed a hand over his face and decided he was awake for keeps.

He said something dreadful about the bird's mother and threw the sheets off to rise. Longarm had a way of moving that tended to make smaller critters thoughtful, so the bird took off, screaming a warning to the neighborhood.

Longarm moved over to the washstand of his furnished room, rinsed his mouth with Maryland rye, and ran a clammy string washrag over his face. He didn't like to shave with cold water but, thanks to the bird, he had plenty of time to let the barber down the street do it right for a change. He ran the rag under his armpits and crotch and decided he was clean enough, considering. As he sat on the bed to dress, the bird came back to perch silently in the open window.

"You sure are a curious little cuss," Longarm said with a grin. "All right, if you must know, the reason you found me alone in bed this A.M. was because I am a pure fool when it comes to women. Given a choice, I always chase the pretty one in a herd. I wasn't invited to the charity ball by Morgana Floyd. I was asked by her dumpy little sidekick, Miss Hewitt."

The bird tilted its head and looked askance at him, so the tall deputy nodded and said, "You're right. It was ornery as hell of me to go after the poor little fat gal's pretty pard, and the hell of it was, I knew I was acting dumb when I done it. Old Morgana Floyd's so stuck up, a man would have to stand on a chair to kiss her, if she kissed at all. She's one of them temperance gals who sing 'Lips That Touch Liquor Shall Never Touch Mine,' and last night I found she don't hold with smoking, either. What threw me off was the fact that I once met a temperance gal who screwed like a mink. I reckoned Morgana had to have some damned vices to balance out all the ones she was so down on. But I was wrong, bird. She don't smoke, she don't chew, she don't drink, she don't screw. I swear, I have seldom met a more tedious person."

Longarm got up again, checked his guns, straightened the fool string tie the government said he had to wear these days,

2

then put on his snuff-brown, flat-crowned Stetson and left the modest digs on the unfashionable side of Cherry Creek. He'd been right about the hour. The streets were nearly deserted as he headed across town for the Federal Building. The few early risers all seemed bright and chipper, like that fool bird. It was a nice morning, Longarm had to admit. He hoped his boss, Marshal Vail, had a job to send him out on. The idea of being cooped up in an office or courtroom on such a glorious summer day made him feel kind of like a kid forced to attend school on one of those days when the fish were sure to be biting down at the creek.

He found the barbershop open and empty, so he sat right down and told old George Masters to shoot the works. He had a trim as well as a shave, and left reeking of bay rum as he smoked one of the cheroots he'd picked up with his change.

He stopped at a beanery on Champa Street and ordered some fried eggs smothered in chili con carne. He had time to dawdle over two extra cups of Arbuckle, and it was still early. He picked his teeth carefully, paid the bill, and moseyed on, checking his pocket watch against the distant chimes of the city hall clock. His watch was keeping good time. It was five minutes later than the Westminster Chimes over at City Hall, and they'd been running five minutes slow as long as he could remember.

He got to the Federal Building just as it was opening. A couple of clerks were gossiping on the marble steps as he came up to them. They both looked surprised to see him. He couldn't see why; he figured they must know by now that he worked here too.

He went upstairs and turned the knob of a door marked UNITED STATES MARSHAL, FIRST DISTRICT COURT OF COLORADO. The door was locked. Longarm sighed and walked back to the stairwell to sit on the steps, muttering about birds.

He'd about consumed an entire cheroot when a shorter, thicker, and older man clumped up the steps, stopped as though thunderstruck, and asked, "What happened, Longarm? Did your landlady throw you out? I told you she wasn't likely to put up with much more of your wild and woolly ways, old son."

"Howdy, Billy," Longarm said. "You're late, and as a tax-paying citizen of these United States I resent it like hell."

U.S. Marshal Billy Vail laughed and said, "As a matter of

3

fact, I'm fifteen minutes early, as usual. Just like you've come in at least half an hour late since the last time I fired you for getting here at noon. What the hell went wrong this morning, Longarm? It's Monday morning, and you don't even look hung over! Were you sick over the weekend or something?"

Longarm rose as Vail moved past him with his keys. "Look," he said, "if it upsets you to see me here so early, I could always go down to the Silver Dollar and kill some time with Madam Ruth and her gals."

Vail said, "Cut the joshing. Washington has just dumped a load of overripe manure on my desk, and since you're so bright and chipper, I'm going to let you spread it."

They went inside, ducked into Vail's inner office, and sat down on opposite sides of his desk as Vail shoved some wanted fliers out of the way and said, "Here she is. We're giving an assist to Treasury. They've been having trouble with a better-than-usual counterfeiting operation. They figure it's a gang. At least one slick and deadly professional gun in addition to the passers and a very skilled coiner."

Longarm lit another cheroot as he muttered, "Coiner, eh? Well, throw her back in the water, Billy. Can't you see Treasury is trying to green us with a petty case they ain't got time to trifle with? Coiners are the punks of counterfeiting. If the Treasury men are too busy to ferret the rascals out, leave 'em be. Justice ain't exactly unemployed out here, you know. Who's working on that train robbery up near Spanish Hat?"

Vail gathered his bushy brows like thunderclouds fixing to rain fire and salt as he snapped, "Goddamm it, Longarm, I find it tedious reminding you who is in charge of this infernal office! I have some men working on that train robbery, and I'm putting you on this counterfeiting case, so pay me some attention. I know most coiners are just drunks with some plaster of paris and a pot of plumber's solder on the kitchen range. But this gang is knocking off twenty-dollar double eagles with a steel die. Take a look."

Veil handed Longarm a shiny new coin. The tall deputy held it up to the light between thumb and forefinger. He nodded and said, "I see what you mean. The mint don't turn 'em out any prettier, and it sure as hell looks like gold. What's this made out of, Billy?"

"Fake gold, of course. It's mostly a copper alloy that jewelers use for them rings that turn a gal's finger green after a

4

rascal's used it to turn her head. It rings like gold and it bites like gold. The only way you can tell it ain't gold is to test it with acid, and not many merchants keep a vial of aqua regia next to the cash register. Treasury thinks the die may have been stolen from the mint. They're checking that out. As you can see, old Bald Eagle has every feather crisp and sassy, and the lettering is sharp and perfect enough to fool a banker."

Longarm put the counterfeit coin in a coat pocket for future reference, and commented, "I can see how putting the critters into circulation could confuse the economy of these United States, but I still don't see it as our worry, Billy. Treasury agents are supposed to be experts on this sort of case. What qualifications did you tell 'em I had?"

Vail smiled thinly. "You stay alive good. I told you the gang has at least one killer on the payroll. So far, Treasury has lost three agents looking for the coiner. Your rep for being hard to kill has come to the attention of Washington. They've chided me some about your unusual views on rough justice, but everybody working for Uncle Sam wants this gang brought to justice, rough or otherwise. So we're sending you after the sons of bitches."

Longarm blew smoke out his nostrils as he said, "Gee, thanks a lot, boss. I've always admired being a tin duck in a shooting gallery, but sometimes I think you overdo me the honors. I'll be proud to shoot the rascals for you, if somebody will just point me the right way. But I don't have the least notion where to begin looking."

Vail shuffled through his papers, found the travel orders he was looking for, and told him, "You're going to San Francisco, for openers. That's where these fake double eagles seem to be surfacing the most."

"Correct me if I'm wrong, Billy, but ain't this the Colorado office I'm supposed to be working out of?"

"You'll still be working out of here, should anybody ask. I don't want you to contact the U.S. marshal in Sacramento. Treasury knows you're on the case, but don't go near the Frisco mint, either, if you can help it."

"Why are we being so sneaky, Billy? Does Washington suspicion that some of the hired help out Frisco way is in on it?"

"Washington don't know," Vail replied. "One of the Treasury men who was killed worked out of the Frisco office. Some others working there haven't been killed, but they can't seem to come up with any leads, either. A couple of special agents were sent out by Washington last month. They reported in to compare notes. Then they wandered off in the Frisco fog and nobody ever saw hide nor hair of either of 'em again."

Longarm whistled softly. "It do make one wonder, don't it?"

"Damned right. Those agents were swept up spooky before they'd had time to stumble over much on their own, so the wise money in Washington figures they were betrayed. I told you they think the gang is using strayed or stolen U.S. Treasury dies, too. You were out there just a while ago on that high-grading case, so you know the area, but you weren't out there long enough for many people there to know *you*, right?"

Longarm studied the ash of his cheroot as he thought about the time he'd spent chasing highgraders in the Mother Lode country, and a more recent case in Southern California, involving government beef. He grimaced. "Well, I'm not a total stranger in California, but the crooks I tangled with are mostly dead, so what the hell. I've been in Frisco a few times, but just in passing. I'd say the odds on meeting anybody embarrassing are a lot lower than here in Denver, but you've given me a rough row to hoe, Billy. How the hell am I to look for leads if I don't go near anybody else who's working on the case?"

Vail looked cheerful as hell, considering, as he said, "I've no idea, old son. That's why sending you on a case can be so interesting. Aside from being hard to kill, you've always been a nosy son of a bitch. You just go on out to Frisco and sniff around until you find your own leads. The boys Uncle Sam has working out there at the moment obviously ain't even warm, or I wouldn't be sending you. So why waste time jawing with folks who're either fools or on the other side?"

Vail handed Longarm his orders. The tall deputy saw he didn't have to catch a train this side of noon, so he figured he had time to protest, "Dammit, Billy, Frisco is one big town, even if I knew my way about it, which I don't. What the hell am I supposed to do, stomp up and down old Market Street, asking folks to let me see the money in their pockets? Hell, Billy, I don't even know where they serve Maryland rye in Frisco!"

Vail chuckled fondly and shook his head. "I have no doubt

you will, before you've been there long enough to matter. If I know you, you'll find out where a lonesome cowboy can meet the friendly gals of Frisco, and in your travels it's only natural you'll either get killed or solve another tough one for your dear old Uncle Sam. So let's say no more about it and get your ass aboard the northbound Burlington, for you've a cross-country flier to catch in Cheyenne, and you can wire me the details, when and if you figure out what the hell you're doing out there."

The train ride was dreadful. Since it was more than a thousand miles and the office was paying, Longarm got himself a Pullman berth. But he had to sleep alone. There was a right interesting Mormon gal riding coach as far as Salt Lake, but he couldn't even get her back to the club car. She said she never drank liquor, and her church even had tedious rules about coffee, tea, and tobacco. She seemed willing to chat with Longarm, but when she said sweetly that his smoking offended her, he decided to let her buy her own infernal dinner.

There was a sassy-looking brunette with bedroom eyes sitting on the observation platform alone when Longarm moseyed back to study the vanishing crossties in the sunset. But he'd just established that she was going all the way to Sacramento when a gent she introduced as her husband came out to join them, looking sort of thoughtfully at Longarm. Longarm jawed about the passing scenery with the husband while the flirty wife sort of laughed at him with her treacherous eyes. As soon as he could retreat gracefully, he did so, muttering to himself. He ate alone, drank alone, slept alone, all the way to Sacramento. He knew a gal in Sacramento, but he was under orders to avoid folks who knew his right name, and what the hell, she'd said no the last time, too. He boarded the steamboat anxious and horny, noticed that the only two gals traveling alone were ugly, and joined a card game in the main salon to pass the time as the boat steamed down through the delta and across San Francisco Bay. One of the other men in the game cheated something awful, but Longarm just cheated back and none of the others seemed to know what was up. He didn't lose big and didn't win big. Life had been like that for the last few days, and it was starting to annoy hell out of him.

Chapter 2

A million years later the steamboat sounded its whistle at the city of San Francisco, so Longarm went to get his possibles and was standing on the foredeck as they approached the slips at the foot of Market Street. He usually traveled with a saddle and a Winchester, but since he'd been sent on a fool's errand to a big city, he was traveling light, with just one carpetbag. He wore the tobacco-brown tweed suit that his office insisted on, but he noticed that he still looked a mite more like a cowboy than the gents around him. Few wore stovepipe boots like his under their sissy britches, and while more than one wore a sensible hat, a lot had derbies and fedoras. One of the homely gals was standing near him, and she cried out, "Oh, I fear I shall be lost if nobody is there to meet me. It's so big. Nobody told me it would be so big."

Longarm knew she was trying to get some gent to escort her off the boat, but if nobody else was dumb enough, he saw no reason why he should be the victim. The approaching shoreline did look impressive. It was getting late, and lights were winking on in the housing plastered over the hillsides to the north and south. The boat was making for a sort of slot between the hills, and when he spotted the tall tower of the Ferry Building, he knew that had to be Market Street, the main drag of Frisco. He could see better now why the locals called Market Street "the Slot." Almost every other street seemed to run up over the hills like a checkered blanket covering a sleepy old gal. That big bulge where her hips lay under the checks would be Nob Hill, if he remembered right. Her head and shoulders lay to the 'north, forming Russian Hill, and that extra pillow in front of her hidden face would be Telegraph Hill. He remembered Telegraph Hill. He'd had a shootout along the docks near Telegraph Hill a while back. Fortunately, the rascal he'd beaten hadn't been connected with the Frisco underworld.

The gal next to him said something about Chinatown. Longarm edged away. He didn't want to take any homely gal to Chinatown, and didn't see what it could have to do with the case he was on, anyway. He'd had time to study the files Billy Vail had given him in Denver. The fake double eagles didn't seem to be turning up in Chinatown. They were being passed in the finer stores and better bars, where a twenty-dollar gold piece didn't attract much attention until they took it to the bank. The coins were so good that Treasury assumed some were banked and recashed without anyone being the wiser. That was another angle Longarm didn't like about the case. He knew his own rough-hewn ways wouldn't stand out in a honkytonk place along the waterfront, but if the coins weren't circulating in such neighborhoods, he'd have to hang out in the sort of joint he felt uncomfortable in. He didn't mind red velvet ropes and potted palms, but he had a hard time staying polite to snooty waiters and the kind of folks who put up with their bullying ways.

The boat nudged her bows into a slip, and the deck crew threw lines ashore. Longarm got out of the way as the other passengers crowded to the head of the gangplank. He figured he could whip most of them in a free-for-all, but the boat didn't appear to be sinking, and he felt sure they'd let him off, even if he wasn't the first man down the gangplank.

He was right. The main herd thundered down to the Embarcadero and fanned out across the cobblestones, shouting for cabs and tripping over one another. Longarm deliberately lit a smoke before he made his way to the head of the gangplank. He saw that a willowy gal he hadn't noticed before was going to reach it at about the same time, so he stepped back, saying, "After you, ma'am."

She nodded demurely, her face half hidden by the black veil she wore over her picture hat, and he enjoyed the view of her hindquarters as he followed her down the gangplank. Her dress was black too, but if she was in widow's weeds, she wore them with a certain flair. Her skirts were gathered over her rump in a sassy Dolly Varden, and she sort of swished when she walked. She carried a small black valise. It seemed dumb to offer to carry such a bitty bag, so he decided not to. What the hell, he was almost ashore, and the whole city offered its female half for flirting, once he got his bearings.

He figured he'd walk up the Slot and check into the first decent-looking hotel before he made any other moves. Evening was coming on, and after he wired Billy that he'd arrived, he could sort of play things by ear. He still thought Washington was loco to send him all this way without any real leads, but he was too horny by now to head back to Denver before he'd at least given old Frisco a chance to make friends.

Longarm wasn't looking at the gal in widow's weeds as he got to the bottom of the gangplank. But he heard her scream, and when he turned her way, he saw a figure scuttling across the cobbles like a big crab, clutching the woman's valise to its chest!

Longarm swore, saw that he couldn't draw his gun, and started running after the snatcher, while others turned to shout questions and get in the way. The tall deputy moved faster than most men his size, and as his boot heels rang on the pavement, the snatcher looked over his shoulder, gasped in surprise, and started running faster, darting between two moving wagons on the crowded Embarcadero roadway that ran the length of the docks. The light was tricky, and Longarm thought he'd lost the bastard as he found another gap in the traffic and tore through at a dead run. A driver cursed loudly as he reined in his team to keep from running Longarm down. Longarm didn't answer. He had the snatcher sighted again. The rascal had made it across to the railroad tracks running parallel to the shore. There were stationary boxcars on all sides. Beyond them rose a fence. If the man he was after made it over the fence, it was adios for sure. The waterfront shanties on the far side of the railyards offered an ideal hidey-hole. The snatcher looked back again, saw that Longarm was gaining, and leaped to grab the top of the fence with one hand, clutching the woman's bag in the other. Longarm grabbed for one of his ankles. The man kicked free with a frightened moan, dropping the valise as he got both hands up to haul himself over. Longarm leaped, missing the snatcher's shoe heel as it whipped over and out of sight. Longarm braced himself to follow, then frowned and muttered, "Easy, old son. Let's study on where we're going."

He bent and picked up the stolen valise. He'd recovered it for the woman, and it was time to quit while he was ahead. The petty thief could have friends in that dimly lit shantytown, and while a Colt double-action .44 could likely handle them, it sure wouldn't be the least conspicuous way to spend his first night in town.

He headed back the way he'd come, crossing the Embarcadero through a break in the traffic. He found the woman and some of the other passengers where he'd left them. Some idiot was shouting for a policeman. A funny-looking old jasper wearing full white whiskers and an admiral's hat had moved to comfort the woman, and as Longarm approached, they both saw that he had her valise. She gasped and moved to meet him as he held it up and called out, "He dropped it, ma'am. I ain't looked inside, but I'm sure it's all here."

The woman took the valise and sobbed, "Oh, how shall I ever be able to thank you, Mr, ah . . . ?"

"Name's Long, ma'am. Custis Long. You don't owe me all that much. I was in need of the exercise after that infernal trip, in any case."

She smiled under her veil, and said, "I'm Calvinia Taylor, and I'm forever in your debt, sir. I've just come from Sacramento with papers pertaining to my late husband's estate, and—"

"You'd best check and make sure they're all there," Longarm cut in, as things started falling into place. He saw now why she'd stayed in her stateroom on the trip down the river.

As Calvinia Taylor opened her valise, the man in the admiral's hat joined them, stared thoughtfully at Longarm, and said, "Kneel, my good fellow."

Longarm looked the older man over thoughtfully and asked soberly, "Ah, is this old gent with you, Miss Calvinia?"

She said, "No, he's the Emperor Norton. All my papers are in order, thank the Lord! Oh, it's such a relief!"

The man in the admiral's hat drew a tinny dress sword from

11

the scabbard at his waist and said, "I told you to kneel, young man. What's the matter with you? Don't you want to be knighted for saving this good woman's life?"

Longarm cocked an eyebrow at the white-whiskered old coot and said, "I hardly ever get knighted, and I never saved anything but her luggage, so if it's all the same to you . . ."

Then he saw the bewilderment in the old man's watery blue eyes. Someone in the crowd laughed and said, "The old maniac's at it again."

Longarm looked to the woman for help, but Calvinia couldn't offer much, with her face so heavily veiled. He stared at the obviously insane old man and said gently, "I'm sorry, sir, but I'm a stranger in town and I don't follow your drift."

The old man sighed and said, "I thought everyone knew me. I am Norton the First, Emperor of the United States and Defender of Mexico. Most of the San Francisco policemen let me knight them, you know."

There was another titter from the crowd. Longarm nodded understandingly and said, "Well, I've always wanted to be knighted, Your Majesty. Just how do we go about it?"

"You have to kneel and let me dub you with my sword. Unless, of course, you'd rather have a medal?"

"Do I get a choice, Your Majesty?"

"Yes, I think you've behaved more bravely than most of my knights this evening. Let's see if we can find something here for you. . . ."

As Longarm watched, bemused, the old man fumbled with the front of his shabby uniform, and now Longarm saw that amid all the frogs and gilt braid, the Emperor Norton had an imposing array of pot-metal geegaws pinned to his chest. He took one off and pinned it to Longarm's lapel, saying, "There. Now if anybody refuses to believe I honored you, you'll have the proof to show them, eh?"

"That's right neighborly of you, Your Majesty," Longarm began, but then he saw that the old lunatic was already losing interest in the odd scene, for Norton suddenly raised his sword and strode out in the traffic, calling, "You there, on that brewery dray! What's the meaning of beating your horse like that? Haven't you read my proclamations regarding cruelty to animals?"

The driver ignored him. As he drove on, the Emperor Norton followed, brandishing his toy sword and ordering him to pull over. Longarm shook his head in wonder and went to pick up his own carpetbag from where he'd dropped it when the excitement started.

It wasn't there.

Longarm stared morosely down at the vacant cobbles and swore long and hard until Calvinia Taylor joined him and asked what was the matter.

He said, "I'm sorry you heard that, ma'am. I don't generally carry on so over fresh socks and such, but it does seem to me I've left my brains somewhere along the Humboldt River. I've seldom done anything so dumb."

"Oh, good heavens, are you saying you've been robbed too?"

"It sure is starting to look that way, ma'am. While I was being a hero with that one rascal, some other rascal slithered off with my carpetbag. By pure good fortune, I didn't happen to be carrying anything as important in my bag as you were in yours, so I reckon we're still ahead, but it sure is getting tedious."

He looked around, saw that the crowd had thinned, and added, "What say we get away from this den of thieves, ma'am? I wasn't headed anyplace in particular, but I'd be proud to drop you off along the way if we can hail us a cab."

She hesitated, then said, "The least I can do is pay for the ride, then. I live on Hyde Street, Nob Hill. Where are you staying here in San Francisco, Mr. Long?"

He saw a hansom cab stopping to let some people out to board the steamboat for its return trip up the river. So he waved at the driver before he told her, "I was fixing to leave my possibles at the nearest hotel. But since I don't have any possibles no more, I'll just run you home and worry about me later."

He took her elbow and walked her to the cab. She gave the driver her address, and Longarm helped her in. They started up, and by now it was really dark, so the interior of the cab alternated light and blackness as they passed street lamps. They seemed to be going up hill, but Longarm was already getting lost, and he said so. Calvinia said, "Finding your way back to the center of things from my place is no problem, if you want to."

He didn't know how to answer that, so he didn't.

"You're a decent man and a kind man," she went on. "You

helped me without thinking, and you were sweet to the poor old crazy Emperor."

"Heck, it wasn't all that much, ma'am."

"I'm not finished. I'm not a giddy virgin, and I know a professional gun when I meet one. I spotted you on the boat. I was watching when you were in that card game. You deal right smartly from the bottom, but my late husband taught me how to play cards Gold Rush style, and I'm good, too."

Longarm laughed. "It's always easier to spot from across the room than at the table. I was only acting in self-defense, by the way."

"I know," she said. "You're not a tinhorn. You play for higher stakes. How much does it cost to hire you and your gun, Custis?"

"Depends on the job," he answered soberly. He'd been taken for a gunslick before, and sometimes it had proven interesting to go along with the notion.

"I don't need a hired gun to kill anybody," she explained. "I need one to keep from getting killed myself, or maybe just robbed. My late husband left a lot of enemies, and I'm a woman alone at a known address. It might surprise a lot of people if you were to spend the next few days—and nights—at my place up the hill."

He muttered noncommittally. The Justice Department hadn't sent him out here to bodyguard widow women whose late husbands might have been mixed up in shady dealings. On the other hand, the folks he was after had to be part of the Frisco underworld. . . .

She'd taken off her hat and veil. As the next street lamp illuminated her features, he was aware that she knew just what she'd been aiming to show him when she did it. Calvinia Taylor was a beautiful woman. Her black hair was piled above perfect cameo features. She was about thirty, as pretty as a Dresden doll, and hard as nails. He was sure he could strike a match anywhere along that firm, stubborn jaw.

She said, "I go with the territory. You're a fine-looking man, and I'm too healthy to be alone so much. From a practical point of view, you'll be a better bodyguard if I keep you as close as possible to my body, don't you agree?"

She wanted somebody killed, he decided. Calvinia Taylor was tough, but not a casual slut. Her voice and breeding betrayed the fact that the added inducement was the weapon of

14

a desperate woman. It made him feel a mite used and abused. Did she really think he was that dumb?

Longarm knew some women found him attractive, praise the Lord. But no well-brought-up Victorian gal came at a man so coldbloodedly unless she was coldblooded indeed. She figured she could wrap him about her finger with a little slap-and-tickle, then have her own domesticated gunhand to aim at folks. But two could play at coldblooded romance, and he knew he'd die of curiosity if he lit out before he found out what her infernal game really was.

He put an arm around her to draw her closer, but Calvinia stiffened and hissed, "Don't paw me in a cab like I was some barmaid, damn it."

Longarm sighed, removed his arm, and said, "It's been nice meeting up with you, ma'am. But I'd best get off at the next corner."

"Wait, I didn't say I wouldn't make love to you, if that's what you need."

"Ma'am, I don't *need* anything. You're the one who started talking about country matters. But I can see you're somewhat confused on the subject, so we'll just say no more about it. You got your bag back and I have you aimed safe at your own door. So this is about where I say adios."

"Custis, you don't understand."

"Sure I do. You just told me you wanted me to guard your body, and you're so hard up for someone to take the job that you offered to throw the body in, but your heart ain't in it, gal."

"Custis, I'm desperate."

"Yeah, so desperate you're acting downright spooky, too. You didn't have to tease me like that, if all you really want to hire is a man about the house. Frisco is a tough old town and there must be hundreds of gents willing to sit in your front parlor with a shotgun across their knees, if that was all you wanted. You wouldn't have to sleep with them, neither. Just tell a straight story, pay the going price, and sleep with whomsoever you want to. Like I said, this is about where I get off. I'll pay the driver for this far."

Longarm reached for the door handle. Calvinia slid off the leather seat to kneel on the floor between his knees. "Don't leave me alone," she sobbed. "I'll do anything you want."

She started to fumble with his fly buttons. He frowned down

15

at her. "Hold on, girl, who said that was what I wanted?"

She fondled the bulge in his trousers teasingly and asked, "Isn't it what all you men want? Boys can't lie about their feelings, if someone's bold enough to feel them."

"When you're right, you're right," he said, sighing. "Women have a cruel advantage over us when it comes to pretending passion. You're a good-looking gal and I'll admit I'd admire rutting with you if you'll be kind enough to let go of my longjohns."

She moved up on the seat beside him and put her head on his shoulder, with one hand still in his lap. "Good. I'm glad we have that settled."

Longarm had settled no such thing, but this was getting interesting as hell—and doubtless illegal. As a lawman he figured it was his duty to go along with her game long enough to find out who she wanted murdered. He doubted she'd be acting like this if all she had in mind was robbing a train.

The cab was going up a godawful slope, so the two of them were lying on the seat back as much as they were sitting on the seat. Longarm put his arm around her. This time she didn't resist, so he raised her chin with his free hand and planted a kiss on her lips. She responded as well as she was able. It felt like kissing two slices of cucumber, fresh from the icebox. She took his wrist and guided his hand to one of her breasts. Between the starched bodice and the whalebone and such under it, he had to take it on pure faith that there was a human tit in there somewhere. But at least she was trying. The cab leveled off and stopped, so Longarm stopped feeling her up. The driver yelled down that they were there, and Longarm opened the door and helped Calvinia down. She insisted on paying, so Longarm let her as he looked around. They were way the hell up in the sky. Hyde Street ran along the crest of Nob Hill. There were frame houses all around, but between the gaps you could see the city and the bay spread out down below, outlined by spiderwebs full of fireflies. Steam tugs moved across the dark water, pulling sailing vessels through the tricky tides of the crowded harbor. Somewhere a foghorn wailed in the night, although the Bay seemed clear enough from up here. As the cab drove off, he commented on the foghorn.

Calvinia said, "There must be a fog bank moving in through the Golden Gate. You can't see it from here. But by midnight the flats down below will be solidly fogged in. Aren't you glad you came?"

Longarm started to say he hadn't, yet, but it sounded sort of country and he'd noticed she didn't share his notions of humor. She unlocked the front door of the tall, narrow house. As he followed her in, he saw that the hall was gaslit, so he didn't have to fumble for a match. Calvinia led him to a lushly furnished parlor and dropped her valise by a cold fireplace carved out of marble that looked like soap. She waved him to a seat on an overstuffed maroon plush sofa and said she would fix them something to eat.

As soon as she left the room, Longarm lit a smoke, picked up her valise, and started going through it.

There were some silk unmentionables, which he set aside, since he already knew what gals wore under their dresses. He found a manila envelope with a Sacramento seal on it. He opened it and was browsing through the papers it contained when Calvinia came back in. She was carrying some sandwiches and a decanter on a silver tray. She'd changed to a sheer dressing gown of burnt-orange shantung, and she'd let her long hair down in raven's wings that helped to cover the nipples under the thin material. She gasped when she saw what he'd been up to. "How dare you go through my belongings?" she sputtered in outrage.

"Oh, wasn't I supposed to?" he replied innocently. "You left the bag here after hinting that folks were out to kill you over what's in it. Seems to me I'd have been sort of an uncaring cuss, had I not had a look-see."

She put the tray down on a teakwood table near the sofa and sat beside him, pouting. "Well, I hope you've satisfied your curiosity," she said.

"Not hardly. There's a probated will giving you control of your dead husband's property, which seems reasonable. You've gotten power as his executrix to foreclose on some mortgages he was holding. Would the Clem Taylor you're aiming to evict from house and home be any kin to the husband you just buried, Calvinia?"

She shrugged and said, "If you must know, Clem Taylor's my brother-in-law, or he was, until my husband, Peter, died after supporting him all these years. That's not a house and home, either. It's a couple of sections of prime barley land, up near Weed. A few years back we staked Clem in a barley-malting operation. You've heard of San Francisco steam beer?"

"Yep. Drunk some the last time I was out this way. It's got a lot of hair on its chest, for beer. You say your brother-in-law makes it?"

"No, he sells malt to the people who do, and they pay well. Clem Taylor's had plenty of time to pay us back the original loan, but every time my poor husband mentioned it, Clem had some excuse."

Longarm nodded. "It happens that way, doing business with one's relations. In other words, whilst your husband was alive, he never saw fit to foreclose on his shiftless brother. But now that he's dead, you've gone and started proceedings to recover what you figure is your own, right?"

"Exactly. The money is mine and I mean to have it. Clem's had plenty of time to pay the estate back, and besides, I've gotten a very good offer for the land."

"I'll bet you have. I don't reckon you saw fit to warn your ex-in-laws that you were fixing to foreclose on 'em, eh?"

"I mentioned the debts at Pete's funeral, and Clem just gave me some soft-soap about talking about it later. He has the money in the bank. He just doesn't want to pay his just debts."

Longarm held up another paper. "Not that you really want him to. 'Fess up," he said. "This offer from the big brewery combine is for three times as much as old Clem ever owed you, ain't it?"

"What if it is? Clem had plenty of chances to pay the debt while his brother was alive."

"Yeah, some brothers are sort of fond of each other, so they don't take things as serious as they might. Your late husband was a rich as well as a generous brother, wasn't he? I see by the will that he left you fixed pretty good, and all old Clem has is the small business holdings up north. You don't reckon old Pete might have seen fit to forgive his brother's debt, do you?"

"Clem seems to feel he should have, but the lawyers I talked to up in Sacramento say I don't have to. Now that Clem's started acting ugly, I feel it's simple justice to teach him a good lesson by selling the property out from under him."

Longarm put the papers back in the valise and asked, "Just what did your brother-in-law do that's so ugly, Calvinia?"

"Isn't it obvious?" she asked, plainly surprised. "He had

18

that man follow me to steal the papers before I could have them served."

Longarm looked disgusted and said, "Sure he did. He sent another thief all the way down from Weed to steal my socks, too! That rascal we tangled with was just a baggage snatcher, girl. He was waiting there when the boat docked, looking for a chance to do what he done! Nobody's gunning for you but your own guilty conscience. You married a rich man, and now that he's dead, you aim to be richer and to hell with his poor relations!"

He stood up. Calvinia asked where he was going, and he answered, "Downhill. The direction don't seem to matter, since we're smack in the middle of town on a high and windy hill."

"You can't leave me alone like this! What if Clem or someone working for him finds me here alone?"

"Call the beat coppers, if you don't want to do right by old Clem. You ain't in danger, your dead husband's relatives are. You're a cold-hearted gal, Calvinia. You might be pretty enough to get some fool to bulge his muscles at the folks you're taking advantage of, but it ain't likely to be me."

She rose in his wake, allowing her gown to fall open and making his heart skip a beat as she pleaded, "Wait, let's talk it over in the morning, darling."

He shook his head. "I ain't your darling, tempting as the sights around me may be. This game of yours is sort of dumb, and I never came to Frisco to play dumb games. So I'll just be on my way."

She followed him out to the hall, and as he put a hand on the doorknob, she called imperiously, "Wait. Turn around."

So he did.

Calvinia Taylor stood facing him without a stitch on, the light from the other room sculpting her perfect curves in bold relief as she cupped one breast in either hand, holding the turgid nipples up to him as she smiled and said, "I dare you to walk out now, you son of a bitch!"

Longarm stared down at her wistfully and sighed. "I'll likely call myself a son of a bitch later tonight, too. But I have always been a sucker for a dare, and damn it, girl, I just don't *like* you!"

He opened the door and stepped out into the cool, damp night, wondering if she aimed to follow him down the hill. He grinned as he considered the image. He closed the door behind him, gently, but it popped open as he walked down the steps and she called out, "Come back here, damn you!"

He never looked back.

It was a good thing he didn't. He'd have been in a hell of a mess with his back to the street when some son of a bitch popped up from behind some trashcans across the way to fire both barrels of a sawed-off shotgun at him!

Fortunately, Longarm was moving to one side as he came down the stairs, and he crabbed the other way instinctively when he saw the sudden blur of motion. The twin charges of number-nine buck spattered on the stone steps and spanged a pockmarked pattern all over Calvinia's front door as Longarm dropped behind a sandstone hitching step to return the fire. But as he threw down on the bushwhacker, the bastard was slithering around a corner like a lizard in the dim light, so that Longarm's one shot might have winged him, and then again it might not have. Longarm didn't hang around to find out. He tore up the steps, dashed into the house he'd just left, and locked the door behind him. He didn't see Calvinia anywhere, but she wasn't the one he was after, so what the hell. He turned off the hall light, ran into the parlor, and doused the lamp before moving to the window overlooking the street. He didn't move the lace curtains as he peered out, gun muzzle raised.

He didn't see any gunmen out there, but the neighbors across the way were out on their front steps, yelling fit to bust as they looked both ways to see if they could determine what all the fuss had been about. Longarm knew the place would soon be crawling with beat coppers, and he didn't want to talk to any lawmen right now. Cursing himself, he holstered his revolver and turned around. In the dim light, Calvinia was moving to join him, still naked as a jaybird. "You see?" she said. "I told you somebody was after me!"

He started to object that the man with the shotgun had been after *him*. But that wouldn't work. He'd only been in Frisco an hour or so, and even if the coiners were laying for him, how the hell could they have known he'd be up here on Nob Hill? He hadn't known himself until a few minutes ago!

"Well," he said, "I stand corrected about old Clem. But if that was him just now, he sure is a moody son of a bitch, for a man who grows barley."

She moved closer and he took her in his arms, not knowing what else to do as she asked, "Are you still angry with little me, you big growly bear?"

20

He was, sort of, but she sure felt good in his arms and he didn't want her yelling her fool head off with coppers responding to gunshots in the neighborhood. The hall light was out, so they likely wouldn't notice the splintered buckshot pattern in the front door. He had to study some before he left these parts for . . . where? It was getting late, and some son of a bitch he hadn't gotten a good look at was gunning for him. The would-be assassin may have started out with this cold-hearted gal in mind, but he'd aimed at Longarm for sure, for whatever reason. So Calvinia's fight seemed to be his, whether he wanted it or not.

She snuggled closer and rubbed her naked body against him like an indecent kitten. So Longarm cupped a hot buttock in each of his palms and kissed her. It felt weird. Calvinia was fire and ice. As she ground her pelvis against his buttoned fly, her lips felt about as enthusiastic as a marble statue's. He came up for air with a grimace of distaste as she asked, "You are going to spend the night with me, aren't you, dear?"

"Reckon so," he said. "Which way's the bedroom?"

She stiffened and said, "You're disgusting!"

"Aw, hell," he muttered. "This is crazier than that poor old Emperor Norton's notion about me being a knight in armor. I ain't noble and I ain't disgusting, girl. I'm a natural man with natural feelings, and this bullshit has to cease and desist!"

He scooped her up and headed for the nearest sofa as she gasped. "What do you think you're doing?"

"*Think,* hell," he said. "I *know* what I'm doing. You're the one who seems a mite confused, Calvinia."

"Put me down this instant," she said in an imperious voice. So Longarm lowered her to the plush sofa and started shucking his gun rig and duds as he wedged her in with his hip and kept shoving her down every time she tried to sit up. "I'll scream if you rape me!" she gasped.

He laughed and said, "Hell, woman, this ain't rape, it's seduction. You been seducing me ever since we met, and I'm just taking you up on it."

She stiffened and sobbed as he leaned forward to press his naked chest against her bare nipples while he ran his free hand down her curves to part the thatch between her thighs with experienced fingers. He could tell she was more than ready, but as he moved to mount her, she gasped, "No, not that! What kind of a girl do you think I am?"

He didn't answer. It would have been rude to tell her she

was a crazy castrating bitch, and fortunately for both of them, Longarm was too hard up to care. She hissed like a snake when he entered her, and even when her hips started moving, her voice dripped venom as she said coldly, "Oh, very well, since I can't stop you, I suppose we'd just better get it over with as quickly as possible."

"Yeah," he agreed. "that's the way us beasts are. I'm sure sorry I neglected to bring along some chloroform. Uh, would you mind raising your knees a mite?"

She wrapped her legs around his waist, and he could feel her throbbing in time to his thrusts as she asked, "There, is that better?"

"It sure is. I hope you ain't in too much pain?"

"Oh, don't mind me. Just satisfy that silly thing and get it out of me, for heaven's sake."

So Longarm did. It was interesting. It felt like he was making love to two women at once. Above the waist, Calvinia was a cruel-tongued ball-breaker while, below her bellybutton, she was pleasuring him just fine. He knew he'd never have been able to keep it up if he had had better luck on that cross-country train. But it felt so good when he came that he decided to go for another, despite her discouraging words.

As he kept moving, she sniffed distastefully and said, "I felt that. Aren't you going to stop, now that you've defiled me?"

"Not hardly," he said. "As long as you're being such a good sport about it, I aim to defile the hell out of you."

She started moving her hips from side to side as she sighed dramatically and said, "Well, for heaven's sake, *do* it, then. Why are you moving so slow?"

"I'm trying to be gentle, knowing how distasteful this is to you."

"I told you I just wanted to get it over with. Can't you move a little faster?"

He grinned and started teasing her even more with long, slow thrusts. She seemed unaware that she was bouncing twice to his once as she said disdainfully, "Honestly, I don't mind if you let yourself go. I know you men have no control, and I can see you really need it."

Obviously she needed it a lot more than she was letting on. But she'd played this game so often it had mixed her pretty head up. So Longarm figured it was time to straighten her out.

22

He raised one of her knees and hooked it over his elbow as he braced a hand against the back of the sofa and got one bare foot on the carpet.

"Oh God," she gasped, "what are you trying to do, open me like a pair of scissors?" And then, as he started to pound, hitting bottom with every stroke, Calvinia pleaded, "Stop! It's too big and too deep and what are you doing and oh Jesus what's happening?"

What was happening was that they were both coming, and while this wasn't exactly a novel experience for Longarm, it must have been for Calvinia, for she spent the next few minutes going crazy. She kept saying that she hated him and loved him, told him to take it out and shove it deeper, and then she screamed aloud in mingled pleasure and surprise as she saw that he meant to keep going while she throbbed in orgasm. She pleaded with him to have mercy while she clawed his back and kissed him hot and heavy from shoulder to shoulder, as she forgot she wasn't supposed to like it.

He swiveled her tailbone on the sofa to kneel with both knees on the carpet. Her bare feet were on the floor and her thighs were spread wide as she sat up against the backrest, eyes wide in wonder as he held her by the waist and pounded her, grinning at her bouncing nipples. "Aren't you ever going to stop?" she asked.

When he answered, "Do you want me to?" she closed her eyes, thrust her pelvis forward even more, and sighed, "No, never! I've never felt it like this, even when my late husband was alive!"

He'd figured as much. Poor old Pete Taylor was doubtless relieved to be dead. It was obvious he'd never tamed this shrew, and the longer they'd been together, the more practiced she'd gotten at making men miserable.

Most men, at any rate. Now that he'd made her come, Calvinia didn't seem to want to hurt his manhood. Her new-found womanhood was enjoying it too much. He stopped a moment in his own shuddering pleasure, and as he discharged his weapon, the floor boards tingled under his knees and he heard the ringing bells.

He frowned and asked, "What was that?"

"Oh, silly, that was just a cable car," Calvinia purred. "The California Street line crosses just down the block."

He said, "Oh, I remember them. Rode one the last time I was here. But speaking of riding, we could do this a lot better in bed, honey."

She hesitated, and he figured she was starting to remember her bitch act. But then she sighed and said, "Yes, I want to try it in bed with you. I want to do it every way with you, darling."

So he picked up the gun rig he'd dropped near the sofa, then picked up Calvinia and carried her out into the hall and up the stairs to where she said the bedroom was. She opened the door for them, and he crossed the threshold with her cuddled in his arms. The room was half lit by a street lamp through the lace curtains, and near the four-poster he spied a Seth Thomas table clock that said it was half past eight. So the evening was younger than he'd thought. That was something to study on. He lowered Calvinia to the covers and hung the gun rig handy as she knelt on hands and knees to turn the covers down, laughing like a little kid swiping apples. He went to the window and looked out. There was nothing stirring in the street, and he could see behind the trashcans that had concealed the bushwhacker. Calvinia asked, "What are you doing, darling? I want you in me again. Come to bed like a good boy."

So he did. And this time she didn't act mean at all. He'd gotten over the worse effects of his celibate train ride, and while she still felt great in his arms, he couldn't see spending a whole night up here. He hadn't been sent out here to get laid, it was still early, and what in thunder did a man do with a tame shrew, once he'd had the fun of taming one?

Chapter 3

Calvinia could have solved the problem by falling asleep like the good little girl he'd made of her. But she didn't. It was just as early for her as it was for Longarm, and orgasms were a novelty to her. Once she'd gotten the hang of it, she wanted to come in every position Longarm could think of and a couple she made up herself. When he finally got her worn down enough to share a cuddle, the damned clock said it was only a little after ten. She was purring contentedly with her head on his shoulder, but he could see she was wide awake and full of beans. He'd done about as much as any man could to settle her nerves, and he knew she was going to be hurt as hell if he just put on his pants and lit out. He owed it to the human race to keep Calvinia convinced that all men didn't aim to just use and abuse her sex like she'd said. Aside from Christian charity, she might not be safe alone here, either. The rascal who'd fired that scattergun at him might or might not be working for her brother-in-law, and while the shooter seemed to have given up his homicidal notions for the moment, the night was young.

As Longarm studied and smoked, Calvinia snuggled closer and asked, "What are you thinking about, Custis? You're so quiet."

25

He blew a smoke ring and said, "We got us a problem with doorways. You have a front door and a back door, and there's only one of me."

"Oh, I was afraid you were having second thoughts about me."

He patted her reassuringly and said, "I am. You're too pretty to get shot full of buckshot. We're going to have to hide you out, Calvinia. This place ain't safe."

"Pooh, I feel safe in your strong arms. You scared that man with the shotgun skinny, and he's probably still running."

"He scared me too," Longarm admitted. "And I've been considering how far he's run. He couldn't have known me, so he was after you. If he wasn't your brother-in-law in the flesh, he was likely somebody old Clem hired. But whoever he is, he knows this address and he's serious about it."

"Couldn't he have just meant to frighten us?"

"He did. But he wasn't funning when he emptied both barrels into where I'd just been strolling. I don't see how he could have mistaken me for you, so he figured you'd hired your own gun and didn't like it much. Did you tell anyone you were fixing to start your own army, Calvinia?"

She thought a moment, then said, "Well, when I got word that Clem was making threats, I might have allowed that two can play at the same game."

He nodded, feeling sort of disgusted. Billy Vail had sent him out here to catch counterfeiters, and here he was, mixed up in an infernal family feud!

He knew Calvinia had started it, but even though it was not a federal offense to shoot a lady trying to foreclose a mortgage on you, he was just a sentimental fool about gals he'd made love to, and it did seem sort of ornery to shotgun a woman, bitchy or not.

He said, "We can't stay here, Calvinia. I was aiming to check into a hotel in the first place. I'd say our best bet would be for you to dress up different, as it might cause comment if I was to check into the Palace with you with you wearing widow's weeds."

"You can't be serious! I could never go to a hotel with a man I wasn't married to! It's downright indecent!"

He didn't answer. She giggled as she ran her hand over his bare belly and added, "I mean, what we've been doing here is hardly a matter of public record."

He said, "At least one gent knows we're in here with the lights out, and by now he could have recruited some help. It ain't like we have to register under our right names, you know."

She shook her head emphatically. "I'm afraid of being found out. What if I were to be recognized, sneaking into a hotel with you like a soiled dove? I'm well known in San Francisco. My picture's been printed on the social pages. My reputation would be ruined forever."

He shrugged. "I know how you society gals value your reps, but you're likely to rate an obituary in the same papers if we don't get you forted up better. They have us at one hell of a disadvantage here."

"Pooh, they'd never get in with you on guard, dear."

"Not while I was awake. But I'm only one man, and any man has to doze off from time to time. They know that. That's why the next time they come, it'll likely be around four in the morning."

She began to fondle him as she suggested, "Don't you think I can keep you awake, darling?"

He laughed. "For now you're doing fine, but the more we make love, the sooner we'll be too tuckered to give the doors and windows our undivided attention. Be serious, girl. We have to study on a safer place for you. If you won't go to a hotel with me, try to think of someplace proper that your moody in-laws don't know about."

"Well," she said after a few moments' thought, "I could always stay with my friend, the widow Doyle. She lives just down the hill, and my in-laws have never met her. I'm sure dear Gwynn would take me in, but there's just one problem."

"She might not understand about me, huh?"

"Heavens, she'd have a fit! She's ever so proper and—well, I don't think she likes men."

"There seems to be a lot of that going around. Did she marry for money, too?"

"Don't be beastly, Custis. I didn't marry Pete because he was rich."

"Do tell? It seems to me that when we first tested the springs of this here bed, you said something about never enjoying it before."

She sighed and said, "I have to learn to keep my mouth shut when I'm making love to you, you brute. All right, I admit my marriage wasn't a happy one. But how was I to know when

I married Pete that he'd be awful to sleep with?"

Longarm grimaced in distaste. He didn't like to bring other men to bed with him, and he'd long since figured out how Calvinia had picked up her annoying habits. "Let's not speak ill of the dead," he said. "If we're to keep you alive, we'd better get you bedded down with your widow-woman friend. I don't reckon they'll be expecting you to move, so it ought to be safe for us to duck out the back way and sneak you in that other house."

"Are you sure you won't mind? You realize it's out of the question for you to visit me alone in Gwynn Doyle's home."

"You told me that already. I'll just have to grit my teeth and bear the frustration for now."

Calvinia sighed and said, "I'm not sure I'll be able to. You seem to have created a monster, darling. I know you don't believe me, but I've never had an orgasm with a man before."

He didn't comment on the unspoken implications of her statement. "Well, we'll do it some more after I get a handle on your family feud. Your in-laws may want to talk sense if I can have a word with them. I may have an edge on them that they didn't suspicion when they blasted at me with that fool scattergun. Since you'll be staying with another widow woman, you may as well put on the duds I shucked you out of. I left mine down there somewhere, so let's go down and get dressed."

"Can we make love one more time?" she asked.

The notion struck Longarm as reasonable. As he snubbed out his smoke, she rolled over and got on her hands and knees, saying, "I want to do it naughty-puppy again. I never knew people could do it like that, too."

So he slid his feet to the floor, took a hipbone in each hand, and went at her, sort of flattered by the way his new pupil responded to his educational efforts. He decided Calvinia wasn't really a natural bitch. She'd just been raised wrong. Queen Victoria and the mothers who raised their daughters according to her fool notions had a lot to answer for. Poor little Calvinia had been taught that a woman wasn't supposed to enjoy it, and then, when she'd married a gent who likely hadn't had much experience, the frustrated gal had just naturally made things worse by mean-mouthing his efforts until he died. As he admired the view of her rollicking rump, he could see how vexing it must have been to live with something as nice as this so close and yet so far away. Her nasty attitude toward her despised husband's relations could be leftover bile, too. Maybe if he got her feeling more friendly, she'd see fit to drop her notions about foreclosing on that mortgage. She didn't need the money. But fair was fair, and while Calvinia hadn't been acting too sisterly, her in-laws had overdone things a mite with that shotgun blast.

He shook his head and buckled down to the job at hand as she chewed the sheets, moaning for more. He had no call to mess in a personal matter like this, damn it. He wasn't here to save Calvinia's ass, pretty as it was. Billy Vail had sent him all this way to track down counterfeiters who gunned federal agents as a sideline, and Billy would have a fit right now if he knew what his chief deputy was doing on Uncle Sam's time!

On the other hand, what Billy and Sam didn't know wouldn't hurt them, and Calvinia said she wanted to turn over and finish right, so they did, and this time she locked her ankles around his neck to take it all with a cry of sheer wonder and delight.

As he exploded and went limp she said "Oh, that was marvelous. I never knew it could be so deep without hurting. Is there any way to get it deeper, darling?"

He said, "No. That's all I was born with. I've been told a few times it's a mite more than required by most gals."

"I'll bet you have, you horrid thing. How many girls have you ruined this way?"

"Hell, I hardly ever *ruin* gals. Most of 'em have allowed they was grateful. Do you feel ruined, Calvinia?"

"No, I feel marvelous. I just wish we didn't have to stop. Maybe if I explained how we felt about each other to poor Gwynn Doyle—"

"Let's not confuse the poor old widow woman, honey," he cut in. "You know it's something you can't hardly explain with words. I had enough trouble convincing *you* it didn't have to be downright disgusting, remember?"

She laughed, then moved her hips teasingly and said, "You're right. It would take a demonstration to convince poor Gwynn, and the shock would probably kill her. She confided in me once that her marriage had been rather grim, too."

He looked over at the clock and said, "You gals can meanmouth us men some more, once I get you there safely. It's time we got going."

So they went downstairs and dressed without lighting the lamps. Longarm finished first and checked the street. It was empty, or at least it looked empty. When Calvinia had her clothes on, she picked up her valise with the valuable papers, and Longarm led the way out the back door. The rear yard was blacker than her widow's weeds, and she protested when he boosted her over a fence, asking why.

He said, "I see a slot where we can come out on the far side of your block. Come on, let's move it. Hoist your skirts if you can't take bigger steps in that fool outfit."

"I feel like a prowler," she said, as he led her past the side windows of the house fronting the next street over. He felt like a prowler too, and he knew the folks in the house would take them for such, if they chose this time to peer out. Fortunately they didn't, and in a moment the two of them were strolling arm in arm along the other street, toward the widow Doyle's.

Calvinia's friend lived in a corner house near the cable car line on California Street. As they crossed the street, Longarm frowned down at the slot between the tracks. It was whispering snake-talk to him. There wasn't a cable car in sight, but he remembered how the things operated. An endless steel cable ran six miles an hour in the slot at all times. When a cable car wanted to go someplace, the driver grabbed the ever-moving cable with a patent doohickey that hung down in the slot. Modern science was getting to be a pure caution. Back East, folks were even talking about streetcars that would run on electricity.

The front entrance of the Doyle house was more imposing than Calvinia's. They went up the steps, and when Calvinia cranked the doorbell handle, Longarm expected a snooty butler to answer. But a snooty woman came to the door instead. She was dressed in black too, and her ash-blond hair was up in a severe bun. She held her head as though she were balancing the ball of hair like a sea lion. When Calvinia introduced him, the widow Doyle looked Longarm over like she'd just noticed dogshit on her walk. But she let them both into the vestibule. As she closed the door, Calvinia explained in a few words that she was afraid to stay at her own place until this "private detective" she'd hired found out who was knocking on her door with shotgun pellets.

Gwynn Doyle nodded and said, "Of course you'll stay here with me, dear heart. You know you're always welcome."

She shot a look at Longarm that told him he was about as welcome as the Apache Nation. The hell of it was, she was a right handsome woman. Not as old as he'd imagined and as pretty as a gal could look, sucking a sour lemon. Her eyes were big and blue, but filled with ill will toward his kind.

If what Calvinia had said about her experience with marriage was true, there had to be something fearsomely wrong with Frisco men. How in hell a man could take a pretty blond to bed and fail to do right by her eluded Longarm. But the way these poor gals had been treated by their menfolk wasn't the mystery he'd been sent to solve. So he told Calvinia he'd come by sometime the next day to let her know how things were. Calvinia seemed sorry to see him go. Gwynn Doyle looked insultingly relieved not to have to serve him tea and biscuits after all.

Longarm started legging downhill, not sure where he was or where he was going, but relieved to be free at last to look for serious trouble. He knew the town of Frisco was down there, no matter which way he left this residential ridge. He followed the cable car tracks, knowing they had to lead somewhere sensible. As he came to a steeper dropoff, he paused, stared down the awesome slope, and muttered, "What the hell?"

He was staring down at pure nothing, or rather the top of a fog bank that blanketed everything as far as he could see. Here and there he saw patches of light glowing ghostly through the fog from the streets below. But he couldn't make out any landmarks he knew. The bay and waterfront had to be somewhere down there in the pea soup, and he knew a big avenue ran toward Market Street across his line of march. He shrugged and headed down, digging in his boot heels as the walk got alarmingly steep. In a short while he was navigating damned near blind. He could sort of see near the street lamps, and the whispering of the cable in the slot to his right told him the tracks were still there. So he kept going.

It got worse. The fog smelled like seaweed and roasting coffee, and made him feel clammy. He touched the handle of his Colt and, sure enough, it was beaded with moisture like it had been left out all night to collect dew. He came to a cross street that seemed broader than most, but there was no traffic moving in the quiet fog. He found his way to a street lamp and peered up at the street sign under the wan gas glow. It said he was on Grant Avenue. The main drag he was looking for was Columbus. So he crossed over and started down another slope. He'd only gone a short way when he heard rough voices and what sounded like a gal in trouble. He frowned and stepped into the doorway of a shop that was closed for the night. What was going on wasn't his business, and if the folks making all the fuss would just leave things that way, it was jake with him. They sounded like a bunch of rowdy drunks.

They were. As Longarm stood invisible in the doorway, a gang of about seven or eight materialized out of the fog, heading his way up the middle of the street and hauling somebody smaller who was kicking and screaming. As they got under a street light, Longarm could see that the gang was a bunch of roughly dressed white men, rawhiding a Chinaman in black pajamas. One of them had the Chinese by his long pigtail, and every time he yanked it the Chinese yelled. They seemed to think this was funny as hell.

Longarm sighed and told himself, "Stay out of it, old son. They've been doing this since long before you got here, and they'll be doing it long after you've left. Billy Vail never sent you here to mend the ways of the Frisco sporting crowd, damn it!"

One of the toughs shouted a suggestion, and the others laughed and threw their oriental victim roughly on the pavement between the tracks. Longarm stiffened but hesitated. At those odds, he'd have to use his gun, and he was trying not to attract attention. They didn't seem to be really out to hurt the poor Chinaman; they were just scaring the shit out of him so far, he hoped. Cowhands had a rough sense of humor too, and he'd learned the hard way not to butt in unless things got really out of hand.

The one holding the Chinaman's pigtail seemed to be trying to stuff it down in the slot between the rails for some reason, and the Chinese didn't find the notion at all appealing, judging from the way he was yelling. Longarm suddenly gasped as he realized what they were trying to do. If the pigtail caught in the rough wire rope, the Chinaman would start moving along the rails at six miles an hour, dragged by his hair!

Longarm stepped out of the doorway and called out, "All right, boys, that's about enough."

There was a pregnant pause. Nobody moved, but the one trying to keelhaul the Chinaman with the cable stopped what he was doing, so Longarm didn't go for his gun.

A burly member of the gang hitched his belt thoughtfully and asked, "Well now, what have we here? You don't look like a Chinaman, me darlin', but if you want to join the dance, we'll be pleased to have you."

"Have you for supper, you son of a bitch," another added, joined by a general growl of agreement.

The Chinese, momentarily neglected, sat up, looked around wild-eyed, and started to rise. But one of the gang kicked him flat and snapped, "Stay put, you slant-eyed bastard! We'll deal with you after we take the measure of your new friend here."

The leader laughed nastily. "Yeah, what makes you so friendly to ching-chongs, stranger? You look like a white man from here. Come a little closer and let's see if your eyes slant."

"Boys," Longarm said, "you are commencing to annoy me a mite. So I seriously suggest you just go on home before your mommas come looking for you."

"Oho! A regular bully of the town, eh? Stand back, boys, I ain't had fresh meat for a month of Sundays, and this one looks like he could use a lesson. How about it, me bucko? Just you and me, fair out?"

"Not hardly. I used to take folks like you up on such fool suggestions, but it got tedious being piled on just as I thought I was winning. I don't fight fair no more. But if you don't cut this bullshit, I'll likely start displaying an awful temper in a minute."

The head tough hesitated, confused as much by Longarm's words as by his size. He said, "Talk sense, man! Do you want a stand-up, man-to-man, or do you want us all to jump you and the hell with it?"

"Neither," Longarm replied. "I'd be dumb to fight you fair, and you'd be even dumber if you rushed me. In case I forgot to mention it, I'm armed."

The one with the big mouth muttered, "Aw, that's not fair," and moved back to consult with his companions. Longarm saw they'd forgotten the Chinese, so he called out, "Hey, you with the pigtail. If you savvy English, move my way, chop-chop!"

The Chinese didn't answer, and Longarm muttered, "Shit," as he saw some other shadowy forms moving thoughtfully into view. No matter who they might be, he doubted they were on his side. This was getting serious. He had five rounds in his revolver and two in his derringer, but the crowd was getting big as well as ugly. He knew that if he started crawfishing right now, they'd probably let him go. But the damn fool Chinaman didn't understand what was going on, and if he left him now, they'd mess him up for sure.

One of the newcomers called out, "What's going on?" and the tough who'd been giving Longarm a hard time said, "Stay out of this, Jimbo. Me and the boys was just having some fun with Fong Sing here, and this stranger stuck his nose in."

The one called Jimbo shook his head and said, "Did he now? Well, and that saves me the trouble of breakin' your back, Seamus Grogan. For I've told you to leave these poor chinks alone on property yez don't belong on."

"Aw, Jimbo, we was just having fun."

"Oh, and it's fun you're for, Grogan? I'll give you fun, you crosseyed son of a bitch! Step clear of your gang and we'll dance a couple of rounds for the sheer enjoyment of it all!"

Grogan shook his head and said, "Garn, you know I'd be a fool to take on one of Buckley's Lambs. Sure and maybe we was lost in this dreadful fog. This is Columbus and Lombard, ain't it, Jimbo?"

Jimbo laughed loudly in the mist. "No, but if you start running now, you'll get there before I spank you, you yellow-bellied North Beacher!"

"Now just who do you think you're talking to like that, Jimbo?"

"You, Seamus Grogan, spawned by a tinker and a crosseyed goat, and about to meet the banshee if you're not out of sight by the time I've counted to ten."

"Aw, Jimbo."

"One, you sniveling pile of cat shit!"

"Come on, boys, Jimbo's not in a friendly mood tonight."

"Two and still counting, you pack of turd-eaters!"

And then the gang was moving off fast, so Longarm stepped over to the frightened Chinaman and helped him to his feet. The one called Jimbo and the three shorter figures with him moved forward. Jimbo took Fong Sing by the other arm and said, "Let me have him. I know where he lives, and he's afraid of strange white men."

"I noticed. Did you say you were one of Buckley's Lambs, Jimbo?"

"No. *They* did. What's it to you?"

"I know Boss Buckley. Met him a while back when I was here in Frisco on other business. I'd like to talk to him again, but you likely know he ain't an easy man to get to."

"Dangerous is what you mean, if he don't want to see you," Jimbo answered. "What did you say your name was, cowboy?"

"I'm Custis Long. Boss Buckley knows me."

"Well, and I'm Jimbo Corbett, and I don't. Come with us while we get this poor old heathen home, and maybe I'll take you to Boss Buckley and maybe I won't. You seem like a decent enough stranger, but you're still a stranger and your name sounds downright Protestant!"

So they fell in together and walked the shivering Chinaman down the street and up a narrow dark alley that doglegged all over creation and smelled like someone was cooking something peculiar. As he opened a gate, Jimbo told Longarm, "His relations will try to reward us. So I'll say right now you're not to take anything but a cup of tea or a rice cake. Fong's Tong has already made their deal with us, and it wouldn't be right to make them pay twice."

Longarm nodded and said, "I know about Buckley's protection racket."

"Bite your tongue! There's no racket about it! The boss keeps order in the streets the police don't see fit to patrol. He's a darling saintly man, and you just saw we give good service."

"Yeah, and if this Fong Sing had been caught by those rascals over in their neighborhood?"

Jimbo shrugged and said, "He'd have no business over by Telegraph Hill. We've agreed that Chinamen don't get roughed up around *here*. Jasus, we can't be everywhere, you know."

The frightened Chinese called out as he recognized his own back door in the murky light. The door opened and the yard filled with shouting sons and daughters of Han. Somehow, Longarm found himself in a well-lit kitchen, and a pretty Chinese gal was filling him with tea while Jimbo explained about the misadventure of Fong Sing. Longarm was surprised when he caught his first good look at Jimbo Corbett in the light. Jimbo was a big tough Irish type, which was only to be expected, but he had the girlish face of a fourteen-year-old boy. The kids with him, now that he could see them, seemed like teenagers too. He wondered how old the other gang had been. He'd pictured them as full-grown toughs back there in the fog, but Jesus, what if he'd gunned a mess of street Arabs? How the hell would that look in an official report?

The Chinese to whom Jimbo had been talking came over to Longarm. He was man of about thirty, and spoke better

English than Longarm as he said, "The Lambs have told me you stepped in to defend my grandfather even before they arrived, Mr. Long. As you may have guessed, Fong Sing is new to this city and confused by its ways. The house of Fong is in your debt."

Longarm raised the cup of tea the pretty gal had served him, and said, "I'd say we're even. I only done what came natural."

The grave Chinese said, "Alas, I know all too well what some Americans find natural when they see a weak old man in a pigtail. Jimbo tells me you are not a member of his group. Please come with me."

So Longarm shrugged, put down the cup, and followed Fong out to a hallway. He noticed Jimbo tailing him, but didn't comment. The grandson led him through a beaded curtain into a dimly lit but luxuriously stocked shop. The glass cases were filled with jewelry and curios of ivory, jade, and gold. The owner turned with a smile and said, "I am Fong Mao, and I can modestly say I deal in better wares than most shops along Grant Avenue. There is nothing here I value more than my poor old grandfather, but if there should be anything in any of these cases you fancy, it is yours."

Longarm saw Jimbo scowling at him from the doorway. He shook his head at Fong and said, "I couldn't hardly do that, sir. I don't know all that much about oriental jewelry, but I can see there ain't anything here worth under a hundred dollars, and I didn't do that much."

Fong looked hurt, slid open a glass case filled with gold jewelry, and said, "Please, a ring for a lady you value? These are modestly priced, I assure you, but they are eighteen-karat gold, made by hand."

Longarm shook his head, then frowned and asked, "Hold on a minute. Are you saying you know a goldsmith personal?"

Fong bowed modestly and said, "I am the goldsmith, Mr. Long. Most of those pieces were cast by me in my basement shop. That is why I suggested one for your reward. It seems more fitting that the hand that saved my grandfather should be paid back by the craft of my own hands in turn."

Longarm said, "I got a better notion, if you insist on being so neighborly, Mr. Fong. I got something here I'd like you to look at."

He took out the fake twenty-dollar gold piece that Billy Vail had given him, and handed it to Fong. The goldsmith looked blankly at it and said, "I don't understand. Why would you want to give me a twenty-dollar coin?"

"I ain't giving it to you. I aim to take it back. It's evidence. Can you tell me why?"

Young Jimbo joined them, scowling, as Fong held the coin up to the light and said, "Evidence? Evidence of what?"

"Are you a lawman, Long?" growled Jimbo.

"Close enough," Longarm admitted. "Let the man look at the play-pretty, son."

Fong fingered the coin, bit it, and said, "It seems a perfectly good twenty-dollar double eagle. Do you mind if I test it?"

"I sure wish you would."

Fong moved along the counter to a flap gate, and stepped through it to open a drawer as Jimbo Corbett insisted, "What's this guff about you being a copper, Long?" Then he frowned at Longarm's lapel and added, "Jasus, I never spotted that in the bad light, but you've been decorated by the Emperor Norton! You must have been wearing your blues when he done it, eh?"

Longarm saw that Fong was taking his time with the vials and touchstone, so he told Jimbo, "I'm not a Frisco copper. I'm a federal agent, and I told you I know Boss Buckley, so keep it under your hat. I'd forgot about this medal. A man in an admiral's hat pinned it on me for some fool reason. Do you know him, Jimbo?"

"Sure, everyone in Frisco knows the Emperor Norton. He's a harmless lunatic. They say he used to be a rich man. An Englishman or something. He lost everything he had in the big crash of the seventies. It drove him crazy and he tried to kill himself. They had him locked up awhile for his own good. And then one morning he calmed down and said it was all a mistake, for it was the Emperor of the United States and Protector of Mexico he was. He's been like that ever since."

"I reckon that feels better than being bankrupt. But how does the old man live, if he lost all his money in the crash?"

Jimbo laughed and said, "Hell, we can't let our emperor starve, can we? Sure, there's not a restaurant in town that won't feed the Emperor Norton. He fancies military dress, so there's a tailor on Montgomery who's honored to provide him with uniforms. A couple of hotels allow him to stay free, when it's cold out, but he mostly wanders about like the poor lost loon he is."

Fong rubbed the counterfeit coin on his touchstone and murmured, "Very good, if it's an alloy. Let us see what the acid tells us."

As Longarm and Jimbo watched, the goldsmith delicately dropped some liquid from a vial onto the edge of the double eagle as it rested on the touchstone.

Fong looked up, his eyes alight with interest. "It's not gold. But I've never seen such a convincing counterfeit. This is a very wicked thing, Mr. Long. I'd probably accept this over the counter as the genuine article, and I'm a goldsmith!"

Longarm nodded and asked, "How do you know you haven't?"

The Chinese started to object. Then he looked stricken and dropped out of sight below the counter, to reappear in a moment with a nondescript metal box. He opened it, took out a dozen gold coins, and spread them on his counter, muttering to himself in Cantonese. Jimbo looked confused, so Longarm said, "The Treasury men think these fakes have only been passed in exclusive shops in fancy parts of town. That might be because damned few waterfront bartenders test like the banks and, as you see, folks in these parts don't use banks all that much."

Fong suddenly cried, "I have been swindled! Look! Three of the double eagles I took in payment are counterfeit, too!"

Longarm nodded sympathetically. "You said I could have anything in your shop, so I'm impounding them as evidence, Mr. Fong. I don't reckon you could say for certain who passed these off on you, eh?"

The Chinese shook his head numbly and replied, "Of course not. There are a week's receipts in this cashbox, and since I sell valuable wares, a twenty-dollar piece doesn't excite me. Or at least it didn't until now! How could I have been such a fool? I handle gold all day!"

"Well, you just said the fakes were good, Mr. Fong."

"They are the work of a devil! If you are a lawman, you must catch the fiends who coined these things, Mr. Long!"

"That's what I'm trying to do. You're the expert on making things out of gold, Mr. Fong. I'd sure admire hearing any ideas you have on how the rascals are doing it so fine."

Fong sighed deeply. "Forgive me, I was terribly shaken to think I'd been taken in like a fool. The alloy is mostly brass, with some German silver. One can obtain it from any jeweler's supply house, and as you see, it's the same shade as ordinary

38

bullion. Let me see what I can tell you of the workmanship."

Fong took out a jeweler's loupe and screwed it in one eye as he held the fake coin Longarm had given him up to the light. "Oh, devilishly good," he said. "It's not a casting." He took a real coin from his cashbox, compared them, and added, "Better than good. It's perfect. But perfection is just not possible."

"Sure it's possible," Longarm said. "You're holding it in your hand. The rascals have copied one of Uncle Sam's dies."

Fong took another coin for comparison as he shook his head and said, "You don't understand. Any jeweler could cast a nearly perfect replica of a double eagle, but these counterfeits are stamped from blank alloy in a steel die. The milled edges have the same number of corrugations. This almost invisible letter near the date is the code of the San Francisco Mint, and— Oh!"

Fong picked up another fake, nodded, and tried his glass on another as Longarm asked, "Find something interesting?"

"Yes," Fong said, looking up and removing the loupe from his eyes. "They are not only stamped from the same pattern, they are stamped from the same set of dies. They are all dated 1878, and there is the same little nick in the numeral 7."

"Then the diemaker who copied some real coin slipped with his tool on the date's seven, right?"

Fong shook his head and said, "I don't think so. I think the counterfeiters are using a real mint die. No master diemaker who could copy that exactly would make such a mistake, nor would he dare to risk exposure by letting such an error pass. A man that good could make an honest fortune without turning to crime."

Fong turned the coin over and studied the obverse long and hard before he nodded and said, "Ah, so, there is a bad scratch on this side. The scratch is in the die, not from wear and tear on the coin itself. The pressed metal is raised instead of depressed. I think I see how they got their hands on the real government die set. The dies are damaged as well as out of date. The mint must have discarded an old set of dies, and the criminals somehow got their hands on them!"

Longarm frowned. "The way I hear it, the mints don't just chuck old dies and plates in the trash out back. Ain't they supposed to be destroyed when Uncle Sam is done with 'em?"

Fong shrugged and asked, "How should I know? I don't

work for the U.S. Mint. I certainly wish they'd been more careful with *this* set of dies! Except for a few tiny imperfections and the fact that they're not gold, these counterfeits are perfect replicas of the real thing!"

Longarm nodded and said, "Yeah, only now that you know what to look for, you'll be able to spot any more as come your way, right?"

"Of course. I'll tell my fellow merchants what to look for, and—"

"I sure wish you wouldn't do that, Mr. Fong," Longarm interrupted. "I don't want to put the rascals out of business just yet. They owe us for three lawmen. By the powers vested in me by these United States, I'm deputizing you as an assistant federal agent. I'll put her in writing for you before I leave."

Fong laughed incredulously and said, "I'm not even a U.S. citizen, if I understand the laws of California rightly."

Longarm said, "Well, I ain't working for the State of California. I'm a deputy U.S. marshal and you're citizen enough for me. What I want you to do if you get any more of these fake coins is to play dumb but remember who passed them on you. If you can get an address, that's even better. Maybe you can offer to deliver or something, right?"

Fong nodded and offered, "I can do better than that. You may have noticed I have many relatives. I will have anyone who offers me a false double eagle followed to his den of thieves!"

"All right, but let's not get carried away and mistake an honest person for a crook. Some folks packing these fake double eagles might have come by them innocent, just like you did."

"I understand. We shall follow them discreetly, and of course I know who my respectable clients are. How will I get word to you if I need to?"

"I'll come by from time to time. Meanwhile, I'll check into the Palace, if only to have a mailing address here in town. I'd best write you up some orders, deputizing you. Jimbo here can witness that I swore you in."

The young Irishman laughed and asked, "Are you serious? You know what I am, don't you?"

Longarm took out his notebook and started writing as he answered, "I told you, I know Boss Buckley. Buckley's Lambs ain't exactly a legal organization, but you ain't a bad gang,

40

and there's no federal wants out on you, so what the hell."

He finished his dubiously legal document and added, "Sign here, where I wrote 'Witness.' I ain't sure how you swear a Chinaman, but as long as we both say I swore him in, the formalities don't matter much."

So Jimbo made his mark and Longarm handed the paper to Fong, saying, "Here, you likely won't need this unless I get killed or something. But if your helping me causes you trouble with the local law, it might help."

Fong gravely folded the paper and put it away, saying, "I am honored to know you trust a man of my race. I find it very unusual too."

"I know what you mean," Longarm said. "I have a Chinese laundryman in Denver who told me about the riots here. We had some bad ones in Denver too. In this particular case, I'd be less likely to trust you if you were white. There's just no way this could be a setup."

"Setup?"

"Folks are always fibbing to me, in my line of work, and it tends to make a man broody and suspicious. But you couldn't have been expecting me, and I doubt like hell you'd risk your poor old granddad just to get to know me, even if you had some crystal ball telling you I was coming down the cableway about the time those punks started pestering him."

Fong gasped and said, "You do think like a chess master, but I assure you—"

"Hold on, that's what I just said. The game's generally more like checkers anyway. But it pays to think sneaky until you mull things over once or twice, and I just done that, so that's why I figure I'm among friends."

He unpinned the medal the Emperor Norton had given him, and added, "While I'm on the subject of covering all bets, what can you tell me about these play-pretties the old lunatic's so free with?"

Fong laughed and said, "Those are well known here in San Francisco, Deputy Long. They're made of cheap pot metal."

"I doubted it was real silver. But how does the old madman make 'em?"

"He doesn't. Some novelty shop makes them for him as a gentle joke."

"Another shop prints money for the Emperor Norton," Jimbo cut in. "No bills worth more than fifty cents, of course.

Sure, and it saves the old man having to beg. Most saloons and beaneries in town will honor his majesty's scrip within reason."

Longarm smiled thinly as he observed, "This sure is a friendly town to lunatics. Do either of you know who makes the Emperor's medals and money?"

They both looked blank. Jimbo said, "Och, it's up the wrong tree you'd be after barking. The stuff's not anything like real."

Fong added, "You can see for yourself this so-called medal is crudely made with the sort of stamp one uses for dog collars and political buttons. I've seen the Emperor's so-called fifty-cent bills. They're run off on a hand press by some job printer."

Longarm put the pot-metal medal away, along with the more dangerous coins he took from the countertop, as he said, "You're both likely right, but I'll ask the Emperor about it the next time I see him. Are you ready to take me to Boss Buckley, Jimbo?"

Jimbo shook his head and said, "Sure, I'd catch me death in lumps if I was to take a lawman to himself uninvited. But I'll tell him you're looking for him, and if he wants to see you, you'll be hearing about it. It's at the Palace you said you was staying?"

Longarm shrugged and said, "I'll hire a box to get mail there, for now. That is, if I can find the infernal place in all this fog."

Jimbo offered to point Longarm in the right direction, so Fong let them out the front way. The street outside was pitch black, even without the fog, and Longarm was disoriented.

Jimbo said, "This is Grant Avenue."

"It can't be," Longarm said. "I crossed it just before I run across that other gang rawhiding old Fong Sing."

Jimbo laughed. "We doubled back through the alleyways. Grant runs north and south, but you can't get to Market on it, for a spur of Nob Hill brings it to a dead end just to the south. They've been talking for years of a tunnel through the hill, but they've been talking of street lamps for Chinatown, too. Come on, I'll put you on California, for it's lit and will take you to Columbus. After that you're on your own, for sure I'm a creature of darkness and Columbus is lit. You just follow it and you'll wind up on Market, close to the Palace."

As they started walking north, Longarm asked Jimbo who he was afraid might spot him in the more civilized parts of

42

town, and Jimbo replied, "Och, it's not the law, for Buckley's Lambs and the coppers have a certain understanding. But if someone from me own neighborhood recognized me and word got back to me sainted mother that I'm not really attending night school like I told her, she'd be after saying three Hail Marys and breakin' a broom over me head!"

Longarm laughed and said, "Mothers are like that. When I rode off to the War, I told mine I was going hunting. It wasn't exactly a lie, but she was sore as hell anyway."

They came to a street lamp and the cableway that Longarm remembered, although the fog seemed even thicker now. Jimbo pointed downhill and said, "It's not far to Columbus. I'll tell Boss Buckley you was asking about his health."

Longarm would have shaken hands on it, but the oversized street Arab had dematerialized in the fog like a ghost. So Longarm shrugged and started down California Street. He'd gone but a few steps when he heard the rapid-fire clanging of a cable car bell as the conveyance crossed an intersection. He peered into the fog and saw a ghostly glow coming up the hill along the tracks. It was making smart time, and he could see how riding one of the fool things would beat walking up that long slope, if and when he ever went back to see how Calvinia and the widow Doyle were getting along. He stopped to admire the wonders of modern science as the cable car rumbled past, its running lights and the coal-oil lamp inside the passenger compartment glowing wanly on the brick walls to either side, thus offering some proof that he was still in a city instead of the Great Dismal Swamp. The car was crowded, despite the hour. He figured nobody else with a lick of sense walked up Nob Hill, either. He lit a smoke as he stared after the cable car, and was about to turn and resume his downslope stroll when he suddenly frowned and ducked into a doorway, shaking out the match. The glow of the cable car's lights had momentarily outlined a figure up the slope, and he doubted it was anyone he knew.

Longarm waited. He'd made his move with the blackness of the foggy street behind him, so the other couldn't know where he was. There was a better-than-even chance he'd been spooked by some innocent pedestrian, for there was no law saying nobody else was allowed to walk down a main street. But it wouldn't hurt to let the fellow just pass on, whoever he might be.

He didn't. Longarm waited, then waited some more, but there were no footsteps coming down the slope. Longarm nodded grimly and muttered, "You're wondering why you stopped hearing my boot heels on the walk, eh? Well, let's see what we can do to reassure you, you son of a bitch!"

Chapter 4

Longarm stayed in the doorway and started marking time in place, like a soldier on parade. He tried to make his footsteps fade after starting out loud, and it must have worked, for, as he stood barely shuffling, he heard a cautious scrape of shoe leather up the slope. This was getting interesting as hell, so Longarm drew his .44 and moved his feet more softly, like he was getting far ahead. It worked. The man trailing him threw caution aside and moved faster to catch up, figuring Longarm was getting away from him.

As the man passed Longarm's doorway, the big lawman stepped out and said, "Freeze or you're a dead man, friend!"

The barely visible figure spun around and tried to hand Longarm a big bouquet of fire and buckshot. But Longarm had been braced for it, and moved sideways after speaking. So the double charge of number-nine buck tore a huge, ragged hole in the woodwork of the doorway as Longarm blew some holes of his own into the figure behind the twin barrels. The shotgunner dropped his weapon one way and thudded his head to the pavement another.

Longarm wearily pushed his Stetson back on his forehead as he addressed the corpse. "I told you you'd be dead, but nobody ever listens."

He cocked his head, his ears still ringing from the gunplay between brick walls. But if anybody in this part of town was interested in the sounds of guns in the night, they didn't seem to be doing much about them. He walked over to the man he'd shot, rolled him on his back with his boot toe, took out a match, and struck it on his thumbnail. The dead face staring up at him looked at peace with the world and belonged to a total stranger. Longarm ran it through the mental file he kept of federal lawbreakers and drew another blank. He holstered his weapon, dropped to one knee, and went through the jasper's pockets, where he found a wallet and some shotgun shells. He pocketed them to look over later. Then he rose, went over to the shotgun, and picked it up.

It was a cheap mail-order twin with both barrels sawed off. Tracing it would be a waste of time. There was a rusty old twelve-gauge like this in damned near any attic. So he gripped it by the barrels and busted it on the pavement before tossing it aside. Then, since nobody hereabouts seemed to want any further discussion of the matter, Longarm walked away, reloading his Colt as he went.

He walked across a few more narrow streets before he came to what had to be Columbus Avenue; there were street lights, and a lonesome dray wagon was moving north towards Fisherman's Wharf. He headed south. He'd only gone a few steps when he heard a distant police whistle.

He sighed and crossed the avenue to cut down a dark side street, muttering, "Some beat copper sure seems nosy about gunshots down the block. If a paddy wagon's coming, it's coming up Columbus, old son."

The ground had leveled out, and he knew he wasn't far from the waterfront now. He knew the broad Embarcadero ran all the way to the foot of Market Street, so he decided that was his best bet. He couldn't see where he was, but it didn't matter. When he came to the Bay, he'd either fall in and drown or find his way to the Palace.

He knew he was right when he came to some railroad tracks and crossed them. He found himself on a broad expanse of cobblestones and stopped to light a smoke and get his bearings. A honkytonk piano was tinkling somewhere in the night, and he homed on the sound, doubting that anybody would be playing a piano in the dark.

A little red glow swam into view in the fog ahead. As he

46

drew closer, the light got brighter and the piano louder. He saw that the source of the glow was a red lantern over a door in the side of what looked like a warehouse. But the light and the piano said it was another kind of house entirely.

Longarm was about to pass on when the door opened and two gents came out, weaving slightly as they held one another up. He'd seen beyond them into a well-lit and crowded barroom, so he knew it was a high-toned whorehouse, like the Silver Dollar in Denver. He needed a fancy gal like he needed a head cold, but he was likely to have the sniffles come morning if he didn't cut this infernal fog in his nose with some decent liquor fumes. So he went to the door and tried the latch. It opened. The madam seemed to be in good with the powers that were.

Nobody paid him much mind as he went inside. As he'd figured, the main room was big and crowded, with a bar running down one wall. The pictures on the wall behind the bar were a mite gamy for saloon art, but otherwise a greenhorn might have taken the place for a local drinking establishment. Some men were playing cards at a table near the piano. The piano player was a gal wearing pink tights and hennaed hair. She played pretty decently, considering the bored look on her painted face. Longarm bellied up to the bar, and the bartender turned out to be a gal too, wearing an apron and not much else. Her hair was canary yellow and she had a French beauty mark pasted to one painted cheek. She asked Longarm what his pleasure might be, and he said, "I'll have Maryland rye, if you got it. How much are the drinks in this place?"

The barmaid said, "Drinks are on the house. What's your pleasure?"

"I just told you, ma'am. Maryland or any old kind of rye."

She looked disgusted, put a hotel tumbler in front of him, and poured a heroic drink, saying, "This is our regular house redeye. I don't know if it was made in Maryland or hell. The booze ain't the pleasure most men come here for. I meant what kind of screwing do you like. Old-fashioned costs two dollars. French is three and Greek is five. We got six white gals, a Mex, a squaw, and two niggers."

"No Chinese?"

"Shit, no, this is a respectable place."

He laughed and took a sip of the godawful stuff she'd served. "I can see that. I'll just set here a spell and be on my way. It's only fair to warn you, I'm only looking for a dry place and a drink, so I'll pay you for this if you like."

She shook her head disdainfully. "I ain't got time for small change, cowboy. You just do whatever you've a mind to. I got others to serve."

Longarm nodded his thanks and turned to lean his back against the bar, the glass in his hand. San Francisco sure was a friendly town. One of the gents playing cards got up to leave. The dealer looked Longarm's way and raised an eyebrow. Longarm shook his head, so the game went on a man short. It was getting late, and playing cards with strangers wasn't the smartest way to kill an evening.

A painted gal in long underwear and a Spanish shawl came down the stairs, looking tired, but she brightened when she spotted the new face in the crowd. She came over smiling, so he smiled right back. It didn't hurt, and she was sort of pretty in a weary way. Her blond hair was black at the roots, and her big brown eyes had seen too much for a gal that young. She walked boldly up to him and put her hands on her hips. "Howdy, handsome," she said. "My name is Barbara, and I'm the best screw on the Barbary Coast."

"I'll bet you are. You can call me Custis and I didn't know this was the Barbary Coast. I thought we was in Frisco."

She laughed and said, "I can see you're a stranger, for I 'spect I've screwed every good-looking gent in Frisco by now. The Barbary Coast ain't exactly a place, it's a state of mind."

"Oh, you mean anywhere rough on the waterfront?"

"Now you got it, handsome. Fisherman's Wharf and the Matson Piers ain't Barbary, even though they're on the water. You look like a brute, but I'm game if you don't want me to do nothing queer. I mean, I might give a French lesson to a friend who's had a bath recent, but I don't go in for cruel stuff and I don't take it in the back door. I'm built sort of small for a gal in this business, as you'll find out upstairs whenever you're ready."

He smiled wistfully. "Your words sure are flattering, Miss Barbara, but I'll have to pass on your offer tonight."

"What's the matter with me? Ain't I pretty enough for you?" she asked, sounding a mite hurt.

"Miss Barbara, you are a vision of love, but I just ain't up to a gal at the moment."

She blinked in surprise. "Well, I never. I took you for a

normal gent, but I might have known you'd heard about that sissy boy we got up in the cribs. He's busy servicing a stevedore right now, but I'll tell him we got another cornholer waiting at the bar when he's done."

"Hold on," Longarm said. "You got me wrong, Miss Barbara. I do it right when I do it at all."

"Oh, you want want to look the other gals over before you make up your mind, huh? That's fair, but you'll see I'm the fairest in the land and I can show you a hell of a good time, too."

"I have no doubt of that, and if there was anybody prettier than you, it would scare me. If I was out to get laid, you'd be my first choice. But, well, if I confess something delicate, will you keep it a secret?"

She looked interested, so he said, "I have been used dreadful by a woman already tonight. I have just escaped her vile clutches and I'm as wrung out as a dishrag. I don't think I could get it up again for Miss Lillian Russell or even you. So please don't take my refusal of your offer personal."

The whore laughed. "You've been to another house already?"

"Worse. I was seduced by a hard-up widow woman who seemed to think I was a circus acrobat. If there is a position I ain't been used in, I ain't never heard of it. But let us say no more about it, for the memory is painful and my poor bones still ache."

She laughed and said, "You're crazy but cute. I could probably show you some positions that rank amateur wouldn't have the nerve to try, but I follow your drift. Gals who do it free do have a way of getting all the good out of a man. But listen, I told you I Frenched, and—"

"I'd be wasting your valuable time and likely feel like a fool," he cut in, reaching in his pocket. He said. "To show you I'm a sport, I'll treat you to some ribbon bows or something, and mayhap another night when I've recovered from my ordeal, we can try it your way."

He handed her one of the fake double eagles. She looked startled and made it vanish as she moved closer and whispered, "Are you crazy? That was twenty dollars!"

He said, "I know. Ain't you worth twenty?"

"Good God, you can get a fancy whore at the Palace for a whole night at those prices!"

"Well, you're mighty fancy looking, Miss Barbara, and some night we'll get to know each other better. Let's call that double eagle a retainer and say no more about it."

She smiled wanly and said, "Jesus, you don't look drunk, but you must be. I ain't about to give it back, but I sure do thank you. Not just for the money, but for the flattery. I know you don't mean it, but it feels nice."

She stood on tiptoe, kissed him on the cheek, and said, "I got to make the rounds. But if you change your mind, remember you've bought a night's worth!"

He chuckled as he watched her walk off, swinging her rump under the longjohns. She wasn't built badly, and he knew that some night alone in a sleeping bag, he'd wonder if he'd missed anything. But even if he'd missed a good lay, it was smart to pass on low-down whores. He'd never caught a dose so far, knock wood, but he knew that half these gals had the pox and the other half could give you blue balls.

He'd given her the counterfeit coin for two reasons. He'd wanted to get rid of her politely and he'd wanted to see if Treasury was right about it being hard to pass fake twenties in this neck of the woods. He saw now that Treasury was too smart for its own good. There were more of the fake double eagles in circulation than Treasury thought, which should cheer hell out of them when he wired it in. Nobody in this place had the know-how to detect mock gold, and the coin would be passed on and on until it wound up in some bank or fancy store that took the trouble to examine its money closely. Figuring they only had to stamp out a score of the counterfeits to make a thousand dollars, the gang was making out pretty good, even if they had a big payroll to meet. That reminded him that they'd just lost a member. Or had they?

He took out the wallet he'd taken off the dead man with the sawed-off scattergun. There were a couple of paper bills and a railroad ticket in it, but no identification. The railroad ticket was likely intended for a quick getaway. It was Southern Pacific to Pueblo de Los Angeles. Calvinia had said her broody inlaws were from Weed, up in northern California. But that didn't mean much, one way or the other. A man on the run didn't head for home if he had a lick of sense. He put the wallet away and took another sip of his awful drink. He didn't read much sign that led anywhere meaningful. Two Treasury agents were just missing and might have been gunned down with anything.

The one found dead on the streets of Frisco had been hulled in the back by a .45, and the shotgunner hadn't worn sidearms. Of course, a man could switch weapons easily enough. A shotgun made a nice killing weapon at night, but tended to attract attention in broad daylight. So the man he'd shot could have been one of the gang, or he could have been working for somebody after Calvinia.

Longarm didn't like it either way. If anybody was after the widow woman, why were they chasing him all over creation? He frowned as he wondered if the two gals were safe up atop Nob Hill. If the jasper with the shotgun had followed him from Calvinia's house after shooting at him earlier, he knew where Calvinia was right now, and— No, he didn't. He was dead. He hadn't gone into the widow Doyle's shooting, for Longarm would have heard it halfway down the slope, and he hadn't. There was no other way a man could get past that frigid Gwynn Doyle's big oak door, either. The gals were likely bedded down by now, and he'd look dumb pounding on the door to make sure at this hour.

He studied the glass and muttered to himself: "Try her this way. He wasn't after Calvinia at all. He followed you from the docks after your boat put in, meaning somebody here was expecting you. A man afoot can follow a hansom cab up a steep hill if he puts his back into it. He saw you go in and hunkered down to see if you were coming out. He missed the first time, ran off a ways, and then cut back to hunker some more. He figured you might go out the back, so he suckered you and trailed you to the other house. But why didn't he— Sure, he wanted to gun you when you was alone. Calvinia would have required at least one barrel of buck, and you just proved two wasn't hardly enough to stop a growed man with a .44 riding his hip. He was trailing you when you mixed with the Chinese business. He couldn't shoot with the Lambs all about, so he just ducked in a doorway and waited, and then, when he had you alone again, he messed up again. His target was you, old son. There's likely nobody gunning at all for Calvinia, but it sure was an interesting experience."

He finished his drink and was about to leave when the whore called Barbara came back, stood next to him, and said quietly, "Don't look around, but there's a man making war talk about you. Are you called Longarm, honey?"

He stiffened but didn't move as he said, "Sometimes. Who's

been using my name in vain, Miss Barbara?"

"Keep your hatbrim low. There's two of them, over in the left-hand corner, seated alone at that table. See 'em?"

Through the haze of cigar smoke he studied the two men she meant, as he said, "I do. Don't know them. But they dress sort of cow, and I've met a lot of folks in passing. You said they knew my name?"

"One of them does. The other says he ain't sure it's you. They was arguing about it as I passed just now. I didn't linger, but from the little I heard, one of 'em thinks he can take you, and his pal's trying to talk him out of it. The one in the gray cowboy hat is the gent who don't like you. The fat one with him said lots of bastards wear brown suits and Colorado hats. Do you want me to get you out the back way? We could link arms like I was taking you up to the cribs, and—"

"No, I want you to get clear of me, Miss Barbara," he told her, adding, "I am much obliged for your warning, and I'm in a good position here. There's nobody behind me and I'm facing them natural. So they're waiting for me to do something dumb, like turning my back on them. I'll just stand pat and you'll be doing us both a favor by staying out of our line of fire. I can't see the barmaid behind me, so get her down the bar a ways, and when it starts getting noisy, duck both your pretty heads."

She moved away slightly as she marveled, "My God, you're cool. I could get the professor to back your play, handsome. He's an old gunhand."

"No, thanks. Just do as I say. I'm an old gunhand too, and this ain't his fight."

Barbara nodded and moved off casually to warn the barmaid.

With seeming nonchalance, Longarm hooked one heel on the brass rail and braced himself to move sideways in a hurry when the time came to move at all. Both of the men in the corner were looking his way as they jawed together. He nodded pleasantly to let them know he saw them. There was no sense taking all night, and it seemed time to fish or cut bait.

The lean and hungry-looking one in the gray Stetson nodded back and rose as if he'd made up his mind. The other one hunkered lower in his seat and called out, "Don't do it, Waco!" in a tone that made the piano player stop playing. The redheaded female pianist turned, saw the gray hat moving as slowly and ominously as lava toward the door, and got up quickly to go powder her nose or something. The sudden silence wasn't lost on the other men in the place, and chairs started scraping on the floor as folks got out of the way. The one called Waco stopped a few paces from Longarm, facing him in a cleared lane of dead silence. After a moment, he spoke.

"They calls you Longarm in Dodge, don't they?"

Longarm said, "In Dodge and lots of places, old son. I disremember meeting you before, though."

"You never met me. You met my cousin, Bang Tail Bob from McLennan County. You remember him, you son of a bitch?"

Longarm nodded pleasantly. "Sure. He called me a son of a bitch too. But that wasn't what the fight was about. Bang Tail Bob sure was a caution when it come to running brands, wasn't he?"

"You killed him. He left a fine woman to mourn for his life, and I told her I'd clean your plow if ever we met up."

"I can see how a man might say such things at such a time, Waco. But your cousin was a cow thief, and getting gunned by lawmen goes with such misguided notions. I sure hope you've had time to reconsider since you made your brag. It ain't like she's watching at the moment, you know."

Waco licked his lips as he studied the cross-draw rig half exposed under Longarm's frock coat. The tall deputy still had both elbows on the bar, hands hanging limp. Waco's own right hand hovered like a hawk near his side-draw S&W as he said, "I wasn't bragging. I meant it. You can slap leather anytime now, Longarm!"

Longarm regarded him mournfully. "You'd best think this through, old son," he said. "Bang Tail Bob was a pro who didn't waste time jawing all night at a man, and I still beat him. They might have forgot to tell you he called me a son of a bitch *after* I shot him, not before. Those were his last words, as a matter of fact. So I'm advising you neighborly to reconsider. You're acting awful dumb, cowboy, but I'm a good-natured cuss, so I won't kill you if I don't have to."

Waco shouted, "You have to *try*, goddamn your eyes!" as he went for the gun at his side. Then the derringer that Longarm had been palming in his right fist barked twice, loudly for such a little gun, and Waco staggered back, dead on his feet, as Longarm dropped the derringer on the floor and whipped out his .44 to see if anybody wanted a serious fight.

The dead man's fat friend was on his feet with both hands in the air as he screamed in a high, girlish voice, "I wasn't in on it, honest to God!"

"I noticed," Longarm said. "Sit down and keep your hands on the table till the local law arrives. The rest of you gents may as well know I'm a deputy U.S. marshal. The man on the floor there was the only rascal here I had reason to suspicion of anything. So it's over as soon as I make a statement for the coppers, and I won't be needing any witnesses if any of you are married gents who might not want to hang about till the constables get here."

A red-faced man in a business suit got up and said, "That's the nicest thing anybody's said to me all evening, and I'm taking you up on it, Marshal."

As he headed for the door, a dozen followed, but some of the regulars stayed to watch. A baldheaded bruiser with a baseball bat in one hand came out from a back room, but before he could say or do anything dumb, the whore called Barbara yelled, "It's all right, Professor. The one on his feet is the law, and a reasonable cuss besides. The one he just gunned started it."

The professor said, "Oh, hell, I do so wish our customers would stick to civilized screwing. Has anybody gone for the law?"

Somebody must have; the door opened just then and two blue-uniformed Frisco coppers came in as Longarm was putting his revolver away and picking up the derringer he'd dropped in the sawdust. One of them spotted the body on the floor and whistled softly. The professor pointed at Longarm and said, "Don't look at me, Ryan. He says he's law, too."

As the coppers approached him warily, Longarm said, "I'm a federal deputy, and what I'm reaching in my coat for is my ID. The gent oozing on the floor was called Waco, and the fight was left over from Dodge City, Kansas. He said he was kin to a cow thief killed resisting arrest back there. Now you know as much about it as I do."

He took out his wallet and opened it to show his ID and badge. The copper called Ryan nodded and said, "Your tale sounds reasonable, stranger. But what's a U.S. deputy doing on the Barbary Coast at this time of night?"

It was a good question, and Longarm was sore as hell that he'd blown his cover. But what the hell, if the gang knew he was in town, there seemed to be little point in sneaking about behind the police force. He kept his cards as close to his vest as common courtesy called for by saying, "I didn't come in here to investigate federal offenses. I'm off duty and I have the same feelings as any other natural man."

Barbara came over and locked an arm through his. "We was talking about his natural feelings when the one in the gray hat got ugly, Ryan." She turned her head and smiled up at Longarm. "You ready to go upstairs now, handsome?"

"Now just simmer down, Barbara," Ryan said. "I got to write this all down in my notebook for the captain before you two run off anywhere. Put your ID here on the bar and let me copy it off, Deputy. Where are you staying, in case the captain wants to talk to you about it in the morning?"

Longarm placed his wallet by the copper's notebook as he said something about the Palace Hotel. He didn't know what he was going to do if they didn't have a room for him there. All this unexpected gunplay was sure making it hard for a man to have some privacy. Billy Vail had ordered him to pussyfoot and not even tell the local federal authorities he was in town, but by morning his fool name would likely be in the newspapers. He'd have to study on some fake reason for being in town. As he answered Ryan's questions in terse sentences, he saw no need to discuss counterfeiting, at any rate.

The beat coppers seemed satisfied with his simple tale, and Ryan turned to ask if anyone in the room knew the late Waco's last name. The man who'd been with him didn't say anything as he stared at Longarm. Longarm didn't say anything, either. The fat boy had said he wanted no part of the action, and the fewer details the coppers reported, the fewer loose ends they'd ask him about later.

Ryan told the professor that the morgue wagon would come by in a spell, and added that he saw no reason to say they'd found the body inside the whorehouse, if the morgue men picked it up out on the Embarcadero. So the professor told Flo to give the coppers free drinks, and added that anything else they wanted was on the house, too. Ryan laughed and said, "Sure, we're on duty and the captain gives us hell for having pecker tracks on our blue pants. But we may remember, later. You still got that French gal working for you?"

The professor nodded and called two swampers from the back to drag the body out and lay fresh sawdust. Ryan handed

Longarm his wallet and said, "I'm sorry we had to be so fussy, but we're paid to keep things tidy in this town. Do you need any help getting back to Market Street?"

Longarm grinned down at Barbara and said, "No, thanks, I wasn't fixing on leaving just yet. You ready, Miss Barbara?"

She squeezed his arm and said, "Been ready for a coon's age, honey. Let's go."

So he let her haul him up the stairs as the folks in the main room tidied up after him. But when they were alone in the rancid hallway between the cribs, he said, "Miss Barbara, I wonder if you'd do me a favor."

"Honey, you got twenty dollars' worth of favors coming."

"You're wrong. Saving my life was worth at least that much. You said before that you could sneak me out a back way. I want to get out of these parts sort of quiet-like."

"Oh, don't you want to have a little fun first?"

"I want to," he lied, "but I ain't got time. A whole mess of gents know where I'm headed, and I aim to get there first and fort myself up proper."

"I understand," she said, "but I've a feeling we're both missing out on something grand. I don't feel the way about you that I'm supposed to feel with a customer."

"Thank you, Miss Barbara. I sort of feel for you too. But I got to go."

She sighed, led him to a rear stairwell, and said, "The back door's down that way. It opens from the inside. Did you mean it when you said you thought I was pretty?"

Longarm took his hat off gravely and said, "I did. More important, Miss Barbara, I think you're a good old gal." Then he bent to kiss her gently, and turned away to drop down the stairs as the little whore held a hand to her painted lips, trying not to cry.

The Palace, off Market Street, was fancied up like a New Orleans whore's dream, and the man behind the desk looked like a sissy. He sniffed suspiciously at Longarm when the tall deputy asked if they had any rooms for hire, and when Longarm allowed that he had no luggage but was willing to pay up front, the clerk said they were full up.

"Damn it," Longarm said, "I told some folks I'd be here, and it's late as hell."

56

"Have you tried the Seaman's Rest, down by the Ferry Building, sir?"

"Let's not rub it in, you snooty son of a bitch. I don't need a shave all that bad, and you are talking to a government official. Has anybody left me any messages?"

"How could they? You're not a guest at this hotel, Mister . . . ?"

"Long. Custis Long. I told some folks they could leave messages here for me. So look in your infernal box."

The room clerk blinked in surprise and asked, "Oh, are you the Deputy Marshal Long we've been expecting?"

"I hope so. But I didn't know I had a reservation."

The clerk turned, took a key from its pigeonhole, and handed it to him with a suddenly oily smile, saying, "Your room's made up, sir. If you'll be good enough to sign in." He opened a big hotel register and pointed at Longarm's name already inked in for room 222.

Longarm scrawled his John Hancock and asked, "How much do I owe you, pard? I'm sorry I fussed at you before."

"The room is already paid for, Deputy Long. You're booked for the next two weeks."

"I am, huh? Well, who in thunder done it? I didn't know I was coming here until recent as hell."

The clerk shrugged and replied, "I'm afraid I can't answer that, sir. The reservation was made earlier this evening, before I came on duty. I'll ring for a boy to take you up to your suite."

"Suite? Hell, I was just looking for a bunk and a place to hang my hat. But hold off on your scouts. I can find it my own self, once I send off some telegrams. Is there a Western Union office handy?"

The clerk pointed at a cross corridor off the lobby, and said the office was down that way. As Longarm headed for the telegraph office, he wondered what was going on in this loco town. His boss wouldn't have reserved him any suite in a fancy hotel and anyway he disremembered telling Billy Vail he planned to stay any particular place.

He found the telegraph office and sent a night letter to Billy Vail. The whole yarn would have been too expensive and wasn't all that important, since he had no more idea now about who was making funny money than he'd had when his boss had sent him out here. He told Vail where he was, and that working undercover wasn't worth a damn, since he'd been expected by the outlaws and questioned by the local law. He said he'd pick up return messages here at this office, and wished his chief a Merry Christmas. It wasn't anywhere near Christmastime, but what the hell.

He went back the way he'd come, part of the way, but he steered clear of the lobby. He found a stairway leading up to the second floor, and moved cautiously down the plush-carpeted hallway, coat open in case he needed to draw. He found 222. It was a corner suite. Pressing his ear to the hardwood panel, he listened sharp and heard the tinkle of ice in a glass.

He hunkered down to peer through the keyhole. He couldn't see anything but some dark red curtains over a window, but he smelled expensive cigar smoke coming from inside. He rose, drew his .44, and turned the knob quietly. The door was unlocked. He opened it and stepped in fast to slide his back along the wall as he covered the portly man seated in an overstuffed chair across the room. The man looked up morosely, with eyes that reminded Longarm of two oysters on the half shell.

Boss Buckley took the cigar from his mouth, raised the glass in his other hand, and said, "It's about time you got here. I've been waiting half the night."

Longarm saw that the old rascal was alone, so he shut the door behind him as he holstered his gun and said, "Howdy, Boss. Are you the one who hired me these rooms?"

Buckley shrugged and said, "I didn't exactly pay for them. Folks here in San Francisco like to do favors for a poor old blind man."

Longarm threw his hat on the bed across the room and moved to pour his own drink from the cut-glass decanter on the table at Buckley's side. The boss wasn't really blind; he could see dimly despite his cataracts, as many a gent who'd tried to take advantage of the tough old mutt had discovered the hard way. But he was a boss, and people did do him favors, whether they liked it or not. Boss Buckley was either the tacit head of the local Democratic machine or the secret head of the San Francisco underworld, depending on who you asked.

Longarm sat down with his own drink, tasted it, and said, "Hot damn, Maryland rye."

Buckley said, "I try to remember things like that. The last time you wanted to see me, it was rough as hell on my furniture and you bent hell out of my bodyguards, so when Jimbo Corbett said you were anxious to see me again, I thought I'd better meet you halfway. I'm not at the headquarters you busted up the last time you were here, by the way."

He took out a business card and handed it across to Longarm. "Here. If you need me, just tell the folks at this office and we'll work it out. What are you doing in my town again, Longarm?"

Longarm knew it would sound stupid to remark that this was a private conversation, so he put his cards on the table faceup by telling the old crook he was after some other crooks. Buckley listened quietly until Longarm had brought him up to date, then he said, "We were wondering who left that jasper with the busted shotgun near Chinatown. Might have known it was you."

"Can you fix it quiet with the police, Boss?"

"Hell, the copper who found the corpse never told anyone else. My Lambs got rid of the body as soon as they reported it to me. I hadn't heard about the shooting in the whorehouse, but don't worry. The precinct captain and me have an understanding. They won't bother you any further about it."

He took a sip of his drink before he added, "I still don't see what you want from me, Longarm. You didn't need a fix from me on either of those idiots who tried to take you. You're a paid-up lawman with a license to gun such rascals. My poor Lambs have to do things like that the hard way."

"It's your Lambs I want to talk to you about, Boss," Longarm said.

"Oh, shit, you don't think any of my boys are passing queer, do you? I've heard about the coiners you're after. That's penny-ante stuff next to *my* graft. My Lambs may have a reputation for playing rough, but they're decent young buckos, despite the Republican papers. Sure, they might bust a few wrong-thinking voters' heads, come election time. They may keep order on the docks with methods the sissies in Sacramento don't approve of, but I don't have thieves or swindlers working for me, damn it!"

"I know," Longarm said. "In your own way, you're a straight-shooting old bastard, and they say you don't break your word as often as the people that folks elect to public office in these parts."

Buckley nodded, mollified, and said, "Damned right. It's

a lesson I learned from old Boss Cameron, back in Penn State. He's the one who said an honest man is a man who stays bought. The newspapers never understood his point, so they treated it like a joke. But it ain't a joking matter, son. You can't run civilization sensible if even the crooks start fibbing to each other. But if you don't think my Lambs have gone into counterfeiting to cut out all the middle men, what do you want with 'em?"

"I'm trying to tell you, damn it. This other set of crooks are giving your fair city a bad name. They've gunned maybe three federal agents, and there's just no telling how complicated your payoffs are likely to get if they keep spreading fake double eagles all about. Washington figures there could be a double-dealer working for Uncle Sam and tipping off the crooks. They sure as hell knew I was coming, and my boss thought it was a secret. I can't be everywhere, and I ain't sure I can trust anybody here in town but you and your rowdy rascals. So I want them to help me."

"I thank you for your vote of confidence, and the boys would doubtless be honored, too. But even my smartest Lambs are bully boys and street brawlers, not detectives, Longarm!"

"I know what they are. They're all over town like a rat pack, and they know every dark alley and no-questions-asked roominghouse like I know the palm of my own hand. They make it their business to know what's going on behind closed doors, too."

"Of course. If it's profitable, we want a cut."

"So I hear, Boss. But the gang I'm after don't fit into sensible graft. They may have bribed some foolish government men, but counterfeiters don't buy police protection or offer to send a local judge's son through college."

"Hell, I know counterfeiting is federal, and you know I never mess with fixing federal crimes. It's too damned complicated and expensive, and look what happened to poor old U. S. Grant's bunch a few years back."

Before Longarm could answer, Boss Buckley took a grip on his cigar with bared teeth and growled, "I don't see the profit in helping you catch the coiners, either. Why the hell should I pull Washington's chestnuts out of the fire? They talk mean as hell about me in Washington."

"I know," Longarm commiserated. "Poor old President Hayes and his reform outfit make me wear this dumb necktie too. I ain't asking you to be patriotic, Boss. It's in your own interest to help me clean up this gang of sneaky moneymakers. I told you I was at least the fourth agent sent in on the q.t. by Uncle Sam, didn't I?"

"Yeah, so what?"

"So what if I fail or they kill me? You know Washington ain't going to just forget it. They'll send more federal men in, and if that don't work they'll send even more. Do you really want all sorts of strange lawmen who don't know you as well as I do writing up all sorts of reports to Washington on the ins and outs of the Frisco underworld?"

Buckley blanched and said, "You do have a way with words, son. You never told me how you worded your official report the time I lent you a helping hand with those highgraders over in the Mother Lode."

Longarm smiled broadly. "I took all the credit myself, Boss. I know it wasn't modest, but somehow I didn't think you wanted your name on any reports going to Washington."

"You are so right! I take it any help we give you this time ain't going to wind up anywhere in some infernal federal file?"

"Now you're starting to follow my drift, Boss. Do we have a deal?"

Buckley finished his drink, put down the glass, and said, "Name your pleasure, cowboy."

Longarm said, "Young Jimbo knows my plan about trailing anybody who's spotted passing queer. Will you tell him it's all right for him to work with me?"

"Sure. He seems to like you."

"Good. Jimbo and his boys can cover a lot more places than I could on my own. If I have need for other Lambs, I may need 'em sudden. So can you clear it so's they take orders from me?"

"Done. But you'll have to do their thinking for them. I don't pick 'em for brains."

"That's all right, I'll do the brain work. I ain't figured out what I'll do with a private army yet, but it's nice to know I have one. How do I get a hold of your young Jimbo when I need him?"

"I'll tell him to get hold of you. His mother is a Holy Mary, so don't ever look for him at home. She thinks he's going to night school to learn bookkeeping."

"I noticed he looked sort of smart for a thug. Ain't he sort of young to be out beating folks up for you, Boss?"

Buckley shrugged and said, "If they're big enough, they're old enough. And wait till you see Jimbo in an alley fight! The kid's still growing, but he's put many a waterfront bully on his back, and if he gets any bigger, he'll even scare me!"

Boss Buckley rose to his feet, and Longarm got up too, to shake on the deal. Longarm knew Billy Vail would have a fit if he ever found out the federal government had enlisted Buckley's Lambs as crime fighters, since even to Longarm it seemed a contradiction in terms. But a man sometimes had to fight fire with fire.

He showed the old boss out, locked the door after him, and started to shuck his duds, feeling tired as hell now that he'd done all he could for the night.

Throwing his things on the bed, he walked naked into the next room to make sure there weren't any surprises, and—wonder of wonders—he found that the suite came with its very own bath! They'd told him the hotel was first-rate, but this was a palace indeed. They even had soap, wrapped in sissified scented paper. He ran a hot tub and got in, and was sort of surprised at how much crud came out of his hide. By the time he'd finished, he was truly having a time staying awake. So he turned down the covers and slid his fresh-scrubbed body between linen sheets that smelled like lavender and felt so smooth they gave him a hard-on.

He laughed incredulously as he stared down at the tipi his pecker was making of the covers. He'd thought, when he left Calvinia, that he was shot for at least a few days, but there the bastard was, acting perky as hell, considering they were all alone in this bed.

He told his tool to cut out the foolishness and turned over to catch some shut-eye. But as he lay there wishing there was somebody else's head on the neighboring pillow, he couldn't help wondering what it would have been like with that friendly whore, Barbara. He caught himself peeling her out of that union suit, and it only followed that since the roots of her blond hair were black, the muff between her thighs would be black too, unless she shaved there, as some whores did to keep from catching crabs. She sure looked interesting with her love box shaved like that.

"Goddamm it, pecker," he said, "you've gone loco from overwork! You could have had that gal while you were awake.

But you have more sense when you're awake, so think about something else, dammit!"

He punched the pillow and turned on his other side, trying to forget what Barbara looked like. He knew he'd get even harder thinking about old Calvinia, so he grinned and pictured that stuck-up widow woman she was staying with instead. Picturing the frosty widow Doyle bareassed should have discouraged any fool erection. But it didn't. *She* looked sort of interesting too, with that severe bun on top of her blond head bobbing up and down like that. He snorted in disgust and muttered, "Oh, hell, if we're going to trifle with gals that the Good Lord knows are plain impossible, let's see how Lillian Russell looks in her birthday suit. You got about as much chance of sleeping with Lillian Russell as you have with that crazy widow woman, and Miss Russell looks a lot friendlier, too!"

Chapter 5

Longarm woke up the next morning with his pecker limp and his legs sort of stiff. He was more a rider than a walker, and the hills of San Francisco were a bitch. So, after he ate breakfast, he went down the street to a livery to see what kind of horseflesh they had for hire.

He didn't like what he saw. It seemed reasonable that mounts intended for a hilly town should be short in the leg and barrel-chested, but he knew he'd feel foolish with his stirrups just clearing the ground, and when he had to chase folks, he liked to chase 'em fast.

So, even though he hadn't originally planned on it, Longarm took a hired hack out to the Presidio, near the Golden Gate, to see if the army remount section had anything on hand that looked more like a horse.

The Presidio was an open post, so they didn't stop him at the gate when he got out of the hack. He asked one of the guards there where the remount depot was, and the trooper said, "Just beyond the parade ground, sir. Take this path and you can't miss it."

Longarm thanked him and walked on, frowning. He didn't feel all that old, but when soldiers started calling him "sir," it made him all too wistfully aware that the War had been fifteen years back.

As he strode along the tree-lined lane, he saw that the Presidio was a bigger post than most. He was afraid he'd gotten lost after walking at least a quarter-mile through nothing much. Then he rounded a bend, and the lane opened up into a big parade ground atop a cliff overlooking the Bay. The man at the gate had said to cross it, but he had to work his way around, since the army was having a dress parade with full flourishes and drums, and he knew how fussy they could get about folks walking through the middle of such goings-on.

The marching troops were all gussied up in full dress blues, and he saw that most of them were red-legs. He knew the Presidio was a Coastal Defense post, so they likely had big guns around here someplace. It was hard to tell. The ridges to the west were forested, and the place looked more like a big park. He got to the far side and stopped to watch as they trooped the colors with the band playing "Hail to the Chief."

Longarm wondered why they were doing that. He'd have heard if President Hayes was in town. Then, as the colors passed a reviewing stand on the far side and dipped in salute, he saw a familiar figure up there with the officers and their ladies. It was the Emperor Norton. The old lunatic had a new ostrich plume in his admiral's hat as he held up a friendly hand to the soldiers marching by.

Longarm wanted to talk to the Emperor, but he didn't think this was a good time. Frisco sure took mighty good care of its pet eccentrics. The CO of this Post had to be a tolerant cuss, for the War Department would have a fit if they knew the Presidio was in the habit of giving full military honors to a certified mental case!

There was a long row of brick barracks beyond the parade ground. Longarm went around them, found himself on non-coms' Row, and asked a passing trooper where the remount was. The trooper pointed west some more, so Longarm kept going, came to a downhill slope, and, sure enough, there were the paddock and stables.

He found a remount sergeant lounging on a ladderbacked chair in a doorway, picking his teeth, and explained who he was and what he wanted. The remount sergeant shook his head and said, "Can't do it, feather merchant. These here horses are federal property."

"I'm federal property too," Longarm said. "I always requisition a mount from the nearest army post when I'm out in the field."

"Not this army post, feather merchant. We ain't a cavalry outfit. We're coastal artillery, and the few riding mounts we have on hand are spoken for by the officers."

Longarm sighed and said, "You're not listening, old son. I'm an officer too. I'm a federal officer. Look it up in your ARs and you'll see that War and Justice have a deal. This may come as a surprise to you, but they both work for the same government."

The sergeant shook his head stubbornly. "I've never issued a mount to a feather merchant, and I doubt like hell I ever will. I don't care what the ARs say, I don't do favors for fucking feather merchants."

Longarm reached down, grabbed a fistful of blue tunic, and hauled the surly sergeant to his feet as he said pleasantly, "Let's try that again. I told you I was a deputy U.S. marshal. That is what you aimed to call me, wasn't it?"

The sergeant blanched and said, "Hey, you're starting to annoy me serious! Nobody is allowed to strike a noncom, damn it!"

"That regulation only applies to army, and you keep reminding me I am not in your army, old son. But I'll tell you what I'm going to do. I'm going to let you go, and then we're going to see about a horse and saddle for me. Ain't that right?"

"Look, I'll get in trouble."

"You're already in trouble. I'll sign for the horse and gear. I've had this discussion before, so I know the rules better than you do."

"You'll have to wait till the parade is over and the remount officer comes back."

"No I won't. They ain't half finished over there, and I'm in a hurry. Do I have to bend your blues some more to convince you of the error of your ways?"

The sergeant looked around, saw that there was no help in sight, and said, "I'll show you a horse, but they ain't going to like this, even if you have authority to sign for one. I told you these mounts was all spoken for."

"You did. Let's see what you have in the stable."

They went inside, the sergeant still bitching, and when Longarm picked a likely-looking roan mare from among the

66

horses in the stalls, the sergeant said, "You can't have that one. The colonel's lady rides her every Sunday."

Longarm said, "Saddle her up anyway. The colonel's lady is a civilian too, and I need a horse serious."

When he saw that the sergeant wasn't moving, he stepped into the adjoining tackroom, picked out a saddle and bridle, and came back to say, "Never mind, I ain't got all day, and I can see you are a slow learner."

"Mister, you're going to get shot if you try to ride out of here on that mare!"

Longarm ignored him as he bridled and saddled the roan. He'd met this kind before. The sergeant was one of those officious cusses who never lifted a finger to do anything and was always in the clear if what he was pissing and moaning about turned out to be against the rules.

Longarm asked the remount sergeant where he kept his requisition forms, and when the sergeant just went on saying he wouldn't be responsible for the mare, Longarm tore a page from his own pocket notebook and wrote an IOU for one mount on it, saying he'd leave the mare in the livery near his hotel when he wasn't riding her. The sergeant didn't want to take it. Longarm shrugged and dropped it near the chair the noncom had been sitting in by the stable door, and said, "You can turn it in to your CO, or you can wipe your ass with it, for all I care. I done my part legal, so adios, you disneighborly cuss."

He mounted up and rode off as the remount sergeant shouted after him that he couldn't do that. As Longarm trotted the mare up the slope toward the parade ground, the sergeant jogged after him, shouting, "Stop that horse thief!" to nobody in particular. Longarm rode back to the parade to find that it was breaking up. The troopers had been dismissed and were heading every which way, so Longarm just cut across, heading for the gate lane. As he approached the reviewing stand, he saw the Emperor Norton jawing with some officers, and headed over to talk to him. As Longarm reined in, a middle-aged bird colonel blinked at his mount and snapped, "That's my wife's horse you're riding, mister! I hope you have a damned good explanation!"

"I do," Longarm replied. "I'm a U.S. deputy and I need a mount to get about. So I'm taking this one."

"The hell you say! Didn't you hear me say that's my wife's horse?"

Longarm shook his head. "Sorry, Colonel, it don't work that way. This mount is federal property. Unless the U.S. Army has started recruiting womenfolk of late, any officer's lady riding it is doing so at the convenience of the government, and I don't find it convenient to walk all over Frisco."

The remount sergeant came running up, panting, to salute and cry out, "It wasn't my fault, Colonel! You can see this maniac is packing a gun, and he took that mare by pure physical threats!"

The colonel turned to a junior officer and said, white-lipped, "You'd better get the OD, Lieutenant. Tell him I want him on the double with a brace of MPs!"

"Now don't get your bowels in an uproar, Colonel," Longarm said. "It may be up for grabs if I'm out of line or not, but you boys don't want to arrest a U.S. deputy. I'd have to testify before the provost marshal, and the next thing you know, some nitpicker would want to know how come you run your post so casual." He tipped his hat to the Emperor Norton and said, "Howdy, Your Majesty. Remember me?"

The old man looked him over, then smiled brightly. "Didn't I knight you a while back?"

"You sure did. Are you headed back to town? I see the parade is over."

"As a matter of fact I am, son. My little pony is over there under the trees." The Emperor's expression saddened abruptly. "I used to have a little dog, but it died."

"Well, Your Majesty, why don't you go get your little pony while I discuss this mare with your friends here?"

Turning to the colonel, the old man said, "It was a fine review this morning, Colonel. Your men do me proud. Should the enemy attempt to make a landing near here, you have your orders."

As the batty old man turned away and headed for a crowbait pony a few yards off, the colonel whispered, "Poor old bastard. But we were talking about that horse, Deputy."

"The part about the horse is settled. I'm riding her until I don't need her anymore. You seem like a nice gent for a bird colonel, so don't you worry about me turning you in. I used to bend the ARs when I was a soldier boy, too."

"Turn *me* in?" the colonel snapped. "For what, goddamm it? I'm not the one who barged in here and helped himself to a prize mount!"

"No you ain't, but you just gave full military honors to a certified lunatic on the government's time. You ain't about to deny that the old man's crazy, are you?"

"Of course he's crazy. Everybody in San Francisco knows that. But he's harmless, and we let him attend our parades just to humor him. You're crazy too, if you think a post commander can't invite anybody he likes to a parade!"

"I agree you're goodhearted and I said I wouldn't tell," Longarm said. "But you did play 'Hail to the Chief' as the Emperor reviewed your troops, and I'll be switched if I see President Hayes around here anywhere."

"Don't be an ass! That was just a little joke the boys were enjoying!"

"I enjoyed it too, and I saw the humor in it. But ain't it a fact that not even the vice-president rates 'Hail to the Chief'? You'd be out of line if you saluted Queen Victoria with that tune, wouldn't you?"

The colonel's face stayed calm, but his neck was turning red. "Goddamm it, this is blackmail and I won't stand for it!"

The Emperor Norton had mounted his little pony and was coming back, so Longarm said, "Sure you will, Colonel. Me and His Majesty have to ride, so we'll just be on our way. It's sure been nice jawing with you. I'll tell the Justice Department how neighborly the army is, out this way."

Neither the colonel nor any of the other officers who were standing around tried to stop Longarm and the Emperor as they rode off side by side.

Longarm asked old Norton where he was headed, and the Emperor replied importantly, "I have to go to police headquarters."

"Oh? You aiming to inspect the police too, Your Majesty?"

"Not today. It's purely a social visit. The chief of police is a loyal subject who worries about me. Unless I drop by every once in a while, he sends his men out looking for me. He's doubtless concerned for my safety. Assassins, you know."

Longarm nodded soberly. "I'd best ride along and guard your flank, then."

The old man said he could, and they trotted along with Longarm thinking and the old man prattling on about his plans for the future of his empire. He seemed to think it would be a grand notion to build a bridge across the Golden Gate. Longarm didn't care one way or the other. He was weighing the

69

possible advantages of dropping all this sneaky stuff and just putting his cards on the table with the other local and federal lawmen in town. The crooks knew he was here. The SFPD did too, thanks to that damned fool Waco forcing his hand in the whorehouse last night. But Billy Vail figured that someone working for Treasury might be in on the counterfeiting. What would happen if he just played dumb for a spell? The rascal couldn't tell his crooked confederates much that they didn't already know, and he might make a slip trying to get the word to them.

They came to a broad avenue, and the Emperor pointed south to say, "The Civic Center is that way, down Van Ness, my good man. What did you say your name was?"

"You can call me Longarm, Your Majesty."

"Ah, yes, Sir Longarm. Didn't I knight you for saving a damsel in distress near the Ferry Building?"

Longarm allowed that that was close enough; he noted that the old man did have some grasp on where he'd been recently. He'd hoped as much. He said, "I understand you have your own money, Your Majesty."

"Oh, do you need some, Sir Longarm? I have a few fifty-cent Imperial Dollars I can give you if you're destitute. It's very unpleasant to be destitute, you know."

"I've heard folks say that, Your Majesty. I don't need any Imperial Dollars just now, but I was wondering where you had yours printed for you."

The Emperor thought for a moment, then answered, "It depends on which color you mean. They print black-and-white money for me on Montgomery Street, and there's a nice young man on Columbus who makes bills for me in red and blue. Red, white, and blue are the colors of my Empire, you see."

Longarm nodded; he did see. The whole town had made a pet of the nice old lunatic. It seemed a lot nicer than locking him up, when you studied on it, but there was little point in suspecting the Emperor of knowing any folks who made serious play money. He asked the Emperor if anybody ever gave him gold or silver money, and the old man said, "Sometimes I get change for my Imperial Dollars in the old coinage the United States used to have before I became Emperor."

Longarm would have dropped it there, but the Emperor Norton reached in a pocket and went on, "I have a pretty double eagle here. A nice young man gave it to me last night, shortly

70

after you and I came to aid of that young woman near the Ferry Building."

He held it out to Longarm. The tall deputy reached across to take it. When he held it up to the light, he saw that it was dated 1878 and had the scratch marks Fong had pointed out to him.

Longarm handed it back and said, "It's real pretty. You say a gent gave it to you on the Embarcadero? The last I saw of you last night, you were chasing a dray driver with your sword out."

The Emperor's tone became grave. "Yes, he ignored my commands and drove off. There are some crazy people in this town who don't know I'm their Emperor, I'm afraid. The man who gave me the pretty coin was a youth I'd spoken to before on the streets. When we met, he asked me to remember I'd not seen him that evening, and when I asked why, he said, 'never mind,' and gave me the double eagle. What do you suppose he meant by that, Sir Longarm?"

"He likely didn't want us to be having this conversation. You say you know him? What did he look like?"

"He was just a young man dressed in a dark suit. He had a carpetbag in his hand, now that I think about it. I suppose he must have been going someplace, don't you think?"

Longarm nodded. He knew where the thief who'd stolen his possibles had been going: off to someplace where he could paw through the contents to check any ID or papers in the infernal carpetbag. Longarm knew something else: his possibles hadn't been stolen by a simple sneak thief.

Could they have taken Calvinia's valise as a ruse, too? She'd thought it was somebody after her legal papers, but what if the gang had just grabbed anything handy off any pretty gal in sight, knowing a fool lawman would be distracted long enough for them to get what they were really after?

Hell, nobody was after Calvinia. They were after him all along! The one who'd grabbed Calvinia's valise hadn't really been all that serious about keeping it, and it had only been sheer luck that she'd had papers of value in the fool thing. He'd been right about the cuss with the shotgun stalking him, and not the gal, so that meant he didn't have to waste any more time with Calvinia. She'd likely cuss him some for loving and leaving her, but Billy Vail hadn't sent him all this way to comfort widow women.

"It's time to eat," the Emperor said. "Let's stop for a bite at yon sausage stand, Sir Longarm."

Longarm saw the umbrella-covered pushcart that the old man was pointing to. It wasn't anywhere near noon yet, but he humored the old man and followed as the Emperor crossed the avenue and reined in to dismount, almost tripping over his dress sword. The burly street vendor looked the eccentric over suspiciously, but when the Emperor said he and his faithful bodyguard would take two sausages, the vendor shrugged and dug them out. Longarm was dismounting as the Emperor paid with his play money, and the sausage dealer asked, "Hey, what's this shit?"

"Don't you recognize coin of the realm, my good fellow?" the Emperor asked, as Longarm sighed and reached in his own pants.

"Sure I do, you old coot," the street vendor answered. "But them sausages are a nickel each and I don't know what the hell this paper is supposed to be."

Longarm tried to catch his eye as he took out two bits. But the Emperor was affronted and drew himself up to his full height as he said coldly, "I can see you're not a U.S. citizen, since you don't know what our money is. I was going to let you keep the change, but since you're so impertinent, I'm only paying ten cents for these sausages, and you must give me back forty pennies!"

"I'll give you the back of my hand, you asshole! What kind of a con are you trying to pull on me, here?"

Longarm moved in and said, "Let me handle it, Your Majesty. Here's two bits, friend. Keep the change, and don't call your elders names no more."

The man pocketed the quarter, still frowning, as the Emperor handed Longarm his sausage and bun. "What's the matter with him?" the vendor asked, and Longarm replied, "Nothing you have call to worry about."

He thought it was over, but then the Emperor was waving his sausage at a beat copper coming along the walk. "Sir Mahoney!" he shouted. "Over here! I want you to arrest this doubtless illegal alien!"

The copper came over, swinging his stick thoughtfully as he took in the situation. He touched the bill of his helmet and said, "Good morning, Your Majesty, what seems to be the trouble here?"

"This old bastard just tried to buy sausages with worthless paper, and I want him arrested too!" the sausage man said.

"Do you, now?" Patrolman Mahoney said. "I haven't seen you on me beat before, friend. I suppose you have a permit for that darlin' cart?"

"Permit? Who says you need a permit to sell sausages on the street?"

"I do, Mahoney in the flesh! If it ain't in the city ordinances, I just put it there, for it's the Emperor Norton himself who's made an official complaint about your criminal conduct on me beat."

"Oh, for God's sake, are you crazy too?"

Winking at Longarm, Mahoney said, "You look like a fine upstanding citizen, whoever you might be. Would you be saying I was crazy, or is this not Norton the First, Emperor of the United States and Defender of Mexico?"

Longarm kept his face sober as he replied, "That's the way I've always heard it. By the way, I just paid this gent two bits for the property in dispute."

Mahoney nodded, turned to old Norton, and asked, "Can I let him off with a warning, Your Majesty? You can see he's a poor foreigner who meant no harm."

Emperor Norton considered. Then he nodded graciously and said, "I'm a merciful autocrat, Sir Mahoney. I'll leave the matter in your hands. Shall we be on our way, Sir Longarm?"

Longarm nodded and they mounted up to ride on, munching sausages, as the indulgent copper explained a few facts of San Francisco life to the confused sausage vendor.

The traffic started getting heavier as they approached the center of town. Most of it was drays and carriages, and most of the others who were riding were mounted on plugs not much taller than the Emperor's pony, for the hills of San Francisco were notorious for what they did to the legs of gals and horses. They said the gals who'd grown up there had the shapeliest calves on earth, if a man could spy them. But hauling loads up the awesome grades had a hell of an effect on a horse's figure. He was having second thoughts about this long-limbed saddle mount he'd requisitioned. The colonel's lady likely rode it over the parklike slopes of the military reservation, and it was shod with steel. Longarm noticed that a lot of the mounts they were passing clumped along on the new patent hard rubber shoes. Some of the dray horses had cleated steel ones that struck sparks now and again on a high cobble.

The Emperor was a nice old cuss, but sort of tedious to listen to, since he never stopped talking and seldom made sense. Longarm made mental notes about some of the places he hung out, for the Emperor got all over and knew almost everyone in town. He'd said the man who'd given him the fake double eagle had been familiar to him. That meant at least one member of the gang was a local. Billy Vail had figured the gang was new to San Francisco. They'd only been passing the queer a short while, but that didn't mean they had to be from out of town. They could be local crooks who'd started a new line of work. That was going to make it tougher to cut their trail. Folks remembered newcomers to the neighborhood, but if they were operating out of a long-established address, that was a horse of a different color.

The Civic Center reminded Longarm a mite of the one in Denver, except that Denver's Capitol Hill was surrounded by flat land, and the one here lay in a hollow surrounded by hills. Longarm saw no need to pay a call on the chief of police with the Emperor, so when the old man pointed out police head-quarters and heeled his pony toward it, Longarm said adios and continued on to the intersection of Market and Van Ness. He saw a copper directing traffic in the middle. The copper had one of the Emperor's medals pinned over his copper badge, so Longarm figured he was a friendly cuss and reined in near him to ask directions to the San Francisco Mint.

"It's 'Frisco,' damn it," the copper said. "We never took Californee from the Mexicans to talk like them. Us native sons call San Diego 'Dago,' and Santa Barbara is 'Santa Bob.'"

Longarm nodded and said, "I stand corrected, but I'm still looking for the goddamned mint."

The cop pointed down Market with his stick and said, "You can't miss her. There's a sign above her door. Them dudes from Washington call it the San Francisco Mint, too."

Longarm thanked him and rode the way he'd pointed, smiling wryly as he remembered the old poem that went:

> The miners come in 'forty-nine,
> The whores in 'fifty-one,
> And when they got together
> They produced the native son!

Folks sure acted odd here by the Golden Gate. They seemed to combine the manners of a jovial bully with a tolerance for eccentric behavior. It made it hard for suspicious characters to stand out. Everybody seemed to act a mite unusual.

He found the big granite building set back across an open space from Market, and rode over to tether his mare out front. He went up the steps and asked a guard where the head man was. The mint director's office was on the second floor, and the man's name was Coogan. He was an older man with a pot belly and a messy head of gray hair. His office was sort of messy too. He sat at a rolltop desk with papers and pasteboard boxes spilling out of it. Longarm showed his ID and Coogan waved him to a bentwood chair, saying, "They told me they were sending an expert from Justice. But they said you'd be working on the sneak. I won't announce this visit to the newspapers if you won't, but this is a mighty public building, Mr. Long."

Longarm took out a cheroot and lit up before he said, "The gang knows I'm in town, so pussyfooting about is just likely to slow me down. I haven't the least notion where to start looking, and for all I know, you and your boys have already narrowed the field a mite. I'd look a fool if I kept tear-assing around while you and yours wrapped the case up, so I thought we'd better bring each other up to date."

Coogan sighed. "I don't have any of my investigators working the case right now. The boys were just running around like chickens with their heads cut off. So when I heard they were sending in agents unknown to the Frisco underworld, I ordered them to get back to work on more routine cases. It isn't as if the folks making those double eagles are the only counterfeiters in California, you know."

Longarm let some smoke trickle out his nose as he digested that. Then he asked, "How do you know the gang I'm after ain't making other queer?"

Coogan reached in a pigeonhole and produced a greenback. "Easy. Take a look at this ten-dollar silver certificate. Isn't that disgusting workmanship?"

Longarm took the bill and turned it over in his hands, then snapped it. "Lousy paper too. Know who's printing these?"

"Sure. We traced the bond paper to a printer in Oakland, across the Bay. His business has been slow and he's living too high for his means. We have his shop staked out so we can pick up his passers when we're ready to move in. You can see, though, why I don't have men to spare on the double-eagle job. Frankly, you're going to have a hell of a time with that gang. Like I said, my boys looked high and low and never turned up a lead."

"One of them must have been getting warm. Tell me about your agent that got killed."

Coogan ran a hand through his unruly hair. "Not much to tell. He was gunned on the street near Telegraph Hill. Shot in the back, in the fog, with no witnesses. It's a tough neighborhood, and it's always possible the killing had nothing to do with the case he was on."

"I ran into a problem like that last night. Did he have some reason for being near Telegraph Hill, or was he just sight-seeing?"

"I'm damned if I know. He lived in the Mission District, and the lead he was supposed to be following had nothing to do with North Beach. His name was Sloter and he was supposed to be checking out an ex-employee of the mint, named Dandolo. Dandolo was Italian and there's a lot of them on Telegraph Hill, but Dandolo lived on Rincon Hill, south of the Slot. After Sloter was gunned, we checked with Dandolo's daughter, and she said Sloter had never come by to ask about her father."

"What did her father say?"

"Nothing. He's been missing since the day he left us without notice. The girl filed a missing-persons report with the police, too. I'd told Sloter to look into it, just in case, but somebody shot him before he ever got near the Dandolo house on Rincon Hill."

Longarm shoved his hat back, took another drag, and asked, "I'd best have the address before I leave. What was the angle about this missing mint worker that Sloter was supposed to ask about?"

"It was just covering all bets," Coogan said. "Dandolo was a skilled diecutter from Venice. He turned up missing shortly before the fake double eagles started hitting the banks, and one of the coins he'd cut dies for was an 1878 double eagle withdrawn from circulation."

Longarm whistled softly. "A thing like that could make one eager to have a word with old Dandolo. You figure he took some work home and maybe went in business for himself?"

Coogan shook his head. "I don't. Washington does. I've known Dandolo for years and I'm a fair judge of character. Besides that, I can count. The entire 1878 series was destroyed."

"You mean you're pretty sure it was, don't you?"

Coogan swore and rose to go over to an office safe. "Let me show you something," he said.

He knelt, opened the safe, and hauled out what looked like a six-inch length of crowbar stock. He handed it to Longarm and sat back down, saying, "That's just half a die for a ten-dollar eagle. It's been yanked from the presses to be recorded and destroyed as soon as headquarters sends back approval. No die is removed or disposed of without a lot more paperwork than it ought to take. Can you see mislaying that, or walking off the job with two of them in your pocket?"

Longarm hefted the heavy bar of tool steel and said, "I might sneak it out in my boots, but I can see how it might be missed. I had no idea these dies were so big."

As Longarm studied the impression on one end of the bar, Coogan said, "They have to be. We're not making waffles, you know. The presses downstairs punch and shape solid metal. The bars are alloy steel, almost as hard as diamond, and they still take a beating. If you'll look closely, you'll see why that one has to go back to the foundry. Some fool allowed a speck of grit to get in the press, and we're supposed to mint clean money."

"I see the scratch," Longarm said. "You say these things go back to some foundry to be melted down again? You may tally them pretty good as they leave, but—"

"You're barking up the wrong tree," Coogan cut in. "We don't just tag 'em and send 'em east. We deface the impression with a grinding wheel before they leave the premises."

"I get it," Longarm said. "So a crook couldn't sidetrack a set of used dies along the way. And you say Washington keeps records too. But if Agent Sloter didn't suspicion this Dandolo of quitting with a set of 'em, what was he looking for him for?"

"It was just routine. The man was a federal employee, and he is listed as a missing person by the police, and he did have the know-how it would take to run off duplicate dies."

"You mean a gent who'd studied on it could maybe make his own set at home?"

"It would be a bitch," Coogan said, "and we know Dandolo didn't have the equipment in his home on Rincon Hill. His daughter's been cooperative about letting us look around. He only had a few home-repair tools in his stable."

"Maybe, but he had the skill, and he ain't around to explain what he's been up to since he quit here. What does a diemaker use to whip these here things up, Mr. Coogan?"

"A machine shop. You want to see where we cut our dies?"

"Time is passing, so I'll take your word for it. Just tell me what sort of gear I might be looking for."

"Well, that steel alloy is too hard to cut with hand tools. We use a pantograph. The original impression is sculpted large in hard plaster. It's about the size of a dinner plate. The diecutter places a smooth stylus on the master impression, and the pantograph arms reduce it to a smaller pattern with a diamond-tipped drill, following the dips and rises as the craftsman traces his stylus over the master. It isn't as easy as it sounds. Every quiver of the craftsman's hand will be cut in the steel forever. You have to have nerves of steel and know what you're doing, even with the machinery doing the hard work."

"I get the picture. How big a table would you need to set the whole mess on?"

"The benches are about six feet long, and connected by overhead pulleys to a steam-driven shaft running the length of the shop."

"I likely won't mistake a diecutter's pantograph for a sewing machine, if ever I should see one. You better write me down that Eye-talian's home address. I'd like a word with his daughter too. What can you tell me about the two undercover agents who preceded me, Mr. Coogan?"

As the mint director scribbled on a sheet of paper, he said, "Nothing. They never reported to me, and nobody here has any idea what might have happened to them. If they went in the Bay, nobody ever will know."

"Do tell? Seems to me that bodies float from time to time."

"Not very many, in Frisco Bay. The water's cold as hell on the bottom, so they tend to stay there long after they'd have bloated and bobbed up anywhere else. There's a hell of a tide running twice a day through the Golden Gate, and the Gate is deep as well. Things sort of squirt out to sea, and if you stand on the cliffs above Baker Beach, you see a lot of shark fins cutting the water. They're out there waiting for the twice-daily servings of garbage, sewage, and anything else that comes bouncing out along the bottom. Sloter was shot down near North Beach. If those other two were killed in that neck of the woods and thrown off a dock, they'll have landed in an almost constant current headed for China."

He handed Longarm the missing mint worker's address. Longarm put it away, saying, "I'll try to stay out of the water."

He reached into the left-hand pocket of his vest and pulled out his Ingersoll watch. It was almost noon. As he put the watch away, the other end of the watch chain came out of the other pocket of his vest. Frowning, Longarm examined the brass clip at the end of the chain.

"What's wrong?" Coogan asked.

"Ain't sure," Longarm replied, reaching into the right-hand vest pocket and withdrawing the derringer he'd used in the fight in the whorehouse. "I generally keep my watch at one end of the chain, with this derringer clipped at the other. I had reason to unclip her last night, but I thought I put her back on the chain right."

Holding the little brass weapon up to the light, he said, "Oh, I see what the trouble is."

He blew a little speck of sawdust from the socket in the butt of the derringer, and clipped the gun to the end of the chain. Then he dropped it back in his pocket and stood up and shook hands with Coogan, thanking him for his help.

As he left, he knew the crooks he was after had gone to more trouble than he'd expected to get the dies they were using. He knew they might have a machine shop somewhere, but that didn't make his morning. There were factories and warehouses all along the shore and on many a side street. The bastards only needed one modest corner to begin with, and now that they had their infernal dies, they might not see fit to go anywhere near where they'd made them. As he went down to remount his mare, he muttered. "Damn you, Billy Vail, this time you've trusted too much to my occasional lucky hunting accidents! I don't even know my way about this infernal city, and I've always worked best in open country to begin with!"

He wondered what Vail would say if he just gave up. He knew he'd never know, for up to now he'd never given up on a case. But it sure was tempting this time.

Chapter 6

Rincon Hill was lower than Nob Hill, and it had been built up earlier, during the Gold Rush, when folks had had more sense and no cable cars. Some of the houses were as grand as a lucky strike called for, but he could see the neighborhood had gone a mite to seed since the nabobs moved to higher quarters over to the northwest. The Dandolos' house sat on a corner lot and had a Steamboat Gothic veranda and a mansard roof. The yard was well tended and the picket fence had been whitewashed recently. He tethered his mare to a horsehead hitching post by the gate and went up to the front door. As he was looking for a bell pull, it opened and a nice-looking blond gal with big brown eyes that matched her cotton house dress opened it and said, "Yes?"

"Are you Angelina Dandolo, ma'am?"

"It's Angela, if you don't mind. I'm an American, even if my father came from Venice."

"Well, I'm American too, and my name is Custis Long. I'm a deputy U.S. marshal, and if I ain't interrupting your noon meal, I got some questions I'd like to ask."

Angela nodded and said, "Come back to the kitchen, then. I just ate, but I've some coffee and cake to offer you."

He followed her back through the house. The hallway smelled of lemon oil and hard work by a house-proud woman. He admired the view as she strode ahead of him. He knew there were blond Italians, of course, but he'd expected anybody named Angelina to look more like that waitress, Gina, at Romero's back in Denver.

As they entered the kitchen, Longarm sniffed and could tell she'd fibbed to him. He could smell the coffeepot on the kitchen range, but she hadn't cooked a meal in here this day. She ushered him to a seat at the plain plank table and poured him a cup of coffee.

"I'm sorry," she said, "I'm fresh out of cream, but there's sugar in that bowl, there. I'll get the cake."

"Don't bother, ma'am. I et some sausages just a spell back, and I ain't hungry."

She looked relieved and sat down, hands folded in her lap, with no coffee cup before her. He figured she might be low on sugar too, so he sipped his coffee black. That is, it would have been black, if it hadn't been mostly water.

"Is there any news about my father?" she asked.

"I'm afraid not, Miss Angela. I was wondering if you had a picture of him. It might help if I knew what he looked like."

She removed a small heart-shaped locket from around her throat, and handed it across to him, saying, "You can look, but I can't let you keep it. I gave the police the only large photograph I had of Papa, and this is all I have left to remember him by."

She looked like she was trying not to cry, but she hung tough as Longarm opened the locket to stare at the tiny face of a man with a little waxed mustache and dark hair parted in the middle. The missing diemaker looked like half the men you passed in the street—a nondescript, middle-aged gent with a mustache he could shave off in a minute if he wanted to look even less interesting. He handed it back, asking, "How tall was your father, ma'am?"

"Was? Don't you mean *is?* You don't know he's dead. He can't be dead!"

"I shouldn't have put it that way, Miss Angela," Longarm apologized. "I wasn't thinking. But we have to consider things grim, hurtful or not. He's been gone quite a spell now."

"I know. I'm sure he'd have written, even if there was some reason for him to drop out of sight like that. You know, of course, that he never came home after leaving the mint that afternoon as usual?"

"Yes, ma'am. I know it wasn't payday and that he wasn't having any trouble with the other workers there. I reckon you'd have known if he'd had other troubles on his mind?"

"He never said anything about them to me. Papa was always so cheerful. He left that morning singing as usual, and I cooked a special supper for him because it was his birthday and—"

"Birthday?" Longarm interrupted with a frown. "Nobody at the mint told me he vanished on his birthday, ma'am."

"I doubt if they knew," she sighed. "But it was. He was exactly fifty the day he never came home. I'd even baked a cake for him with fifty candles on it, like they do here in America."

Longarm chose his next words with care. "You and your father lived alone here, right?"

"Yes, my mother died years ago. We have no relatives here in California. My mother was an American. Papa met her back East when he first came to this country from Venice. Sometimes I think he missed Venice. I've never learned much Italian, and I think he was lonely for the sounds of his birthplace."

"Ain't there lots of Eye-talian folk living over on Telegraph Hill, Miss Angela?"

"Heavens, they're Sicilian fisher folk. Papa was Venetian and from a proud old family. He used to brag about one of his ancestors being a Doge of Venice."

"Do tell? I think they might have named a town in Kansas after some old Dodge. You don't get over to Telegraph Hill much, then, Miss Angela?"

"I've never been there. It's a very rough neighborhood, and I told you I only know a few words of Italian."

Longarm sipped some more weak coffee as he considered that Treasury Agent Sloter might have been suspicious about the social life of a healthy widower with a decent income who was likely uncomfortable pestering gals in English. But he didn't think Angela would understand about the needs her daddy might have felt on a lonesome Frisco evening. He knew if he was stuck in Italy and heard about a neighborhood of bawdy Americans, he'd likely wind up visiting it, and visiting it regularly if there was an English-speaking gal there who wanted to be friendly. It was still just a guess, of course, but Sloter had probably followed up on it, and Sloter was dead!

He figured he'd drunk as much of the insipid brew as politeness called for, so he set the cup down and said, "I hope you won't take this personal, ma'am. But if you're a single woman, your father's vanishment leaves you with no visible means."

"I was just discussing that with the grocer down the street," she said. "We own this house, but I can't sell or even rent it without my father's permission, for the property is in his name." She pushed a strand of hair from her brow as she added brightly, "Oh, well, it could be worse. At least I have a roof over my head and I've been to several job interviews."

"You look like a hard worker, ma'am, but meanwhile you have to eat. I couldn't help noticing you ain't been cooking today, and I'd be proud to grubstake you till you find a job."

"Oh no, I couldn't!" she gasped. "What sort of a girl do you take me for?"

"A hungry one. Look, it ain't like it's my own money. I'm on an expense account. I could put it down to paying for vital information or something."

She looked down and shook her head. "Thank you, sir, but I'm not a charity case. Papa always said nobody needed to beg in America if they were willing to work, and I'll not dishonor him by making a liar out of him!"

Longarm thanked her for the coffee and the little she'd told him, and she led him out. He mounted up and headed back for the Slot. But a block downhill he came upon a corner grocery, reined in, and stepped inside. He told the scrawny old cuss behind the counter to fill a pasteboard box with staples. As the grocer put in flour, beans, sugar, coffee, and such, Longarm pointed to a big glass jar of penny candy and said to fill a paper bag with the same. He bought a ham and a mason jar of pickles to top the load, and paid the grocer. Then he took out a ten-dollar bill and wedged it between the ham and beans. He went out and remounted, with the bulky box braced on one hip, and rode back to Angela's house, where he got down, sneaked up to the veranda, and put the box by the door. Then he rang the bell and ran like hell, grinning like a kid playing a Halloween trick. He was on his mare and almost out of sight when he heard the girl call out his name. He didn't look back. He didn't aim to fuss with proud dumb gals, and he knew she was set for at least a week. Ten dollars was top wages for a week of herding cows, and she'd said she had some jobs lined up. He knew Billy Vail was going to think he'd paid a street informant outrageous when the office got his bills, but a man who'd leave a bereaved gal with nothing in her pantry deserved a horse-whipping.

The missing diemaker had to be dead. Nobody raised a daughter to be a fine young woman and then left her to starve alone. Sloter had thought the same way and had started looking near Telegraph Hill. Maybe there was a smarter way to find out if the old man had had a mistress on the sly over there. He'd have to study on it.

When he arrived at the livery near the Palace, he told the groom to rub the mare down and give her some oats, then he went to see if there were any messages for him at the hotel.

There were. Western Union had delivered a wire from his home office that just told him to be careful and keep in touch, damn it. The desk clerk handed him a scented envelope with just his name on it in a woman's hand. He went in the hotel bar to wash away the taste of that weak coffee while he opened and read the mysterious message. It was from Calvinia Taylor. She said she was scared and wanted to know why he hadn't come back to the widow Doyle's as he'd promised. That part didn't puzzle Longarm. What he wondered about was how she'd known he was staying here. Had he told her he'd check into the Palace? He couldn't remember.

He helped himself to a bologna sandwich at the free-lunch counter and went up to his rooms to study his next moves in comfort. When he got to the door, he saw that his old trick with the matchstem had caught somebody. Longarm liked to leave a length of matchstick wedged between the door and the jam when he went out.

This afternoon it lay on the rug near the bottom hinge. Either a hotel maid or somebody else had opened his door while he was out. Maids were one thing, but uninvited visitors were another, so he moved down to the adjacent door, knowing there was more than one way to get in the double suite. That match was still in place. So he unlocked the door silently, drew his revolver, and let himself in. The extra room Boss Buckley had sprung for was empty, save for the made-up bed. Longarm crossed the plush rug on the balls of his feet and eased open the connecting door to the room he'd been using. A blond gal was sitting, stiff-backed, on his made-up bed. He'd just left another blond, but the resemblance ended there. It was that

84

snooty-looking widow Doyle, staring at the door he was supposed to come in, looking like she was trying not to vomit. He stepped into the room and holstered his sidearm as she shied like a spooked horse.

"Oh, it's you!" she gasped. "You startled me!"

"You startled me some yourself, ma'am. How'd you get in here, and while we're on the subject, how did you know this was my hired digs?"

The widow Doyle said, "I asked at several hotels along Market, knowing you had to be in one of them. I was downtown anyway, and wanted to talk to you."

"I'm listening, ma'am. That door was locked when I went out."

"No it wasn't. When the room clerk told me your key wasn't in the box, I came up and knocked, assuming you were in. I received no answer and took the liberty of trying the knob. It was open. I assumed you had just stepped out for a moment, and I've been waiting here for maybe twenty minutes."

"I generally keep my keys handy, in case I get home late," he said. Then he stepped to the desk across the room, tried the drawer, and muttered, "Might have known, damn it."

"Don't swear with ladies present, sir. What might you have known? I assure you I have not been going through drawers and closets while you were out!"

"Somebody has," he said. "I tucked a sliver under that desk drawer. I'm sort of sneaky that way. They didn't find anything, because I never left anything valuable here. But unless the maid dusts like a maniac, somebody's been snooping about, likely before you got here. They were in a hurry and forgot to lock up after themselves, too."

"Heavens! I thought poor Calvinia was being overdramatic about her ex-in-laws. But maybe there is something to her story after all!"

He pulled a chair from near the desk and sat down, removing his hat to be polite. He skimmed it over to the plush chair in the corner, and though it was his place and not hers, he asked if she minded if he smoked.

She sniffed and said, "If you must." So he decided not to.

"You allowed you wanted to talk to me, ma'am," he said.

"Yes, I did, but now I'm a bit confused," she replied. "You see, I thought Calvinia was being silly about her brother-in-law sending people to bother her. Now I'm not so sure."

"To tell the truth," he said, "I think she's suffering more from a guilty conscience than anything else. I'm pretty sure the rascal skulking about up there was after me, not her. You gals didn't have anybody prowling about after I left, did you?"

"Lord, no. I'd have called the police. I have a telephone, you know."

"I heard that some of the finer homes are getting them things in, and you do live high on the hog as well as on Nob Hill, no offense. I'm glad you have a telephone as well as a stout-looking front door. It means I don't have to worry about Calvinia, even if there's an outside chance her relatives are sore enough at her to pester her."

"Oh? Then you're not going to trifle with her anymore?"

Longarm raised an eyebrow and said, "I ain't sure what you mean by that, ma'am. She said she wanted to hire me as a bodyguard, only I don't reckon she needs one."

Gwynn Doyle's face went pink as she looked down, lips pursed, and said, "I'm afraid Calvinia was in a talkative mood after you brought her to my place last night, Custis."

He grinned sheepishly and said, "Some gals do like to talk. I hope she didn't say anything shocking."

"It was shocking indeed, and, if you ask me, impossible as well. You had no right to take advantage of a poor widow woman like that!"

"Well, ma'am, who took advantage of whom ain't exactly clear in my head, and in any case what did or didn't happen ain't for you to say. You're too young to be her mother, so this conversation is bordering on nosey, and I'd like to get down to what you come for."

She was even redder now, as she stammered, "I just wanted to know if you were coming back up the hill this evening. Calvinia thinks you are, and she made a very shocking suggestion about it to me."

"I got a note from her, inviting me to your house. I won't come if it upsets you, ma'am."

She started twisting the glove in her hands as she said, "Oh, dear, I'm trying to be sophisticated and broad-minded about this. I'm not a child, and I know how poor dear Calvinia suffered when she was married to that boor. I was married to a boor too, and—oh Lord, what am I saying?"

"I've no idea, ma'am. You look all lathered up. Are you running a fever?"

"I don't know. I'm perspiring like a horse in these weeds,

and it's not a warm day. What I was trying to say is that if you and poor Calvinia really need to be together, I don't want to be a prude about it. I may look like a dried-up old thing, but I understand about such matters."

"You don't look so dried up, Miss Gwynn," he reassured her. "You're glowing sort of pretty. That's a handsome offer you just made, and I can see what it took out of you. But we both know Calvinia's likely safe to go back to her own place now. So if I should get up that way, I see no need for us to abuse your hospitality."

"Oh? I, uh, wouldn't really mind. It seems to have done wonders for Calvinia."

Longarm said, tongue in cheek, "It's my duty as a Christian to help ladies feel good, Miss Gwynn. You look sort of feverish yourself, right now. I got a bathtub next door. Would you like to sort of cool off for a spell?"

She looked up, startled, and forgot to purse her lips as she gasped, "That's a terrible thing to say to a woman in my condition! Do you think I could disrobe in a strange man's bath?"

"Might help. There's a lock on the door."

"Oh, I thought . . . Never mind. Calvinia was right. You are an animal."

He shrugged and admitted, "You're both likely right. But I disremember coming to call on you, Miss Gwynn. It was your notion to bust in here, talking about country matters. I offered you a soak in cold water as the politest thing I could think of for what ails you. You can take a bath or take a walk or do anything you want to. I haven't done or said a thing for you to mean-mouth me about."

Suddenly she started to cry. "I know," she sobbed. "I've behaved insanely. I don't know why I even came here, and I've no right to hurt you."

"Hell, I ain't hurt. Puzzled, mayhaps, but I ain't in pain. Are you sure you come here to play Miss Matchmaker for your friend, or did you have other things in mind?"

"Whatever are you suggesting, sir?"

"I ain't suggesting a thing. You're the one who keeps talking country. Meaning no disrespect, ma'am, you strike me as a natural woman who's having trouble with her natural feelings."

"Don't be ridiculous! I'll bet Calvinia told you I was, uh, cool to men."

"She did say something about it. You've been throwing fire

and ice at me since I got here. I can't come up with any polite suggestions about your condition, but, honest, a cold bath helps a lot. If you don't want to do that with your hot and bothered flesh, I suggest you head on home, for, to tell the truth, I'm starting to feel the need of a cold tub myself, and I'm trying to be decent."

"Pooh," she scoffed, "I'm not the sort of woman that inflames men to passion . . . am I?"

He said, "You're a she-male with a pretty face and a decent figure. I wonder what you'd look like with your hair down."

He stood up, stepped over to her, and pulled the pins from the severe bun atop her head as she gasped, "Stop that! What are you doing?" Then the long blond hair cascaded down around her shoulders, softening her looks as he raised her chin and said soberly, "Hell, you're beautiful. Why do you wear that dumb black dress?"

"I'm a lonesome widow," she replied with a sigh. Then she took Longarm's hand in both of hers. She pressed it to her cheek and sobbed, "Oh, if only you knew how lonely, Custis."

He petted her hair with his free hand as he said gently, "You don't have to be, Gwynn. You're a young and handsome gal of independent means. Just come down out of that ivory tower and give the world a chance to know you better."

"I can't. I'm afraid of men."

"Are you afraid of me, Gwynn?"

"Yes. Can't you hear my heart pounding? I know you're just a drifter and a perfect choice for a casual affair, but even though I came here to see if Calvinia was right, now that I'm here I'm frightened."

He sat on the bed beside her and put an arm around her waist. "What did Calvinia say that got you so hot and bothered, Gwynn?"

"Oh, you know. She said you knew how to pleasure a woman right, and that she could trust you neither to talk nor make a scandalous bother."

"Was it her notion for you to see if I could serve you the same way?"

"She said she was sure you could, you know. I got so excited just thinking about it, and now I feel like such a perfect fool!"

He fell back across the bed with her and said, "You'll feel even dumber now, if you back out." Then he kissed her and ran his hand down over the stiff black poplin to feel whether those curves were real or whalebone. She wore next to nothing under her widow's weeds, and by the time he cupped her groin through the material, the poplin wasn't all that was stiff. She twisted her mouth to one side and panted, "Stop! I said I couldn't go through with it!"

He didn't take his hand away, but he didn't force her or hold her helpless. As she saw that she was likely to get free if she struggled too hard, she went limp and sighed, "Oh, you're too strong for me."

So he pulled her skirts up and went on kissing her as she rubbed her legs together like she was trying to run in place. She'd been smart enough not to wear pantaloons, and he parted her warm blond thatch with his fingers.

She sobbed, "Oh, you should be ashamed of yourself, taking advantage of my helplessness like this."

He didn't answer. It wasn't nice to laugh at a gal while she was moving her hips like that. He still had his coat and gunbelt on, so getting it out and in was a bitch, but he managed, knowing she'd go prune-faced again if he stopped to undress either of them. As he entered her, she spread her legs wide and protested, "You're touching me! You mustn't! Take that terrible thing out this instant and . . . Good Christ! You *are* hung like a horse!"

She raised her knees and locked her high-button shoes across his rump. "This is disgusting," she said. "We're still fully dressed. What on earth do you have in your vest pockets?"

He cupped one of her breasts through the stiff bodice and said, "Watch on one side and a derringer on the other. You got nice things in your own vest, honey. But fair is fair, and this would be nicer with our duds off. Can I trust you to play fair if I stop a second?"

"Let me up, damn you! I could never disrobe in front of a strange man in broad daylight. You're behaving just awful and I'll never speak to you again after this and . . . Oh Jesus, what are you *doing* to me?"

He thought it was mighty obvious, but as he felt her contractions, he started moving faster.

"You still want me to stop, honey?" he asked.

"Yes. I mean, *no*. I don't know what I mean, and . . . Ohhh, faster, Custis! Faster, harder, deeper and don't ever stop and . . . Jeeeesus!"

Of course he did stop, once he'd come himself, for it was

uncomfortable as hell in his sweaty duds. He rolled off her. She didn't resist at first, as he shucked her out of the dress. But as he started rolling down her cotton stockings she opened her eyes and said, "I'm naked! How did that happen? What are you doing with your own clothes? I don't want to face you naked!"

"Close your eyes and pretend it's dark."

So she did, protesting, "Don't look at me. Even my late husband never saw me naked like this!"

He figured that was likely half the trouble, and as he rolled back on her, nude and slick with perspiration, she hissed, "Oh, you're all naked and sticky!" He flattened her erect nipples against his bare chest and entered her once more, belly to belly, as she giggled and said, "Heavens, it feels so different this way!"

Then they both went crazy for a while, and by the time she'd come again, the cool-looking blond had gotten over her shyness enough to open her eyes and look down between them as he moved in and out, braced above her on stiff arms.

"I can see us!" she gasped. "It's so dirty I can't bear it! Now I know why people are supposed to wear nightgowns. It looks so terribly naked and . . . No, don't stay deep like that. It's awful but exciting to see that long wet shaft treating me so naughty. Do you like being naughty with me, Custis?"

He laughed, rolled her over, and mounted her dog-style.

He was starting to understand Gwynn, now. She was one of those gals who liked her sex hot and earthy, but she'd been raised too proper to admit as much to any man. The poor old gent she'd married had likely been raised proper too, so they'd spent night after night together, sleeping back to back and horny, but too polite to suggest doing much about it.

When he rolled off to enjoy a breather and a smoke, Gwynn sat up and started dressing, insisting she had to get home. So he let her. He offered to escort her downstairs if she'd give him time to haul on his duds, but she said she had to think of her reputation and that it would never do for her to be seen in the Palace lobby with a man like him.

But when he rose to kiss her goodbye, she made him promise to come up the hill that night, even if he was just awful.

He let her out, locked the door after her, and dressed, taking his time. Then he checked his guns, put on his hat, and went out again. While this had been fun, he was supposed to be working on a case, and he'd screwed away more than an hour of Uncle Sam's time. At the moment, the notion of going to bed with two publicly proper and privately depraved widow women sounded sort of fatiguing. But he knew that if nobody shot him, he'd likely wind up at the Doyle house later. He was as weak-natured as most men when it came to womenkind.

Down in the lobby, a familiar figure rose from a chair to meet him. It was young Jimbo Corbett. The youth said, "I've been waiting here since I came to your door and found you was entertaining company. Sure and she was a grand-looking lady, Longarm."

"Do you peek through keyholes, Jimbo?"

"Hell, yes, don't you? Don't worry, I won't tell anyone what I saw you doing in there. Jesus, walking through the lobby just now, she looked as proper as a saint."

"Never mind about that, you rascal. What brings you here?"

"Oh, Boss Buckley said you might be after needing me. So it's here I am, and who do you want me to beat up for you?"

"I got a task that'll likely put more strain on you, Jimbo. Do you know how to read and write? I noticed you signed with an X the other night."

Jimbo grinned and said, "I'd be the fool to sign me name for a lawman. But I can write a grand copper-plate hand if the need should arise. Why?"

"Want to give you some names and send you out to gather gossip, Jimbo. Folks are more likely to talk over a backyard fence to you than to me. Let's go over to yonder desk."

He led the youth to a writing desk under a lamp and potted palm, and tore a sheet from his notebook to scribble the names he wanted checked. He said, "I was aiming to get the vital statistics out of the dry and dusty files at the Hall of Records. But folks seldom certify what they've been up to on the sly. The most important name here is old Enrico Dandolo. He dropped out of sight just as he was turning a doubtless nervous fifty, and it's my notion he might have had a few drinks on the way home and gone to get some consolation. There's reason to suspicion he had a woman on the side over to Telegraph Hill. Do you know your way about over there?"

"It's not me turf," Jimbo said, "but there are still some dacent Irish on the hill. It used to be *all* Irish until the dago fishermen started moving in and blowing garlic in the faces of paple who prefer the smell of cabbage. This girl the old Eye-talian would have been after seeing would have to be his own kind if he was visiting her on Telegraph Hill, for the boyos would never have stood for him trifling with a dacent Irish girl."

Longarm said, "That sounds reasonable. But I don't much care if she was an Eskimo or a Swede, as long as I can talk to her. So see what you can find out. I'm going out, too. Where do you want to meet up, say along about sundown?"

Jimbo pondered briefly, then said, "Sure this hotel is a mortal walk from Telegraph Hill. Why don't I wait for you at Dirty Mary's? It's near the hill on the waterfront, between the Matson Piers and Fisherman's Wharf. Just go along the Embarcadero and you can't miss it."

"Is Dirty Mary's a whorehouse or a saloon?" Longarm asked.

Jimbo laughed and said, "That depends on whether you like it upstairs or downstairs. I'll be bellied up to the bar if I get there before you, for I've never had to pay for me loving. It's a safe place to meet, for a truce line between us and the North Beachers runs right through Dirty Mary's."

Longarm agreed and told the young tough to look for him at sundown or a few minutes either way. They split up, and Longarm headed for Saint Francis Square, in a nicer part of town. The banks were closing for the day, and he had plenty of reports from banks to read. They all told much the same tale. All the counterfeit double eagles the banks had detected had been turned in by regular customers. The passers weren't bold enough to cash them in at banks, it seemed.

Gump's Department Store, near the square, was supposed to be about the fanciest one in Frisco, and they'd been hit bad by the gang more than once. When Longarm moseyed in, he could see why. The store was big and crowded with well-dressed folk who looked like they spent gold coinage on a regular basis. He eyed the fancy merchandise in the glass cases. Gump's sold mighty fancy dinnerware, jewelry, and play-pretties for spreading about the house to let the neighbors know you'd made it to the top of the dungheap. He stopped to admire a big marble Venus with a clock set in her naked belly, and a pretty salesgal asked him if she could do anything for him. Longarm didn't think she'd do what he'd admire most, so he asked how much the clock cost. She said it was "only" five hundred dollars.

"That sounds fair," he said, "but I already got an Ingersoll that keeps fair time. To tell the truth, ma'am, I ain't here shopping. I'm the law. I'm a deputy U.S. marshal and I wanted to jaw with somebody here about the fake money you folks say you've been stuck with. Am I guessing right that it ain't unusual for a customer to lay down twenty or more for most of your wares?"

She smiled sort of snootily and said, "Heavens, we have knickknacks for as little as five dollars, in the gift section."

She sounded like she thought five dollars was not a lot of money, so she likely hadn't been reared on a farm. It was damn near a third of a soldier's monthly wages, and enough to hire a trail herder for a week. But he could see they were used to throwing the stuff about, here. He said, "If I made a sort of average purchase and paid with two or three double eagles, you'd give me back fifteen or sixteen dollars in change without any fuss, right?"

She nodded, but said, "We've been instructed to watch out for double eagles dated 1878, though. We're not to make change for them without showing them to Mr. Kilbride, our floorwalker."

Longarm said he'd like to talk with the man, and the gal pointed at a fussy little gent in a Prince Albert coat with a carnation in the lapel. The floorwalker saw that they were talking about him and came their way, with his eyebrows raised and his nose wrinkled suspiciously. Longarm could see that it was a drinking man's nose, too. But Kilbride was one of those gents who either didn't drink on the job or just got more dignified as he did.

Longarm introduced himself, and the floorwalker said, "You're a little late. The scoundrels have given up on Gump's. We haven't had anyone try a mock double eagle on us for a couple of days now."

"For your sake, I hope you're right," Longarm said. "But they could be laying low, for they know I'm here looking for them."

Kilbride smiled at the salesgirl as though he thought that was funny, and said, "You must have quite a reputation, Deputy. None of the other treasury men have been able to stop them."

"Well, I ain't Treasury. But I didn't come to brag. The young lady here says you're the final say on who can change gold coins here and who can't. Do you test suspicious coins with acid or what?"

Kilbride sniffed and said, "I don't have to. The fakes are good, but nothing looks and feels like gold if you're really used to handling it. I used to have my own jewelry business, before the Bank of California failed back in the seventies. I got wiped out along with everyone else, but I still know my trade. That's why I'm working here at one of the better stores. You just can't fool an old jeweler with red brass!"

Longarm frowned. "Do tell? I talked to a Chinese goldsmith the other night about the queer twenties. He had to test with acid before he could be sure."

Kilbride sniffed again and said, "Oh, what would a China-man know about real value? He's probably never dealt in anything but fourteen-carat gold."

"Maybe. Fill me in on them carrots."

Kilbride said, "Twenty-four carats would be pure gold. But of course pure gold is too soft, so it's alloyed with copper to harden it. The lower the number, the more base metal in the alloy. Fourteen-carat gold is really almost half copper or even zinc. Decent jewelry and gold coinage is eighteen carat, three quarters pure. If I had one of the fakes to show you next to a real double eagle, even you would be able to see the fine distinction in the color."

Longarm took out one of his fakes and said, "You're on. I got one here."

Kilbride nodded and asked the girl to fetch him a real double eagle from the cash drawer. When she did he laid them side by side on the glass top of her counter. He said, "There. See how much redder the counterfeit is?"

Longarm saw no such thing. He knew by the date and scratch which one he'd taken from his pocket, but he couldn't see much difference between them. They both looked like gold to him, and he said so.

Kilbride shrugged and said, "I was wondering why you wore that string tie with that shirt. It takes a trained eye, but I assure you I can see the difference."

"I reckon it's like the way a bank teller gets to know how a real silver certificate snaps," Longarm said. "Most of us don't handle enough money in a lifetime to get that good. But I'll take your word for it. I'm staying at the Palace and I'm counting on you to let me know the minute you spy another one being cashed here. Do you get many folks just in off the street, or do you mostly deal with regular customers?"

Kilbride thought and said, "Well, of course we deal mostly with the carriage trade from Nob Hill. But Gump's is a famous store. Naturally, many vistors to San Francisco shop here."

"Rích visitors, you mean? You'd notice folks who looked like they was more used to shopping in less expensive necks of the woods?"

Kilbride looked Longarm's tweed suit over and said, "Quite," while the salesgirl looked away, trying not to smile. Longarm decided he didn't want to kiss her after all.

He told Kilbride, "I've noticed a mar or two on every one of these fake gold coins. You likely noticed the way the die they use is scratched a mite?"

"Of course," Kilbride said. "But I don't think they've been coining them that way. I think they're casting them with the lost-wax method."

"You do, huh? What's this lost-wax notion, Mister Kilbride? I never heard of it."

Kilbride wrinkled his puffy red nose and said, "Naturally. You're not a jeweler. You'd need a heavy hydraulic press to stamp these coins the way the mint does. That brass alloy is harder than eighteen-carat gold, too. In my opinion, they're using a two-step process. They made a simple set of impressions by pressing two fist-sized lumps of dentist's moulage against both sides of a real double eagle. That would give them very good impressions in nearly perfect detail, but of course it would be too soft to use on cold metal."

"I can see that. Where does the wax come in?"

"Simple. They make a bunch of soft beeswax coins between the dental molds. Then they set them on edge in a tray of plaster. When the plaster sets, they heat the slab and the wax melts and runs out, leaving hollow spaces in the shape of milled and stamped coins. Need I go on?"

Longarm shook his head. "I can see how you could pour a ladle of melted alloy into the empty holes, let the metal cool, and just bust the plaster up to free them. There'd be no casting seams, and it'd only take a little work with a rat-tail file to get rid of the pinhole stems the process would leave. But ain't that a lot of work to go to, next to having a press and set of dies?"

"Work is a relative term, Deputy. Using that old jeweler's trick to make small parts is time-consuming, next to owning a mint. But one could easily coin a thousand dollars or more in a few hours that way, using equipment anyone might have about the house."

Longarm frowned, pocketing his evidence, and said, "You're right. It would be awesomely hard to find a neighbor who'd noticed somebody coming home with a few things in a paper sack, while the pantograph and press that everybody's been looking for might draw more than a little attention. I'd like to tell you you've brightened my day, but you never. If they're using this lost-wax notion, it means almost anybody could be doing it in any house in town!"

Chapter 7

On the way back to his hotel, Longarm picked up a city directory to study later. He went to the Western Union to let Billy Vail know he was still alive and to send a wire to Sacramento about Calvinia Taylor's brother-in-law, just in case she wasn't crazy. Folks seldom started gunning for folks in middle age, after living innocently most of their lives, and he wanted to know if Clem Taylor had a record. As long as he was about it, he asked the state records department to fill him in on her dead husband, Pete. Calvinia hadn't said how she'd gotten to be a widow, but Longarm knew her husband had been rich, and he figured he might as well find out if he'd gotten that way honest. As he left, he was already having second thoughts about sticking his nose in Calvinia's family feud. But he knew that if he went up there later to stick anything else in her, Calvinia would likely start up again about it, and he wanted to know if she was really worrying needfully or just flapping her mouth. Gwynn had seemed to need a lot of excuses just to do what came natural, too. He was pretty sure they were just a pair of secret bawds who liked it with a safe stranger. He was mighty ashamed of himself for even considering a return match with the two of them, but he expected he'd weaken before midnight.

He went to the livery and got the mare. It was a mite early to meet Jimbo, but he meant to jaw with folks along the way. So he rode down Market to the Ferry Building and turned left to follow the Embarcadero, passing the place where he'd lost his carpetbag the other night. He wasn't too surprised to see that nobody had seen fit to put it back on the cobbles where they'd stolen it.

San Francisco was the busiest port on the Pacific Coast, so the Embarcadero was crowded as he reined the mare in and out of the heavy traffic. The army mount seemed upset to meet so many social inferiors, and he was sorry he'd picked such a high-strung, sissy mare by the time she'd shied a couple of times. He patted her neck and said, "Simmer down, girl. That brewery team wasn't trying to rape you. Couldn't you see they was geldings? That mule coming at us ain't a wolf about to bite you, either, so let's cut the bullshit."

Some idiot stevedore rolled a barrel across the cobbles in front of them about then, and the mare reared back, showing the whites of her eyes as her rider cussed and said, "I said steady, damn it! I've a good mind to take you back to the army and just walk about this infernal town. But it's too damned big, so cut the funning and behave like a lady, damn it."

His voice seemed to calm the mare as they moved on. She danced about a bit, sideways, but didn't try to throw him as he looked around. To their left lay railroad tracks, warehouses, factories, and such. To the right, the bowsprits of oceangoing ships stuck out over the passing throng like the limbs of trees. The day was winding down, but you could hardly tell it from the way folks were rolling and shoving cargoes on and off ship. He saw a big loading shed built out over the water on pilings, and said, "Well, so that's where Arbuckle Coffee comes ashore, huh? Funny, I've drunk it in many a cow camp, but I never pictured it in the hold of a clipper."

He knew Levi Strauss had a factory around here somewhere too, and it didn't seem right that pants intended for the High Plains should be made in such a nautical neck of the woods.

He saw a job printer next to a ropewalk, and stopped to see what they had to say about the Emperor Norton's money. When he said he worked for Uncle Sam and allowed that printing money could be considered a federal offense in some picky quarters, the shop foreman laughed and said he pleaded innocent to the charge of counterfeiting for old Norton in the first place, and that it wasn't likely a crime in the second. While the old lunatic cashed his fifty-cent bills all over town, nobody ever passed them on. They just tore them up. The foreman said, "You might consider that scrip a license to beg, as well as a harmless joke, Deputy. The poor old Emperor is too proud to ask for a free meal, but the city can't let him starve. He lost everything he had in the crash of the seventies."

Longarm nodded, but said, "A lot of folks got wiped out in that same crash. How come nobody worries about them?"

"Don't know. Mayhaps 'cause not many of the others went as crazy. I lost my bank account when things fell apart in that scandal, too. But as you can see, I can still hold a job. Most of us managed one way or the other, for it's a tough old town and we're tough folk. But the Emperor was raised genteel, in England, and he's just never been able to get his wits back together again."

Longarm said he noticed, and left.

He spied a foundry and stopped there too, to talk about what sort of gear a man would need to cast metal. They told him the lost-wax business was a sissified artistic notion, and that they cast anchors and such in plain sand molds. But he found out brass couldn't be melted in a kitchen range. They said to melt it you needed at least a blacksmith's forge, with an air blast playing on the retort. They showed him a new patent blower they used on small jobs. It worked with a crank instead of a bellows, and while it was small enough to carry in a Saratoga trunk, it wasn't the sort of thing you could pack in your pocket. They said a pot of molten brass would be heavy and dangerous as hell to handle, too, so he could expect anyone using it to have a chain hoist. He thanked them and left, satisfied that while somebody might be coining in a home workshop, it had to be a lot more elaborate than Kilbride's notion about a kitchen range.

He rode around a bend and spotted the rise of Telegraph Hill ahead. It stood isolated in the middle of the North Beach slums, with more slums rising like a shabby wedding cake on its flanks. It was called Telegraph Hill because back in the Gold Rush days a semaphore tower had stood atop the hill to signal the folks downtown when a ship came in the Golden Gate. He didn't know why they called it Telegraph Hill instead of Semaphore Hill. Folks out here did everything sort of strange.

By now he'd passed the busiest stretch of the waterfront. The hiring of a pier got dearer the closer you were to the center of town. The ships along this stretch petered out to schooners and copra tramps from the Sandwich Islands. He knew that beyond the hill it got cheap enough for little fishing boats to tie up; that was why the Sicilian crab fleet had made North Beach its headquarters. They lived on Telegraph Hill because, without a cable car up it, it was one bitch to climb, and rich folks didn't want to be bothered. He started looking for some sign of Dirty Mary's, but the most interesting sight in view was some construction work going on along the water's edge. A floating piledriver lay anchored a hundred yards offshore, and they'd been dumping sandfill out to make another pierage. The work crew had knocked off for the day, for it was late and the sky was pink to the west, with Telegraph Hill outlined like ink against the gloaming. As he rode past the empty construction site, a gang of about a dozen men moved across his path from the sand pile they'd been concealed behind. They ranged in age from their teens to thirty or so, and none of them looked friendly.

Longarm reined in and said, "Howdy. I'm looking for Dirty Mary's. Am I headed the right way?"

The obvious leader, a thug of about thirty with a patch over one eye, said, "Give us some money, cowboy."

"I ain't a cowboy," Longarm said evenly, "and I ain't going to give you dime one. You're blocking my way, friend."

Longarm's mount reared back as the thug grabbed for her bridle and shouted something mean as hell. Longarm swore and reached for his .44 just as some other son of a bitch drove a hatpin in the mare's rump and sent her in the general direction of the moon!

Longarm hadn't been expecting her to go in two directions at once, and he realized that he'd lost his seat as another thug whipped out a length of chain to lash her across the beast while a sidekick smacked her rump with a plank studded with nails. So there Longarm was, sitting on air as the screaming mare went out from under him. He tried to finish his draw on the way down, but he landed flat on his back on the hard cobbles, and as they piled on him, one of them kicked his .44 off across the paving to God knew where, while somebody else was kicking him in the head.

After that, they started to get rough, but Longarm was partly saved by the fact that there were so many that they tended to get in each other's way, while he was free to kick and punch in any direction.

Somebody yelled, "Jasus, hold him!" as Longarm doubled up, got one hand in somebody's eye and the other on the ground, and came up fighting. He grunted in satisfaction as he landed a solid punch on somebody or other, bulled clear of the main press, and got his derringer out. He said, "I'm starting to get mighty peeved, boys."

Since they paid him no mind, he shoved the muzzle of the derringer in someone's gut and pulled the trigger.

Nothing happened. The goddamned derringer was jammed, he knew, for he'd thought to clean and reload it last night. He let it fall to the end of its chain as he backhanded his intended victim off instead. This was no time to pick sawdust out of the fool belly gun. His hat flew off as another one landed a nasty punch over Longarm's ear. He grabbed at random, picked a gang member up, and threw him ass over teakettle into the pack to clear himself some room. One of his sleeves was out at the shoulder, and his nose was bleeding. But things began to look up as he dropped into a fighting crouch to face the three closer ones as they charged together. He decked one with a left hook. Then somebody hit him across the back with a length of plank and staggered him. As he fought to regain his balance, a cobblestone smacked into his gut and sent him reeling backward as little white stars pinwheeled before his eyes and he tried to remember which way the infernal Bay was.

He found out when somebody smashed a two-by-four against his skull and sent him off the bulkhead to land in Frisco Bay with a mighty splash!

He went down and down and down some more, holding his breath until he hit the muddy bottom with his hands and pushed off to go the other way. They'd been right about the water being as cold as ice, and while it cleared his head some, he could feel the current sweeping along the bulkhead, and when his head broke the surface, he was a good hundred feet closer to the Golden Gate. He didn't want to go there, so he started swimming for a ladder running down the piling of the bulkhead. It wasn't easy; his water-filled boots and soaked clothing weighed a ton. But he caught the rungs and held on to study the situation. He didn't see anybody above him yet, but he'd be in one hell of a spot if somebody decided to drop another cobblestone over the side about now!

Nobody did, and since it seemed just as dumb to stay where he was, Longarm started climbing. As he got near the top, he heard the sounds of mortal fisticuffs. No member of the gang had yet seen fit to gaze over the edge to see if they'd drowned him or not. He got to the top, risked a peek, and saw young Jimbo Corbett doing a lonesome war dance in a circle of fallen foes. They weren't all down yet, but as Longarm grinned and came over the edge, Jimbo did a funny little jig with his feet and suddenly landed a fist at impossible range in the center of a burly thug's face. It looked too pretty to hurt, but the thug went down and hit the ground as limp as a dishrag.

Longarm ran to join the fray, but when the survivors saw him coming, they lost heart and took off in every direction. Longarm saw another boy, younger than Jimbo, holding his army mare over near the railroad tracks as Jimbo said, "Oh, there you are. I thought they'd drowned you."

"I thought so too. I left a sixgun and a hat around here somewhere. Where did you boys come from, Jimbo?"

"We was on our way to Dirty Mary's when we saw what was going on over here. There's your gun, over there by that unconscious North Beacher in the ragged jeans. I'll get your hat."

Longarm limped over to retrieve his gun, squishing in his waterlogged boots and duds. He picked it up, checked the action, and saw that the fall hadn't damaged it. He holstered it, broke open the derringer dangling uselessly down his vest front, and saw that he'd been right. It was loaded, but a sliver of wood was jamming the hammer. He put it back in his wet vest pocket. His Ingersoll was still ticking. He'd have to have it cleaned before the saltwater dried in the works, but he didn't care what time it was.

Jimbo handed him his Stetson and he said, "Thanks. That's the only dry thing I own." He took out his wallet and added, "Oh, shit." The ink hadn't run on his ID, and he hadn't lost his badge, but unless he spread everything out to dry on a flat surface, folks were sure going to think he was messy. Jimbo led him over to the boy holding the skittish mare and introduced him as Mario. "He's Eye-talian, but a dacent fella. He says he knows a woman up the hill who can tell you who's been sleeping with who in these parts."

Mario said, "She's called La Strega, and you'll have to cross her palm with silver, but La Strega knows everything."

"I'll worry about that later," Longarm said. "I got to get dried off some damned way."

Jimbo said, "Lead the horse, Mario. We'll go to Dirty Mary's and get some beer in us while she takes care of this poor drowned rat."

That sounded fair to Longarm, so the three of them left the battered gang to recover as best they could. Jimbo pointed to a large frame building near the tracks running around the base of Telegraph Hill, and Longarm saw why he'd missed the sign. There wasn't any. Dirty Mary's was one of those places you had to know your way to.

As they approached the plain door, he asked Jimbo, "Are you sure this is supposed to be neutral territory, Jimbo?"

The youth said said, "Oh, that was No-Nose Brannigan you tangled with. Him and his ratpack don't own no turf. They're just footpads free-lancing, you might say. You'd have been in trouble if you'd tangled with a *real* Barbary Coast gang."

"Remind me never to do that, Jimbo. You box pretty good. I wouldn't want to tangle with you myself. Where did you pick up that fancy footwork?"

"Oh, Father Murphy at Fourteen Holy Martyrs has an athletic program, and I've had a few lessons. There's a Jesuit brother there who likes to keep abreast of modern science, and he showed me some of the basic moves that professional fighters use."

"He showed you more than the basics, Jimbo. You're good. I'd match you against that gent they call the Boston Strong Boy, now that I've seen you both box."

Jimbo actually blushed. "Go on with your blarney! Nobody could beat the great John L. But is it true you've seen Sullivan in the flesh?" he asked in an awed tone.

"Sure. Last year in Leadville, he whipped the miners' favorite. He's bigger than you, but a lot slower. I hear he's on his way to England to take the world championship away from some boxer named Queensbury."

"Well, he'll win it, then, for no Englishman born of mortal woman could lick John L. Sullivan. But be off with your flattery. Let's see what Dirty Mary can do about your condition."

Mario tethered the mare as Jimbo led Longarm inside. The main room of the place was as big as a warehouse. But Dirty Mary was a pleasant surprise. They found her behind the bar, dressed in red satin, with her long black hair piled atop her head. Her skin looked clean enough to eat off of, and she was pretty, if a mite plumper than Longarm cared for. Dirty Mary looked them over and said, "Jimbo, I've told you before, you're too young to be served here."

"Hell," Jimbo said, "I never asked to be served. I only drink your steam beer. This is my friend Longarm, and he's all wet."

Dirty Mary said, "So I see. It ain't raining out, is it?"

"One of No-Nose Brannigan's lot shoved him in the Bay, Dirty Mary. He came here to dry off."

Dirty Mary laughed uproariously. "Well, and that's one of the most unusual requests we've ever gotten here. What kind of ladies suit your fancy, Longarm? We've got blonds, brunettes, and redheads, fat, skinny, and in between. But no colored or Chinese, for it's a respectable place I'm after running."

Longarm said, "I can see that, ma'am. But why do I need a gal to dry me off? I can do it my own self if you'll give me a towel and someplace to spread my duds out for a spell."

Mario came in to join them as Dirty Mary was pouring their beers. She frowned at Mario and said, "It's root beer for you, me lad, and I'll brook no argument! Jasus, Mary and Joseph, me place is crawling with children and impotent cowboys!"

She slid the three glasses toward them and yelled so loud that it startled Longarm. A wan, pretty girl in long white underwear and a Topsy ribbon in her blond curls came out from the back, and Dirty Mary said, "Take the big one to your crib and dry him off, Sally. Stuff his boots with newspaper and soak his duds in fresh water before you run a sadiron over them to steam 'em dry. For he'll smell like fish and shit together if the Bay dries in that tweed."

"I'm no damned Chinese laundry, Dirty Mary," Sally pouted.

Dirty Mary said, "Faith, I know what you are, Sally, and if he wants your usual services, take care of him while you're about it. Go with her, Longarm. I know she's not pretty, but she's a caution with a sadiron."

Longarm nodded and asked, "How much do I owe you, Miss Mary?"

The madam snorted and said, "Don't talk like a sailor. You came in here with Buckley's Lambs, didn't you? What's you last name, handsome? Sure, them shoulders say you're a Donegal man."

Longarm grinned sheepishly. "It's Long, and I'm afraid I ain't exactly Irish, Miss Mary."

Dirty Mary shrugged off his protestation. "You have to be Irish. You're too cute to be anything else. But it's soaking wet you are, and we'll talk about it after Sally takes care of you."

So he went with the blond. Sally muttered to herself all the way to her crib. When they got there, he saw that it was an eight-by-ten-foot cubicle occupied mostly by a bed. The crib smelled cleaner than most, and the sheets had been recently changed. He started taking things from his pockets and spreading them out to dry on the orange-crate dressing table in the corner.

Sally said, "Don't sit on my bed in them duds. You smell awful."

He agreed with her and stood well clear of her pristine sheets as he peeled out of the wet clothing, which smelled like seaweed with a sewage aftertaste. He felt sort of dumb, undressing in front of a gal he'd just met, but Sally was likely used to any sights he had to show her, so he stripped to the buff. She took his things and said, "I'm taking these to the kitchen. If you want a bath, it's down the hall, but wrap this towel around your middle, for Pete's sake. What kind of a place do you think this is?"

He didn't think he'd better answer that. Sally flounced out with his duds, and he stood up to wrap a towel about his waist as he stared morosely down at the gear he'd spread on the dresser. His sixgun hadn't been in the Bay, but the leather of its cross-draw rig had, and he hadn't know what the salt would do to it. He strapped the gun rig on over the towel, picked up his wallet, watch, and derringer, and went exploring.

He found the bath down at the end of the hall, as Sally had said. There was a sign above the door saying a bath was two bits to the public. He went in anyway. A naked redhead was in the tub already, so he said, "Oops, I'm sorry, ma'am."

"It's all right," she replied calmly. "I'm about finished anyway. You want to use my water, or shall I pull the plug? I got it just right, and it's full of rosepetal bath salts."

He said, "I'd best run a fresh tub, ma'am. Folks would think I was a sissy if I got out smelling like roses."

So the redheaded whore pulled the plug and rose from the tub like Venus from the waves. That is, if Venus had been an Irish redhead all over. This sure was a friendly, down-home place. Dirty Mary didn't go in for frills, but he could see she served the best in beer and bawds. It was surprising to find the place so empty. But it was suppertime, so things would likely liven up in a little while.

The redhead said her name was Colleen, and asked him if he wanted to come to her crib when he was finished. He said he sure would, but that he'd take a rain check, since he was in a hurry. She shrugged and sat on the edge of the tub, drying herself with another towel as Longarm ran a fresh tub and hung his gun rig and watch chain over a nearby towel rack. Colleen didn't seem to find it unusual that he packed a gun even when naked.

She said, "Get in and I'll soap your back before I go."

So he took off his towel, feeling dumb but relieved that his feelings hadn't started to show yet, and lowered himself into the shallow water. He didn't have time for a long soak, with the two Lambs waiting for him in the bar. But he could tell, the moment the water hit his itchy butt, that he'd made a good move.

"You have a nice body," Colleen said, as she knelt naked on the tile floor to run the soap bar over his back. He said she had a nice body too, as he started getting hard below the waterline. Hell, it wasn't like the two young rascals would get bored, waiting in a place like this. But when the redhead said, "There, I got to get dressed," he let her go. Even a freshly scrubbed whore was a mite distasteful, and it wasn't as though he had no friends in Frisco.

He lathered himself as the tub kept filling. He dunked his watch and derringer, and quickly took them out to let them dry off. He figured they wouldn't corrode too badly, now that he had the salt off the metal. He reached for the sixgun rig, took the .44 out, and dropped the leather in the fresh water, swishing it about.

He'd just hung it to drip dry when the door opened and Dirty Mary came in. She said, "I told Mario to rub your horse down and stable her out back with my carriage team."

"That was neighborly of you, Miss Mary. I wonder if I could leave her here for the night. I just learned the hard way that a skittish mount on stone paving ain't the best thing to be aboard in a rough part of town, and I have to go up some hills later."

"Sure and you can bed down here yourself," Dirty Mary said. "I was right about them Donegal shoulders. The Vikings

106

got into Donegal a lot, they say. Sally's steaming out your clothes with her sadiron in the kitchen. It's going to take her some time, I'm thinking. Why don't we go to my room and enjoy a smoke or something while we wait, handsome?"

Longarm wasn't sure he ought to, but he didn't want to be impolite to a right friendly gal like this, and he knew the cheroots he'd left in Sally's crib were no longer fit for smoking, even if his waterproof matches still worked. So he asked what about the boy, and when Dirty Mary said they were occupied at the moment with some other gals, he decided to take his beating like a man.

He tried to wrap the towel about his hips too fast for her to notice his erection as he rose from the tub, but Dirty Mary laughed and said, "Sure, ain't it grand how great minds run in the same channels?"

He laughed too, and they went to her room down the hall.

Dirty Mary's room was large, furnished with lace curtains and red satin counterpanes on the four-poster. She turned the covers down, and the sheets were red satin too. As she started to shuck her red dress, she said, "I hope you don't mind if I leave me hair up, for it's a bother to pin up, and we've only a few minutes. I like to be behind the bar when the boyos start drifting in after dark."

"Well, look," he said, "if you want to skip it for now, it's all right with me." But he didn't mean it. He saw how Dirty Mary looked in nothing but black stockings and frilly red garters. She was Rubenesque but solid. Her ample breasts rode high on her ribs in defiance of gravity, and he could see that the hills of Frisco had done wonders for her legs and round white rump. She reclined on the red satin sheets and smiled up at him to say, "Sure and you look foolish wearing a gun at a time like this."

So he took it off, and the towel off too, and joined her.

"Jasus," she said, "it ain't only your shoulders that run to size. Be gentle with me, will you? I know what you think I am, but I don't work the cribs no more, and to tell the truth, I haven't been with a man in almost a week."

He took her in his arms to kiss her as he ran his hands over her firm, plump curves. She reached for his shaft, sighed, and rolled on her back to welcome him, saying, "We don't need to have a romance. I've been wanting this in me since you came through me door."

So he mounted her and started moving gently, surprised at

how small she was built where it mattered. She said he was too big and then started moving her hips to swallow him alive, so he let himself go.

It was better than he'd expected. Nobody did it like an experienced whore doing it just for fun. Gals like Dirty Mary were funny that way. They seemed to feel contempt for the men who paid them, but a man who wouldn't pay made them feel romantic or something. He could tell she was trying to prove how wrong he'd been to dismiss her charms as a take-it-or-leave-it notion, so he went sort of wild to reassure her, and she let herself go too. She likely got a boot out of not having to maintain her usual professional control.

They both came hard and fast, being experts who saw no need to hold back, and when she saw that he didn't mean to stop at one climax, she raised her legs, let her arms go limp above her head on the red sheets, and sighed, "Oh, that's a grand tool you've got in me, and I love the way you use it. But let's save some of it for later, for I have to get back to work. You're staying the night, of course?"

He stopped, halfway there, and said, "I have to go out a spell, but I'll likely be back to, uh, make sure my horse is all right."

"You could probably serve that mare if she needed it, you brute. But it's me you'll be after screwing to sleep in this very bed, after business slows down in the wee smalls. Either come or take it out, darling. I have expenses to think about, and business has been dreadful of late."

He rolled off and wiped himself on the towel as he asked her why her business was slow, considering what a nice place she had.

"This town's just recovering from the terrible depression of the seventies, and even those with steady work are inclined to bank their wages. Sure it's unsettling to be broke, and the crash put a lot of men off their feed."

"I noticed," he said. "Do you accept the Emperor's scrip here, Miss Mary?"

"He's older than God and needs no pleasure stronger than beer," she replied. "He's been in me bar a few times, for if there's a bar in town that the old lunatic hasn't visited by now, it must serve watered drinks. But His Majesty is too dignified to visit the cribs."

"Well, everybody agrees he's crazy. I'm interested in another gent you might know, Miss Mary. Middle-aged mint worker named Enrico Dandolo. Does the name ring a bell?"

The whore sat up, frowning, and said, "Never heard of him. Why would he be after visiting a place so far from the mint?"

"Another gent working for my outfit thought he might spend time in these parts, and from the way he was gunned in the back, he must have had reason for his suspicions. Dandolo was Eye-talian and might have felt more at home near Fisherman's Wharf. He was a widower with a grown daughter he sheltered from the facts of life, so he wouldn't have trifled close to his home on Rincon Hill. I thought he might have been better known in this neck of the woods. But I'll take your word he wasn't one of your regulars here."

Dirty Mary frowned thoughtfully and said, "Sure an Italian might have felt more comfortable with his own kind, and while we have a French girl, most of the others are Irish, or Yankee Protestants. If he was visiting a girl near Telegraph Hill, she was probably a *signora*."

"That sounds reasonable. Is there a house like this where they serve meatballs, Miss Mary?"

Dirty Mary shook her head. "Not a regular cathouse. Them Old Country dagoes are sort of prim, being heathens. I've heard of some local Italian girls selling semi-pro up on the hill, but only to their own kind, and even then, it ain't safe for a stranger to wink at a woman on Telegraph Hill. Sicilians are like A-rabs when it comes to their women. You mess with a crab fisher's wife, sister, or daughter, and he tends to act mighty wild about it. If this Dandolo you're looking for had a girl on the hill, she was his steady. She'd be a widow or an orphan, with no men of her tribe guarding her reputation."

He nodded and thanked her for the tip. She'd narrowed down the field, and her words made sense. Dirty Mary said she wanted to douche, so he went back to Sally's crib and found his duds laid out on the other bed. They were damp, but dry enough to put on. The hickory shirt and longjohns were all right, but his socks had shrunk and his tweed pants, vest and coat smelled like wet blankets.

He put them on and discovered they'd only shrunk about an inch all around. They'd likely fall back into shape as he moved about in them. He took the newspapers out of his boots and hauled them on. When he stood in them, they sort of squished, but what the hell. The stuff he'd spread on the dresser was still damp, but he filled his pockets. The watch was still ticking. He unloaded the derringer and dry-fired it a couple of times. The hammer was working again, so that wood shaving had been the culprit. He reloaded and dropped the belly gun in its vest pocket, cussing himself for missing that sliver when he'd reloaded after the gunfight in the other whorehouse.

He spilled his sixgun ammo on Sally's bed and checked the Colt's action before he tried a couple of quick draws from the damp holster. The waxed holster hadn't lost its shape, and if he was careful about leaning it on anything before it dried completely, it would be all right if and when he needed to fill his hand. He reloaded and headed for the main bar, feeling a lot more useful.

He found the two boys with Dirty Mary in the bar. A couple of stevedores were nursing beers down at the other end. He told Mario he was ready to meet La Strega, and promised Dirty Mary he'd say howdy some more when he came back for his horse.

As they left, he asked Jimbo how come everything had been on the house, and Jimbo explained that the Lambs made sure no other gangs shook Dirty Mary down for protection money.

Longarm asked how much the Lambs got, and Jimbo said, "Nothing. Dirty Mary and her girls vote as a block for Boss Buckley's machine, and as you see, they treat us dacent. Us Irish stick together." He nudged Mario and added, "Even when our mothers didn't come from Cork. How was it, Mario? Did you lose your cherry to that redhead?"

"A man of the world doesn't boast of his conquests," Mario said loftily. "But that Dirty Mary makes me mad. She says liquor might stunt my growth and she never lets me have none. It seems to me that a man old enough to get laid is old enough to drink. What do you think, Longarm?"

"It could be worse," Longarm replied. "What if they served you beer and wouldn't let you at the gals? How far is this Strega woman's place, Mario?"

The Sicilian youth pointed at a wooden stairway running up between the shacks ahead and said, "We have some climbing. I'd better take the lead. Jimbo, keep your voice down as we go. That loud brogue makes some of my people nervous, and I don't want to get hit with a slop bucket again."

They started up the steps Indian file. It was starting to get dark and, as in Chinatown, the city fathers hadn't seen fit to

be free with street lamps. The steps twisted confusingly between the overhanging eaves on either side, and he knew he'd
hate like hell to have to find his way through here on his own
after dark. They came to a steep cinder path, followed it around
a big hairpin, and wound up climbing another, steeper flight
of crooked steps. Mario led them to a sort of inclined alley and
said, "Wait here while I see if La Strega will talk to you."

He left, and Longarm asked Jimbo if he knew La Strega.

Jimbo said, "No, but I heard about her. La Strega means
'the witch' in dago. She helps women with family problems
like unfaithful husbands and unwanted babies. So she knows
everything that's going on up here."

Longarm reached for a smoke, then remembered he'd aban-
doned his soaked cheroots, and bummed a smoke off Jimbo.
They'd half consumed his cheap cigarillos when Mario came
back and said La Strega would see Longarm—alone. So Jimbo
said he'd scout Longarm up later, and headed back down to
the Barbary Coast, where he likely felt more comfortable.

Mario led Longarm up the alley to a gate covered over with
grapevines, and they went through a little herb garden to a
frame house squatting like a big gray toad, its tin roof lower
than the ones on either side. Mario said, "You go in alone.
My folks would have a fit if they heard I'd visited La Strega.
They'd think the stories about me and the Tancredi girl are
true."

Longarm thanked the youth and ducked under the low ov-
erhang of the door, which stood open, save for a bead curtain.
It was as dark as a cave inside, and smelled like somebody had
been burning bats and incense. He stood there blinking in the
dark and said, "Ma'am?" uncertainly.

He heard a wild, mad cackle, and then La Strega removed
the cloth from a votive candle in a red jar. He could see in the
hellfire that the walls were covered with cheap imitations of
Persian rugs, and that La Strega was likely as crazy as the
Emperor Norton, for she was dressed like an A-rab princess,
or maybe a Gypsy dancing gal. But she was a mite long in the
tooth to be either a princess or a dancing gal. She sat on a pile
of cushions near a low-slung table covered with black velvet
and Tarot cards. She was maybe sixty, and he could see she'd
been a reasonably decent-looking gal at one time.

She pointed to more cushions across from her and said,
"The boy said you wanted a reading."

Longarm sat down and placed a silver dollar on the velvet before he replied, "I don't need card tricks, ma'am. I just wanted to gossip with you about an Eye-talian gent who hasn't been seen around town of late."

"Enrico Dandolo, from Rincon Hill," the woman said matter-of-factly. "He thought he was important with his Lombardy accent and waxed mustache. But all men are the same when they are naked and in bed, eh?"

"Did you know him, ma'am?"

"No. We never met. But I have ways of finding out what is going on in the dark around me. You think I am a fake, eh?"

"No, ma'am. Not a fake at finding things out. Mario spoke respectful of your powers, and that's good enough for me."

La Strega started playing with her cards as she said, "I know who you are. You don't have to tell me. You are an agent for the Treasury, like that other who was looking for Enrico Dandolo. I did not like him. He did not cross my palm with silver, but said I had to tell him everything I knew. Who do you think shot him?"

Longarm frowned down at the cards and answered, "Don't know, ma'am. Likely somebody as didn't like him asking questions about Dandolo. He may have acted a mite pushy. Is that cartwheel enough, or should I sweeten the pot before we get down to brass tacks?"

La Strega didn't answer, so he put another dollar down and she cackled, "You are a wise young man. I like you. You do not threaten and you do not bluster. You treat me with respect. So let us forget about the silver. What is it you wish to know about Enrico Dandolo?"

"I know better than to ask where he's buried, but can I assume your powers don't extend that far, ma'am?"

La Strega shrugged. "He was not harmed by anyone I know. He had a woman on the hill. She did not live here either. They kept private rooms over the winery of Papa Guido. Do not search for him there. Papa Guido and his sons might get upset if a federal man poked about their, ah, informal winery."

"I follow your drift. I take it the love nest is empty now. But what can you tell me about it, ma'am?"

"A love nest is a love nest, eh? It was clean, isolated, discreet. Enrico Dandolo was a widower who did not wish to take his lover home to meet his friends and family on fancy Rincon Hill. The woman was probably married to someone else too. She wore a wedding band, and she never got it from Enrico Dandolo, I'm sure. They thought they were so smart, but the other women around them knew what was going on."

Longarm knew that was how La Strega knew too. "What can you tell me about this sneaky gal he was seeing, ma'am? Was she Eye-talian too?"

"Italian? Of course she was Italian. Would he be keeping a Greek on Telegraph Hill?"

"I don't see why not, ma'am. You said they was meeting on the sly and both come from other parts. What did she look like, or don't you know?"

"Hah, of course I know. I know everything. She was nice looking and well dressed. She was dark and they spoke Italian to each other. Mr. Know-it-all. They both had fancy accents, like they thought they were aristocrats. But he worked with his hands just the same, in spite of his waxed mustache, eh? *Dio carne,* I don't know what this country does to our people. Give an Italian peasant a shirt and tie, and he wants you to call him a Don! The woman was a snob too. She snubbed the other women of the hill when she got down from her fine carriage in a back alley to meet her lover. But she was just acting big. They rutted just like anyone else in that love nest over the winery, eh?"

"I take it they was careless with the window blinds?" Longarm asked smiling.

La Strega smiled back and said, "No, but the walls were thin, and she was a hellcat with a shrill voice. They made love like caged tigers, and when they weren't tearing at each other's bodies, they fought like cats and dogs, very loud. They had a terrible spat the last night they used the place. It was about the time that other lawman said he vanished. Eh, it must have been. They never came back again. But don't pester Papa Guido about blood spots and bullet holes. They left together, both alive, and drove off in her carriage. He'd said something about having to go to a party. I think that was what the fight must have been about. Rosa Francetti, across the way, was listening. She couldn't help it. The man said he had to go to this party and the woman was insisting he go somewhere else with her. Rosa says she's sure they left before they'd had time to make love. The fight started right after he joined her, and they left shortly after sunset."

"That ties in with what his daughter told me," Longarm

said. "It was his birthday and he wanted to go home. But he never got there."

"He went with his lover, then. She was young and pretty, and all men are putty in the hands of a stubborn wench."

"I've noticed, ma'am. But if he went with that gal, he never left the place she took him. If she was married, I doubt it could have been to her own home, wherever that might be. You reckon he got killed in a lover's quarrel?"

"Such things happen commonly," La Strega said. "They may have been caught by her husband. On the other hand, she may have killed Enrico, or Enrico may have killed her. In either case, the victim has been disposed of and the other is still hiding, since it was not too long ago, eh?"

Longarm pulled at the end of his mustache as he thought briefly, then said, "You said they tended to be passionate. There's something I don't savvy about the whole thing, though. You say this Eye-talian lady was pretty and high-toned, right?"

"I know what you are saying. She was young enough to be his daughter, and he could not have made much money working at the mint. Bored married women do not have affairs with middle-aged men of average means. They want a strong young Casanova or a rich sugar daddy, no?"

"We're both smart, ma'am. Dandolo was a short, uninteresting gent of fifty, waxed mustache or no. It seems to me a nice-looking spitfire with her own carriage and team could likely do a mite better, unless he had something she wanted."

La Strega said, "Well, he was Italian at least. Maybe she was not comfortable flirting in English. Maybe there was more to Enrico Dandolo than the neighbor women could judge, with his pants on, eh?"

They were starting to talk in a circle as well as dirty. Longarm had traced the missing mint worker a mite farther than anyone else now, but La Strega had told him Dandolo left the neighborhood alive. So he decided to try the same deal. He thanked the old gal for her help and let himself out. It was black as hell now, and he had a chore getting out the gate in the dark.

He moved off a ways and holed up in a pool of shadow to get his bearings and see if anybody was tailing him. Nobody was. He heard folks fussing in Eye-talian in a nearby house, but La Strega hadn't played him false, as far as he could tell. He hadn't expected her to, but a man in his line had to cover all bets, and the last federal lawman who'd jawed with folks up here about the missing mint worker had been gunned in the back.

So Longarm's back sort of itched as he felt his way downhill toward the west. He felt out of place in this transplanted hunk of Sicily. But nobody bothered him as he worked his way down to the United States. Stepping into the first flatland doorway he came to, he waited some more to see if he was being tailed. Nothing happened, so he shrugged and headed for some bright lights in the middle distance.

He came to an open, cobbled space where folks were cooking crabs in big pots, and bitty sailboats bobbed alongside the broad, paved Fisherman's Wharf. He asked a colored man rolling a big barrel where he could catch a cable car to Nob Hill, and the stevedore pointed south along a lit-up street. Longarm thanked him and headed that way, stopping at the first shop with a wooden Indian out front to stock up on cheroots. He spied folks ahead standing near a big wooden turntable in the middle of the street. There were tracks leading on and off the turntable, so he didn't ask if this was where you caught yourself a cable car. He went over to a street vendor's pushcart and bought himself a hot tamale for supper. It tasted good but made him thirsty. He looked about for someplace that served beer, but then he saw the cable car coming down the tracks and decided he could wait.

Chapter 8

The dinky car was about half the size of a Denver streetcar. It looked strange and a mite magical, rolling onto the turntable without the aid of horses. The passengers on board disembarked, and those waiting to go the other way joined in to help the conductor as he got down to swing the cable car around on the turntable. Longarm walked over, got a hand on a side post, and helped. They got her aimed the other way and the conductor thanked them and said to climb aboard. So they all did. The car had a closed compartment in the middle, with open platforms fore and aft. Longarm sat down on a hardwood bench up front, near the driver, and asked him to let him know when they got to California Street, atop Nob Hill. The driver said he would, clanged the bell with his foot pedal, and lowered the cable shoe to start out with a lurch. Longarm wondered if you rode these things free until the conductor moved forward along the open platform and took a nickel off him. It seemed a right reasonable price to pay as the street went mad and started up Russian Hill at an impossible grade. He was glad he'd left the mare at the whorehouse. It looked like they were headed for the moon, and she'd have never made it on steel shoes.

They clanged along with folks jumping on and off, for the

cable car didn't seem to stop anywhere, but just clanged a warning through every intersection as it kept going. There were lots of folks out walking, this early, but few horsedrawn vehicles on the higher slopes. Nobody drove on the ridges of Russian Hill and Nob Hill unless they had a good reason and it was past delivery and going-home times.

They reached the crest of Russian Hill and tooled along flat for a spell as he admired the view down the side streets. It was a clear night, and the lights below winked like the stars were in the wrong place tonight. Then they dropped into the saddle between Russian and Nob Hill and started going even higher. The driver dinged his gong and yelled to Longarm that his stop was coming up. Only he never stopped, so Longarm took a deep breath, stood up, and dropped off running. The cobbles were slick and his boot heels were still damp, so he slid some before he staggered to a more dignified walk in the wake of the merry cable car. He looked about to get his bearings, and sure enough, there was the other cable car line, crossing the one he'd been on. A car was coming up from Chinatown, so he stood on the corner to admire it as it passed, dinging away. It crossed over the ridge without stopping and dropped off to the west at an alarming angle, but nobody screamed. They were likely used to getting about like that.

He found Gwynn Doyle's stoop lit up like she was expecting company, even though he was hours early. He went up the steps and rang the doorbell. The widow Doyle came to the door and looked surprised to see him. She said, "Oh, Custis, you said you were coming around midnight."

He said, "I know. I finished early. I'll go off again if I'm disturbing anybody."

"Don't be silly. Calvinia's as anxious as I am. But watch your mouth, darling. I have company, and I told you my reputation is important to me."

She led him into the parlor, where Calvinia was presiding over a mostly male guest list and a sideboard covered with booze and buffet. All but one of the men were sort of stuffy gents of the sort he'd expect to meet on Nob Hill. But Calvinia was serving smoked oysters to Kilbride, the floorwalker from Gump's Department store.

The fat was in the fire and he was thirsty, so he went over to help himself to a drink, fixing himself a rye and water while Kilbride asked him if he'd found out anything more about the counterfeit double eagles. Calvinia seemed surprised as she realized Longarm was a federal agent, and when she asked him why he hadn't mentioned it, he shrugged and said, "Must have slipped my mind. Are you sore about it?"

Calvinia shot him a knowing look and said, "I don't see what difference it makes. Ah, Gwynn told you we wanted to talk to you privately after the others leave, didn't she?"

"Yes, ma'am. She said it was a pressing matter requiring my full attention."

The saucy-eyed brunette turned away before Kilbride could catch the gleam in her eye. So Longarm was stuck with talking to him, and Kilbride wanted to talk about fake money.

"I said I don't who's been doing it," Longarm told him. "I didn't know you lived around here, Kilbride."

The floorwalker looked about wistfully and said, "I wish. Actually, I'm living on the wrong side of the Slot, these days. Roominghouse in Noè Valley. I came to appraise some jewelry for Mrs. Doyle, earlier, and she was kind enough to invite me to stay awhile."

Longarm nodded and sipped his drink. He saw now why the ex-jeweler wasn't being accepted by the stuffed shirts around them. Neither Gwynn nor Calvinia saw fit to introduce Longarm around, and that was jake with him. From snatches of conversation that drifted his way, he got the idea they were bankers, lawyers, and other tedious types. He caught one looking at him like there was something funny about the way he looked. Hell, he'd hung his hat, and his suit was store-bought and totally dry now. His hickory shirt wasn't starched, and he'd only paid two bits for the string tie they made him wear, but this wasn't a wedding or a wake, and he thought he looked elegant enough to drink with anybody at an infernal buffet at a private home.

Kilbride must have felt unwanted too. He left in about five minutes, leaving Longarm alone in a corner. After she'd shown Kilbride out, Gwynn joined him there and asked if he was having a good time. He said he'd rather be herding sheep and asked what this party was about.

She lowered her voice and said, "Strictly business, you jealous thing. As you know, the stock market has recovered and business is getting better, now that dear President Hayes has cleaned up the mess that old drunk Grant left behind."

"You playing the stock market, Gwynn?"

"I am. And the men you see about you are leading lights

of the West Coast business world. That's Collis Huntington over there, looking down the front of Calvinia's dress. He's the Central Pacific and he just gave me a good tip on irrigation bonds. Don't look at him so mean, dear. I assure you we haven't slept with anyone in this room but you."

He grinned sheepishly. "I wasn't looking at him mean, just sort of thoughtful. You don't see many men in the flesh who can say they took on Jay Gould in a financial war and won. I had no idea you traveled in such company, Gwynn, no offense."

"Well, this is Nob Hill, dear. But there's not a man here who's as, ah, impressive to me in other ways."

He felt mollified as she wandered off to pump more business secrets out of some old goat with a gray beard. But it was boring as hell, even eating and drinking, and he was looking forward to the two gals alone. He took out his watch and checked the time. A million years later he did so again, and the minute hand hadn't moved. He held the Ingersoll up to his ear and swore under his breath. The fool watch had stopped.

He put down his glass to build himself a sandwich, and another man came over to join him, asking Longarm to pass the mustard. He seemed friendlier and more relaxed than most of the other guests, and had a young but somewhat grizzled face of the sort that Longarm was used to seeing on cowboys. When he spoke, he had a slight accent, which Longarm realized after a few moments was Scandinavian. As they talked, the man said he'd been a sea captain—which explained his weatherbeaten appearance—but that he'd give up the life of the open sea to start his own shipping line. His name was Matson.

Longarm asked if he was the Matson who ran ships to the Sandwich Islands, and the fellow admitted modestly that he was.

"And you, Mr. Long," he said. "I understand you're some kind of lawman."

"That's pretty much right," Longarm said. "I'm a deputy U.S. marshal. But I don't work out of the local office. I'm here to investigate some funny double eagles that some rascal's been making in your fair city."

Matson nodded. "I've heard there's a lot of queer going around. But I'm afraid I can't help you. I only know how to get from here to Honolulu and back."

"I was admiring some of your clippers earlier today. Noticed you're starting to put funnels on 'em. I don't want to go to Honolulu, but I'd like to hear about this boom everyone's talking about. I knew the price of beef was up, back East. Knew silver was up too. But ain't it a mite early for everyone to start playing the stock market again? Last time it got exciting, the whole country damn near went bust."

"As it will again, Deputy Long. For what goes up must come down, and it will ever be boom and bust in a free economy. The depression of the seventies was a long and hard one, though, so the coming boom should see new heights. You're right about it being early. That's when the smart money gets on the bull. By the time the mass of investors can see that the market's rising, it's generally too late to make a killing. Do you have a few thousand to risk on some dirt-cheap blue chips that have to rise within the year?"

"Not hardly. I'm going to have to cheat on my expense account to make it through next payday."

Matson sighed. "Pity," he said. "I know a dozen good buys you could make right now if you had the liquidity."

Longarm said some more rye and water would be about as much liquid as he could manage. So they both laughed and he built the shipowner a drink while he was at it. Matson wandered off with his sandwich to tell somebody else how to get rich as Longarm sipped his drink, feeling left out. Everyone in the room was richer than he was, and he could sense the greed in them as they jawed about bonds and the new Edison of Jersey stock now coming on the market. Longarm knew he wasn't likely to die rich. But if getting rich meant coming to many affairs like this, he wasn't sure he was missing out on all that much. Uncle Sam paid him decently enough, and he'd have a pension to keep from starving in his old age, if nobody gunned him before he had to retire. By then, if Matson was right, he'd likely have lived through a couple more booms and busts, so maybe he was better off not thinking too hard about money. Money did funny things to folks' heads.

He'd eaten all he could, and didn't want to get drunk with two love-starved women waiting, if only he could keep from turning into a pumpkin before they got rid of their stuffy business associates. Nobody seemed interested in him, so he drifted out with his drink and sat down alone in the empty study to enjoy one of his new smokes. He was beginning to feel the effects of that brawl on the Embarcadero, and caught himself nodding off. He stood up and went over to a bookcase to see if there was a good book to read. Either Gwynn was more intellectual than she let on with her clothes off or, more likely, her husband had been a bookworm—which explained a lot, when you studied on it. The shelves were full of stuffy non-fiction tomes about law, history, and economics. There were some language books, and right now he was sort of interested in Italian. He spoke fair Border Mex, and the two lingos sounded sort of related. But they didn't have an Italian dictionary. They had French, German, Greek, and even Spanish, but nothing he was interested in right now. He took down a book about the Union Pacific scandal that had nearly put Vice-President Colfax in jail, carried it back to the sofa, and cracked it open. He knew what the watered UP stocks had done in Colorado, but he wanted to check on California. The book was dry as hell, and he gave up after reading a few dates. California had made it through the first big mess, since most local investors had bought rail stock off the better-run Central Pacific when they were wedding the rails. Folks out here had made out decently until a delayed reaction broke the Bank of California in the mid-seventies. So Matson was right about its being time for another boom. But he was out here to catch counterfeiters, not to play the stock market, and, Jesus H. Christ, what time was it getting to be?

He'd lost track of how many cheroots he'd smoked. He was lighting another when Gwynn came in, unpinning her long blond hair as she sighed and said, "I thought they'd never go. Are you ready, Custis?"

He grinned and said, "Been ready for a coon's age. But shouldn't we start in a bedroom?"

"Calvinia's undressing in the bedroom, dear. I want a private moment with you before we join her."

That seemed a mite selfish to Longarm, but since he wasn't the one getting left out, and since Gwynn was peeling off her black dress in any case, he stood up and started shucking. Naturally, she beat him to it, since she'd not only had a head start but wasn't wearing as much to begin with. He'd been just a mite concerned about his weak moment with Dirty Mary, but as he saw the widow Doyle's cool, lean body in the soft light of the study, he started rising to the occasion. When she lay back on the sofa to open her thighs in welcome, he was sure glad he'd stopped early in the game with the plump Irish gal.

"Hurry," she gasped. "I can't wait another second!"

So he joined her on the sofa to enter her with no foreplay. She wrapped her arms and legs around him hungrily and they kissed as he touched bottom in her.

She certainly had been thinking ahead to this moment, for she started going crazy as soon as he was in her, and came ahead of him. He didn't even slow down as she climaxed and she sobbed, "Oh God, you're better than I remembered, and I've been remembering you all afternoon!"

He didn't answer. Between the earlier session at his hotel and the unexpected romp with Dirty Mary, he wasn't as anxious as he might have been, and while he knew he was good for a few more times, he'd have to pace himself if they both wanted this. He rode in her saddle like a rider cantering back to camp after a hard day herding cows, reasonably anxious to get there, but not hysterical and lathered up about it.

The long, steady strokes drove her wild and she gasped, "Oh my God, it's happening again!"

Sure enough, he could tell by her throbbings that it was. She went limp under him and pleaded, "Have mercy, darling. I'm too sensitive to bear it so passionately."

So he faked an orgasm and stopped, breathing hard. It was only fair to play a trick so many gals had played on him, wasn't it?

Few gals knew that men could play at the same game, so when they got up and she saw that it was still at half-mast, she gasped and said, "Lord have mercy. You really are a primitive brute. Let's join Calvinia. I see you're just too much for any one poor girl to handle."

She led him by the hand out of the room. He felt sort of dumb, leaving his duds and possibles in the study like that, but she seemed anxious, and she swore the front door was locked. He felt even dumber when they walked in on Calvinia hand in hand, all three of them stark naked and the coal-oil lamp by the bed reflected over and over in the mirrors on both sides. The smaller brunette lay on pristine white linen sheets, but the mirrors made the setup more shocking than in Dirty Mary's red satin four-poster.

Shocking was what they had in mind. As he climbed in bed with them, the two widow women were all over him at once. He wound up on his back, with one of them trying to shove her breast down his throat, while somebody got aboard his poor

122

tool and started riding up and down like they thought he was a merry-go-around. When he glanced sideways at the mirrors, he saw that Calvinia was screwing him while Gwynn made love to his top half. He'd thought it felt different inside her. Calvinia leaned forward to get in on the kissing as Gwynn made room for her.

It got sort of confusing after that.

As the two of them took turns satisfying Longarm and each other, with their images in the facing mirrors on both sides of the bed duplicating their acts endlessly, Longarm no longer regretted his digression at Dirty Mary's. A man who hadn't practiced for this evening would have come like a schoolboy in two seconds. As it was, the two widow women took nearly ten minutes to damn near knock him out.

After that, nobody had much to say for a spell. When the heavy breathing had quieted down some, Longarm extricated himself from between them.

"I hate to admit defeat, ladies," he said wearily, "but I'm afraid there ain't no more where that came from."

Calvinia seemed to be asleep already, but Gwynn replied, "I'd say we've about exhausted all the possibilities for now. Let's all get some sleep and start fresh in the morning."

Longarm yawned widely and shook his head. "Right now," he said, "sleep sounds better than being President of these United States, honey. But I can't stay the night. Aside from what your neighbors would say if I should go tippy-toeing out of here in the cold gray light of dawn, I want to get back down the hill and see if there's any answers to some wires I sent."

"You'll have to let yourself out, then. I'm too worn out to move from this bed. Have you found anything about poor Calvinia's in-laws?"

He glanced at the sleeping brunette and said, "Not yet, but I mean to check her notion out, just in case there's anything to it. Have you gals received any threats or noticed anybody skulking about?"

She shook her head and he said, "There you go, then. So far, all the mean folk in Frisco seem to be after *me*. So it'll likely be safer for both of you if I stay at my hotel than if I'm up here, drawing fire from God knows who."

As he sat up, Gwynn asked him why anyone would be after him, and he ducked the question by rising. He hadn't talked to the gals about the counterfeit double eagles and didn't have time to go into it now. He bent to kiss her and left to go down and get his duds. She didn't follow. He dressed and armed himself, found his hat in the hall, and let himself out.

He went down the steps, starting to reach for his watch and then remembering it was out of order. But it hardly mattered what time it was, for all he needed to do was find his way back to the Palace and sleep a million years.

He didn't see how it could be midnight yet, but when he got to the corner and looked down at the flats below, there wasn't a light showing. Another fog bank had run in through the Golden Gate like like cobweb syrup, and it looked worse than the fog the night before. But this time Longarm knew the way back to his hotel.

He stood a few minutes to see if a cable car was clanging along anywhere down there in the pea soup. Then he shrugged and headed east, downhill. Despite what the two crazy widow women had put him through, he could still walk downhill, and once he made it to Columbus, at the bottom of the slope, it wasn't far to his hotel if he didn't take side trips to odd corners of the Barbary Coast. He made the first cross with no trouble, but then, as he saw that the fog had risen higher than before on Nob Hill, the going got a mite tricky. The wan light of the occasional street lamps only served to make everything look like dirty cotton wool instead of plain old blackness. He slowed down and navigated by the sibilant hiss of the invisible cables running down the center of the street to his right. The stone walk underfoot was wet from the drifting fog, and the odd hissing of the cables sounded more spooky than reassuring. His wet boot heels hardly made a sound, and he seemed to be alone in the fog. Undoubtedly, normal Frisco folk preferred to wait for the cable cars if they had to be out at all in this infernal fog.

He figured he was somewhere in Chinatown again when he smelled something funny cooking and off in the night some gal seemed to be singing a high sad song through her nose, to the accompaniment of twanging of rubber bands. He came to a street lamp and looked up for a street sign. There wasn't any. He shrugged and trudged on into the blackness. But when he brought his heel down, there wasn't any sidewalk there; he'd walked off a change in slope that pitched him forward and nearly spilled him on his nose. He cursed and staggered down the treacherous walk like a drunk on ice, and just as he was getting his balance, a gun went off behind him and something hummed by his left ear like a pissed-off bumblebee!

Longarm let himself drop to the wet paving and slid on his butt for a spell as he hauled out his sixgun, dug in a heel, and swiveled around to face upslope on his belly, his Colt trained the same way.

There wasn't anything to shoot at. The street lamp that he'd stopped under like a greenhorn spread a faint glow as illuminating as a firefly's fart, high in the middle of the air. Everything else was as black as a process server's heart, and you couldn't tell whether the fog was moving about up there or whether something more solid was shifting position. The only sound was the hiss of the cable to his left and the beating of his heart on the cold wet walk. The only bright spot was that the bushwhacker had no way of knowing whether Longarm had been hit or just fallen on his ass after tripping over his own feet in the fog. He knew no lights silhouetted him from behind, down the slope, unless a cable car chose such an inconvenient moment to come up California Street. He tried to remember how often they ran late at night. But he hadn't asked, so he didn't know.

He tried to put himself in the other's boots. He didn't go in for shooting folks in the back without warning, but if he did, and had seen a man go down just as he fired, there were two ways to finish the play. You could move in to make sure, or you could quit while you were ahead. Longarm was sure the stalker in the fog was after him personal, so the shooter likely knew his victim's rep. Longarm knew he'd have to feel brave as hell to walk blind into total darkness after a man he had pegged as a tolerable shot.

But then he saw the ghostly outline of a man on the edge of the dropoff, walking quiet as a cat with his sidearm raised and ready to throw down on any likely target, as he looked for the man he hoped he had put a bullet in.

Longarm saw no need to discuss the matter further; the bastard had not seen fit to call out when *he'd* fired. Longarm slowly squeezed off a round—then gasped in dismay as the hammer clicked uselessly.

He was already rolling when the other fired at the cricketlike chirp of his crippled sixgun, so the son of a bitch missed again, but not by much, for his bullet spanged off the walk near Longarm's hip, to sing its life away in the fog downslope.

Didn't they have anyone in Frisco who paid mind to the sound of gunplay at night? Longarm was smack in the middle of town, and not a creature was stirring except that son of a bitch up there, throwing lead at the lawman as he slithered like a reptile on the wet cobblestones, snapping his useless gun back at him!

As he rolled over the cableway, Longarm saw that the other was crabbing sideways along the crest, growing fainter as he tried to improve his aim. Nobody could miss forever, and as he saw that his clicks were giving his position away, Longarm stopped, took off his hat, and rolled back the other way as he skimmed the Stetson like a pie plate the way he'd been going. As the gunman spotted the movement and fired at it, Longarm let go of the sixgun and drew his derringer. This time the little bastard behaved itself when he pulled the trigger, twice. The other staggered as the two .44s slammed into him. Then he fell in the center of the roadway and Longarm heard his gun sliding down the cobbles his way. When it got to him, he grabbed it and got up, holstering his own out-of-order gun as he transferred the big Patterson Conversion .45 to his gunhand and headed gingerly upslope, figuring there were two or three rounds left in it, depending on whether the other had started with six or five in the chambers. One would do, if he could just spot the bastard. But when he reached the crest, the other wasn't there.

"What the hell?" he whispered, and then, as he heard what sounded like something dragging and moaning at the same time, he caught on and ran up the cableway, yelling, "Dammit, come back here!"

As he chased the cableway higher, the fog started thinning again, and now he could see what looked like a bundle of rags going six miles an hour up the middle of the street. The man he'd put on the ground had caught his belt or tie or something in the moving steel rope under the street, and the cable was dragging him along on his face!

There was no telling where the hell the erstwhile bush-whacker might have wound up, had not the California Street cable crossed the Powell Street cable at right angles.

Something snapped, and the man he'd shot just lay there oozing, in the center of the intersection. Longarm moved in, covering him, and asked him how he felt as he dropped to one knee. The man didn't answer, and when Longarm rolled him over he could why. The long drag over the granite cobbles had scraped his face off, and the rest of him was mighty messy too. It was a waste of time to feel his pulse, but Longarm did anyway, and then he started going through the dead man's pockets.

He'd just put the man's wallet in his side pocket when he heard the sound of a police whistle and running footsteps. So he put the bushwhacker's gun back in its holster and stood up to call out, "Over here, Officer."

The beat copper materialized out of the fog near him, looked down, and said, "Oh, Jasus, not another dragging! I heard shots just now. Did you?"

Longarm said, "I sure did. I moved toward them and found this gent laying here like this. He might have fired his gun for help when the cable caught him, don't you reckon?"

The copper wasn't that dumb. "Sure he did," he snorted. "Then he put the darlin' gun back in its holster while the cable dragged him to death. I see you're wearing a gun, while we're on the subject. Do you have a reason for walking the streets of our fair city wearing a sidearm?"

"Doesn't everybody? I got a permit, though. I'm a deputy U.S. marshal, and local gun laws don't apply to me. You want to see my ID?"

"No offense, but I'd rather see if your gun's been fired recently."

Longarm grinned, drew his sixgun butt first to keep from spooking the copper, and handed it over. The copper sniffed, held it up to the light, and said, "Well, I see the shots I heard never came from you. What happened to your hat?"

"Lost it down the slope a ways. It fell off as I was running up here to see what was going on."

The copper considered this, then said, "Well, and why don't you go look for your darlin' hat, then? We don't need feds butting in for glory we can use ourselves. This is my beat and my case, if you follow me meaning, Uncle Sam."

Longarm grinned and said, "I was just trying to be helpful. But he's all yours. You'll be taking him to the city morgue, right?"

"Faith, I'd hardly be taking home to me wife and kids. What's it to you?"

Longarm said the copper had a point, and left him to clean up the mess. Frisco sure was a friendly town. He'd just avoided a lot of tedious paperwork and doubtless some long hours jawing with the local law. It would be interesting to see how this case was reported, and who might be surprised to see him again the next time they met. He went back down into the fog, scouted up his Stetson, and walked back to his hotel with no further incident.

He was dead tired when he got to his room. But before he turned in, he disassembled his Colt on the bed. The extra ammo he'd taken into the bay might have gotten wet inside its brass. But he hadn't dunked the sixgun and he hadn't reloaded it since it had been knocked from his hand on the waterfront, and the derringer ammo worked fine after taking a couple of baths with him. He picked up a .44-40 round from the Colt and held it up to the light. The firing pin hadn't dented the cap, so the ammo wasn't the problem. It was his hammer. The damned firing pin had been snapped off clean. Bouncing over the cobbles hadn't done much other damage to the weapon, as far as he could see. There was a nick on the grips that he didn't remember being there the last time he'd cleaned it, but that was it, save for a few scratches. He cursed himself for not noticing the broken firing pin when he'd dry-fired after reloading in the whorehouse.

He put things back together, muttering, "You're getting sloppy in your old age, Custis, my boy. A man who can't see that his firing pin ain't there when he reloads has no business packing a shooting iron."

He put the useless gun back in its holster and reloaded the derringer, saying, "At least you were there when I needed you, pard. This town is sure hard on hardware. Got to find me a watchmaker in the morning, too."

He put the derringer under his pillow, shucked his clothes, and was fast asleep a couple of minutes later. Frisco had been a mite rough on *him* that day, too.

Chapter 9

San Francisco woke Longarm up early as it went to work, noisy as hell. He figured it was time he buckled down to work too, so he got up. The few hours' sleep had cleared his head and, as he dressed, he made a mental list of things he ought to do that day. It got so long that he was tempted to go back to bed. He was as hungry as a bitch wolf, but being lightly armed put him off his feed. So he only ate half a dozen flapjacks in the coffee shop downstairs, as he read the morning papers and the wallet he'd taken off the jasper up the hill.

Like the wallet that had belonged to the shotgunner, this one had nothing in it to identify its owner—just some ten-dollar bills and another railroad ticket, a coach ticket you could use anytime for the coast train south. Ten-dollar bills didn't jibe with the nondescript way the bushwhacker had been dressed last night. A working man might have one on him, but twelve at a time seemed sort of fancy.

Longarm snapped the bills and rubbed them on a damp napkin. They were real. They were his now, too, for there was no sense turning them in as evidence to a sometimes ungrateful Uncle Sam. Longarm needed no proof that the rascal had been up to no good, and it wasn't likely he'd ever stand trial now.

The extra money would do wonders for his expense account, too. Billy Vail was never going to believe how folks spent money out here, but the extra hundred and twenty he had to play with gave Longarm a freer hand.

The paper told a tale of "another cableway accident," and the cable car company was mad as hell. It had issued a statement demanding an autopsy, no matter how the police reported the dragging on Nob Hill. The folks who ran the cables under the streets of Frisco said a man who lay down in its right-of-way and stuffed the tail of his coat down the cable slot had to have been unusually drunk or full of opium from Chinatown.

Longarm could see they had a point. The autopsy might identify the bastard while they dug the bullets out of him. He'd ask about it discreetly, later in the day.

The financial page said the gossip about the market that he'd heard the night before hadn't gotten around among the peasants yet. Beef and blue chips were up from where they'd been a spell back, but most stocks were rising moderately, and he saw that the irrigation bonds they'd been talking about were still to be had at par. It made his extra funds seem sort of modest when he wistfully concluded that a hundred-odd wasn't enough to take advantage of that tip he'd heard last night.

He left to find a gunsmith, and by the time he did find one, he'd figured out that the mysterious ten-dollar bills added up to a passer of bogus double eagles. A merchant changing a twenty-dollar gold piece for a ten-dollar purchase wouldn't be as apt to worry as he handed you your purchase and a good ten-dollar bill. That meant the rascal lurking near the Doyle house was a member of the gang he was after, and not one of Calvinia's relatives.

The gunsmith examined his broken .44 and told Longarm he ought to be ashamed of himself, adding, "I see you busted off your front sight as well."

Longarm said, "No. I sawed off the barrel and the sight along with it in case I ever had to draw sudden. All I need fixed is that firing pin. How long will it take?"

"Only take a minute to just replace the hammer, pin and all," the gunsmith said. "You sure you don't want me to replate her? You've marred the nickel plate awful, and though I see you keep her oiled, a new finish would protect the steel better. I plate heavier than the Colt folks start out with."

Longarm shook his head, but asked, "What do you do, dip the gun in melted nickel?"

The gunsmith snorted, "Hell, no. Nickel's got a high melting point, as well as being hard as steel. That's the whole point of plating a gun. I plate electric, out back. You know how electroplating works, don't you?"

Longarm thought and said, "Sort of."

He didn't have time for a lecture, but the gunsmith gave him one anyhow as he found the replacement hammer and put it in the gun for Longarm. Longarm found it dull as well as technical. But halfway through, he frowned and asked, "I know how the current running through the acid deposits a thin layer of whatever on the metal on the receiving end of the circuit. But tell me, could you electroplate brass with gold?"

"Of course you could. How do you think they make cheap jewelry? The electroplating process will plate any metal with any other. All it takes is a battery of wet cells and some patience."

Patience was in short supply right now, so Longarm paid for the repairs to his .44 and left, feeling more comfortable with a real gun on his hip again. As he walked west he ran into Jimbo, coming the other way.

The youth fell in with Longarm and said, "I was on me way to your hotel to see if you needed me. How did you make out with La Strega?"

"She told me a few interesting things, and I do have a chore for you, Jimbo. I have discovered that the streets of Frisco ain't made for any horse I wouldn't feel foolish riding. I want you to fetch that mare from Dirty Mary's and drop her off at the Presidio for me. Tell the remount sergeant I'm sorry as hell about the nail holes in her hide. Don't worry if he acts tough. He's really a sissy."

Jimbo said he'd take care of it, and handed Longarm a folded paper, saying, "I asked at party headquarters about the people you was interested in. The ones who vote Democrat are on file with anything the boss can use against them. That Dandolo dago must have been a Republican, though. We don't even have an address on him."

"That's all right. I do. And I know where he was meeting an Eye-talian lady with more of an allowance than them fishermen's wives on Telegraph Hill. You might see what you can find out there, Jimbo. How many high-toned Eye-talian ladies can there be in Frisco?"

Jimbo snorted. "A lot. What if some dago gal married a well-heeled Yank who don't keep a good eye on her?"

Longarm sighed and said, "Dammit, Jimbo. I wish you weren't so smart. You're right. She wouldn't even be listed under an Eye-talian name in the city directory. A good-looking fisherman's daughter who could comfort old Enrico Dandolo in his own lingo could be sitting in her private opera box under the name of Smith or Jones."

"More likely a Crocker or a Stanford, if she's Frisco society. But I'll ask around. Somebody might remember an old Gold Rusher marrying a pretty gal who chews garlic."

They split up and Longarm went on to Gump's Department Store. He went in and asked the snooty young thing from the day before where Kilbride was this morning. The salesgirl sniffed and said, "Mister Kilbride is no longer with Gump's, sir."

"Oh? Did he quit?"

She glanced about and confided quietly, "He was dismissed. He may not know it yet. But I'm to tell him, should he show his face here again. He's been warned about coming to work late. I suspect he has a drinking problem."

Longarm nodded and said, "I noticed the nose. He said something about a roominghouse in Noe Valley. Do you know the address?"

"No. Noe Valley's on the wrong side of the Slot."

"Oh, forgive me for mentioning places south of Market in the company of a lady. You reckon the manager would be able to tell me where I could find Kilbride? I want a word with him, drunk or sober."

The girl said that the manager wasn't in yet, but that she'd tell him when he arrived that a U.S. deputy was looking for the fired floorwalker. She said she got half an hour off for lunch, but Longarm let the hint pass over his head. She looked too snooty, and the last thing he needed in Frisco was another girlfriend, snooty or otherwise. He said he'd try to get back that afternoon, and she said she got off at six, sending smoke signals with her eyes despite her lofty nose.

Having given any night letters Billy Vail might have sent time to arrive, Longarm backtracked to the Western Union office. They had a couple of wires for him, so he took them up the street to a watchmaker, and while he had his Ingersoll cleaned and oiled, he read them.

Denver was just fussing at him for sending so little news. The night letter from the state capital in Sacramento was more interesting. The late Pete Taylor's baby brother, Clem, was a pure caution when it came to losing his temper. He'd been arrested a dozen times for brawling, and a hung jury had barely let him off, the time he'd stood trial for gunning a man in Weed for no particular reason. The plea had been self-defense, which seemed a mite thin when you considered that the stranger he'd gunned after a heated political discussion had been shot in the back.

The law in Sacramento said the rascal was up north raising hell as well as barley, and that they'd be proud to arrest him if Longarm had a charge he thought might stick. He decided not to wire back one way or the other just yet. Calvinia wasn't just making up mean things about the man she meant to evict from his holdings, and he could see how a man who shot strangers casually could present a menace to a relative trying to put him out of his only business. But damn it to hell, he hadn't come out here to protect even friendly gals from unpleasant in-laws. Maybe the best bet for her would be a peace bond and a hired guard, after all. He wondered if one of Buckley's Lambs needed extra income. Jimbo was a mite young for that mirrored room, but he'd probably be forever grateful for the opportunity. Longarm put the matter aside for now. He didn't think he was up to another Nob Hill orgy. But on the other hand, he always felt sensible this early in the day.

The watchmaker handed him back his watch, as good as new, and charged him enough to buy a new one. When Longarm pointed that out, the watchmaker said, "It's just as hard to repair a cheap watch as an expensive one. It's not my fault you gummed up the works with soap and salt. I oiled it with whale oil, for I see you're an active man. It ought to keep fair time until you beat hell out of it and give it another bath."

Longarm paid, pocketed the watch, and left to head for Chinatown. He was halfway there when he cussed himself for not thinking to ask Fong about a good oriental watchmaker.

Chinatown looked a lot more cheerful by daylight. Grant Avenue was crowded with folks, Cantonese and Californian. He passed a couple of right interesting China dolls along the way, but he remembered that they were sort of shy, and that the hatchet men of the Tongs could get sort of moody about white men messing with their womenfolk. So he behaved himself.

The goldsmith acted glad to see him. Fong said nobody had passed any queer on Grant Avenue lately, and he seemed to think Longarm had something to do with it.

Longarm said, "It's more likely they know folks are catching on to the date and that mar on the coins they've been circulating. They're laying doggo until the heat dies down or they can run off a new set. I got me a couple of goldsmithing questions to ask you, Mr. Fong. A gent I met at Gump's says he thinks those coins were made with a lost-wax something or other."

The Chinese shook his head and replied flatly, "Impossible. I told you those coins were stamped from cold metal, not cast. There's a different patina to cast brass, and the process is terribly slow."

"I'll buy that. This other jeweler said something about patina too. He said he could tell gold from red brass at a glance, and that he didn't need to test it with acid."

"He has a better eye than I do, then," Fong said. "That jewelry alloy was intended to pass for gold when they rolled it. The factory is run by jewelers, too. What is the name of this so-called expert?"

"Kilbride. Used to have his own jewelry shop, and now he's been fired by Gump's for brooding about it too often with strong drink. Listen, can you give me a few addresses on the folks who make this fake gold for junk jewelry, Mr. Fong?"

"Of course. I have some catalogues you can have. I remember the name Kilbride. You are right about his being a heavy drinker. He was a crooked jeweler, too."

"Do tell? He said he lost his business in the stock market crash."

Fong smiled thinly. "He'd hardly want anyone to know what really put him out of business. He's an expert on artificial gold, indeed. He almost went to jail when some very prominent San Francisco society ladies noticed that their fingers were turning green. They say the dowager Hopkins was dreadfully upset to awaken one morning with green ear lobes, too!"

"I noticed the folks up on Nob Hill sort of snubbed him the other night," Longarm said. "I thought they were just being snobs. But I was told he was up there appraising jewelry for a rich lady. Do you reckon he could be crooking her?"

Fong thought about this. "Maybe not. Kilbride's not a bad goldsmith, when he's sober. An appraiser is paid a percentage, but doesn't usually buy or sell the jewelry involved."

"What if he was to switch, say, a gold ring for one made of dross?"

"Anything's possible. But it would be awfully complicated. He'd have to have an impression in advance of the jewelry he intended to steal."

"Yeah, you're right. Why sneak it off to a hidden shop and then not just keep it? He said he lived in a roominghouse. Could a man do goldsmithing in a rented room without folks noticing?"

"Of course not. Gold and silver have high melting points. You need a furnace as well as a workbench."

"Yeah, the landlady would likely notice when she cleaned the room. Of course, he could have been fibbing. I'll find out when I pay a call on him. I got another question for you, Mr. Fong. Do you do any electroplating?"

The Chinese said, "No. I only deal in real jewelry. But I know a little about it. Why?"

"Ain't sure. I got a couple of half-ass notions cooking in my head. If somebody was to gold-plate one of those fake double eagles, it would stand up to the acid test, wouldn't it?"

Fong's eyes widened as he said, "That's a nasty thought! But the gold-plating would have to be unusually thick, and that would take a lot of time, blur some of the detail, and use up a considerable amount of real gold."

"Yeah. It starts getting diseconomical when you study on it. By the time you cover every bet, you wind up coining with solid gold, which sort of misses the point of counterfeiting. Tell me about this blurring business anyway."

Fong said, "The object being plated attracts gold or silver atoms from the electrified solution and they build rather like paint, but of course as solid metal. The more you plate and the thicker it gets, the more the new metal tends to smooth out, so—"

"I get you," Longarm cut in. "It's sort of like dipping a coin or whatever in chocolate. But just for the hell of it, could you plate gold with some cheaper metal?"

"Of course, but that would be a strange thing to do, Deputy Long. What would you do with gold jewelry or coinage covered with base metal?"

"Ain't sure. I told you I'm still cooking it in my head. You got a flier or catalogue that tells about electroplating? I want to know what sort of gear I'm looking for, in case I stumble over it in my travels."

Fong nodded, moved down the counter, and reached under it to get Longarm a handful of thin booklets. As the tall deputy stowed them in a side pocket, the Chinese said, "I don't see why anyone would be using electroplating. I told you those fake coins were stamped from sheet red brass with a steel die."

"I don't doubt your word," Longarm reassured him. "But tell me something else. If I had me a set of dies, would I really need a hydraulic press, or could I maybe just hammer the two together with a blank brass betwixt 'em?"

Fong said, "That's the way they used to do it. It wouldn't be nearly as fast as the powered machinery at the mint, but we know they're not making quite as many double eagles as the mint, either."

Longarm smiled thinly. "I was hoping you'd say that, Mr. Fong. I thank you, and now I'd better get it on down the road."

Fong showed him out. He headed back toward the American part of town, and came to California Street just as a cable car clanked and clanged its way by to climb Nob Hill. It sure looked a lot less spooky around here in the daylight. It was hard to picture the way it had been in the fog and dark. He stared up at the distant crest, wondering if Gwynn and Calvinia were up yet and whether they were eating ham and eggs or one another for breakfast. He grimaced and told himself it was too early in the day to consider such matters. He viewed revisiting the sassy gals with mixed emotions. They were a mite rich for his blood, but now that he knew Calvinia's brother-in-law could really turn out dangerous, he figured he owed it to her to warn her.

He laughed at himself for starting to think sneaky again. Calvinia had told him the first night they met that her brother-in-law was out to get her and that she needed protecting. If he never went near her again, she'd find her own protecting. It didn't look like Clem Taylor had sent all those rascals after him, even if they had laid for him near the widow woman's house.

He frowned and stared up the steep slope from Chinatown to the fashionable high country as he ran through that notion a second time. The gunman last night hadn't been waiting outside Gwynn's door. It had been clear and well lit in the first place, and he'd made a good target of his fool self in the second. The rascal had been set up farther down the slope in the fog. But how in hell had he recognized his intended victim? Almost anybody could be coming down the slope at night, and he hadn't told even the gals when he intended to leave. Could one of the men at the earlier party have told somebody he was there? He knew that at least Kilbride was a crook, and the ex-jeweler had known he was a federal man looking for counterfeiters. The man who'd tried to ambush him had smelled like a queer-passer too. That all dovetailed together. But how could they have known when he'd leave, and which way he'd head out? There were four ways to walk from Gwynn's corner lot. He shrugged and muttered, "Mayhaps *four* gunmen laying for you would cover all bets. It ain't like they're short-handed."

As he crossed the street, he heard someone call his name. It was Jimbo and another of Buckley's Lambs. They were nailing a poster on a telephone pole when he joined them. It was in Chinese. He nodded at the Irish kid and said, "Sure is a small world, Jimbo. You take care of that mare for me?"

Jimbo nodded. "Sure, and you were right about that sergeant being a sissy. I just got back from the Presidio by cable. Me and McCarthy here are getting out the Chinese vote for the boss."

"Do tell? What does that Chinese writing say, Jimbo?"

"Beats the shit out of me. But if the next mayor of Chinatown ain't the man Boss Buckley picked, I'll be mighty surprised."

Longarm grinned and said, "So will I. Keep up the good work, boys. How do I get to the city morgue from here?"

"Jasus, what a dreadful place to spend a sunny morning. It's near police headquarters, by the Civic Center, Longarm. Who do we know that might be there?"

"I doubt it's anybody you Lambs know. Fellow tried to gun me up that slope last night, and I'd sort of like to know who he might have been."

"Oh, was that you tied the darlin' man to the cable, like I read in the papers? I told that army sergeant not to mess with you, either. That's twice they've tried to do you near the same place, ain't it?"

"Yeah, and it's getting tedious as hell. I'll see you later."

He went on his way. But he'd only gone a few paces when a man fell in on either side of him. They were both big, but dressed sort of prissy for Chinatown.

One of them asked, "Are you Longarm?"

Longarm said he was and asked who they might be.

The one on his left said, "U.S. Treasury, and you're beginning to annoy hell out of us, Colorado. Since you've hit town, they've started picking bodies off the streets, and so far you've not seen fit to even pay us a courtesy call."

"I'm sorry if you have sore toes, boys," Longarm said, "but I have my own row to hoe. I did pay a call on the mint director, which is doubtless how you know I'm in town."

The one on his right said, "The mint didn't say anything to us about it. We got your name off the police blotter. Aside from that gunfight on the Barbary Coast the other night, the copper who reported the body dragged to chopped liver on the cableway described you as a witness. By the way, at his autopsy they found the two .44 slugs you put in him. I suppose you mean to say you don't pack a .44?"

"I cannot tell a lie," Longarm said. "I done it with my little derringer. I hope you boys don't mean to arrest me over a little interservice rivalry? I'll beat the charge, but it could be a bother."

The other one snorted in annoyance and said, "The federal government can wash its own linen. But we sure would like to hear about you shooting that queer-passer, Longarm."

Longarm told them the little he knew, leaving out the part about the widow women, of course, and asked, "How do you know he was a queer-passer, boys?"

The one on the right said, "Yeah, we noticed what happened to his face, and you didn't leave his wallet on him. Fortunately he had a tattoo we had on file from the last time he got out of Leavenworth. His name was Bleeker and he had an arrest record going back to desertion during the War. He was a gunslick as well as a check forger and passer of counterfeit. So we can't say you did Uncle Sam a disservice by putting him in the box. But, for Chrissake, you might have seen fit to tell us about it!"

"I was aiming to," Longarm lied, adding, "You just saved me a trip to the morgue, and I was going to drop by the mint as soon as I found out who the rascal was."

"Sure you were. Then you were going to flap your arms and fly around the bay with the seagulls. No shit, Longarm, it's not polite to work another lawman's case without letting him in on it, and we could be working at cross purposes."

"You're right, boys," Longarm admitted. "But what can I tell you? My boss in Denver ordered me to be sneaky out here."

"What are you talking about? Does somebody up the totem pole suspect us Frisco agents of being crooked?"

Longarm didn't think it would comfort them to hear the truth, so he said, "Nobody mentioned crooked agents. But don't it make you thoughtful that the gang's spotted at least three gents on our side before they could find anything out?"

The one on his left said, "All right, maybe somebody working around the flagpole talks too much. But we're both known as Treasury men, and they sure as hell know you're in town. So this secrecy shit is confusing *us* a lot more than it's confusing *them!*"

Longarm said fair was fair, and suggested they belly up to a bar and put all the cards on the table. The three of them found a corner saloon and had some beer while they compared notes. The atmosphere got friendlier, but they soon saw they all knew much the same things, and that none of them made much sense. The Treasury men turned out to be named O'Hanlon and Coletti. When he picked up on the Italian name, Longarm asked Agent Coletti how he felt about a society gal of Latin background.

Coletti growled, "I've been working on that. I know about the love nest the missing mint worker had on Telegraph Hill. More than one Italian girl has married well in Frisco. But it's not a big list, and none of them pan out as Dandolo's mistress. The ones who fit the description have alibis. The ones who could have been there with him the night he vanished don't happen to be young and petite, with an aristocratic accent."

"Try her this way," Longarm said. "The gal didn't have to come from Frisco. She could just be an Eye-talian lady from other parts, living expensive with maybe Smith as her given name. I wouldn't have known you were Eye-talian if you'd given me another handle to call you. If she came from a high-toned family, her English might be as good as mine."

"You have a point," Coletti said. "We could be wrong in assuming she was a married woman meeting Dandolo on the sly. If she was a gang member, she'd have wanted to meet him secretly, no matter what her marital status may be. What do you figure happened after they left Telegraph Hill screaming at one another, Longarm?"

Longarm took a sip of steam beer and said, "I'd know better

if I knew what she wanted off him. She wanted something. He was just a middle-aged and middle-waged gent who'd been living quiet till she come into his life."

O'Hanlon said, "We've checked and double-checked the idea that he might have swiped some withdrawn dies for his lady love. We know he was living beyond his means. It's understandable that a man whom fortune had passed by till he was pushing fifty might be tempted from the straight and narrow by a glamorous beauty. But, dammit, Dandolo never left the mint with a set of dies. Every die they ever used while he was working there has been accounted for. More than once."

"I know how tedious double-checking is," Longarm said. "I'll take your word that the poor dupe never left work with a big, heavy set of mint dies under his shirt. But Dandolo was a man who *made* dies, remember?"

Coletti said, "We remember, and we've made sure the master molds are all accounted for, too. Dandolo was a machinist, not a sculptor who could model a plate-sized coin in bas-relief from scratch."

"Why couldn't he use a real coin and a pantograph, off in some secret machine shop the gang owns?"

"We thought of that. The experts say no. You cut a die from a larger model because you lose detail in the process, and the difference in scale makes up the difference. If you started with a life-sized coin, the die would be just a blur. The dies the gang's used even show mars and scratches from the issue they copied. It's a perfect impression even under a magnifying glass."

Longarm took another sip of beer and said, "I don't know how he did it the first time, boys. But I suspicion they killed him when he refused to do it twice. Dandolo had a lovely daughter to think about and a pension to protect, and the bloom is off the rose once a man's had a gal in every position more than once. You're right about the imperfections in the first set of dies he made. They wanted him to run off a new series. But he was coming to his senses. The gal they used to tempt him may have been the bee's knees starting out, but the honeymoon was winding down as he discovered she had a nasty temper. And they likely didn't give him as big a share as promised, either, for he left his daughter flat-ass busted on his birthday. That birthday may have been what triggered the showdown. Men staring fifty in the face tend to either get dumber or smarter, depending on their natures. The neighbors on the hill thought they were hearing a lover's quarrel. It was more like one crook trying to blackmail another into wading deeper in the mud. Dandolo wouldn't go along with making the new dies, but he was dumb enough to accept a ride back to civilization with her. Along the way they killed him, and if we ever find his body, I'll be surprised as hell."

Coletti said, "I like the sound of your theory. But where are the facts to base it on, Longarm?"

Longarm said, "Fact one: The gang never got the new dies they wanted, for the old coins keep turning up. I might have made them withdraw them from circulation for a spell by making them even more nervous. But if Dandolo was alive, they'd have new dies, he'd be at work acting innocent, and I wouldn't have had to buy groceries for his daughter. Fact two: They keep trying to kill me, which they wouldn't have to do if they had new dies and felt safer. Fact three: They mean to stay in business, new dies or no. They need the money too bad to just lay low like sensible folk, with all of us looking for them. Oh, yeah, another fact. There's some reason they can't leave town, which would be another sensible move."

The two agents exchanged thoughtful glances and O'Hanlon said, "I admire a man who thinks on his feet. You figure they have an elaborate setup they can't carry around easily, right?"

"Don't know. But there must be a good reason to stay in Frisco with Uncle Sam breathing so close to their mousehole. They could be using an established workshop. They could have built up too good a front to abandon. Hell, boys, if I knew *why* they were standing pat, I'd know who they were!"

The treasury agents agreed, and the three of them finished their beers. O'Hanlon gave Longarm his card and said to keep in touch. Coletti said he aimed to visit the Italian consulate to see if any aristocratic ladies from the north of Italy were known to them. Out on Columbus Avenue, the three of them parted more friendly than they'd met, and Longarm went back to his hotel.

There were no messages waiting for him. But Angela Dandolo was. She was seated by a potted lobby palm, dressed up in her Sunday-go-to-meeting duds and looking as comfortable as a coyote in a trap.

He howdied her and suggested they go into the coffee shop to see what they were serving this noon. She let him take her there, but as they took a booth together, she dabbed at her eyes with her white gloves, and he saw that they were red-rimmed. He asked her what was fretting her, and Angela said, "You are. How on earth am I ever to pay you back? I was just turned down for the job I went to see about."

"You need more money, ma'am?"

"My God, no! I've food enough at the house to feed an army, and I still have most of the money you left. You have to take it back, Custis."

He waited until he'd ordered them coffee and cake, and sent the waitress off to fetch it before he smiled at her and said, "You sure talk dumb for a gal who hasn't got a job, Miss Angela. Can you play a typewriter? I might stumble over something as I wander about."

"I'm going to another job interview this afternoon. I know I'll find a position sooner or later. But whatever possessed you to leave that food and money on my doorstep? Surely I never said anything to give you a false impression of my, uh, nature?"

"Don't talk silly. Any man with eyes can see you're a lady. Can see you're in bad shape too. What possessed me, if you must know, was called Christianity. I know that a lot of folks who go to church more regular than me can't quite get the hang of what the Good Book means, but my folks raised me simple. I tend to forget who begat whom, and I take walking on water with a grain of salt. But the Sermon on the Mount sunk in, and it's ornery to let folks go hungry when a man can afford a few staples."

"Yes, but the money, nearly a week's wages!"

"Hush, girl, you can't buy a ride on the cable with bread or beans. I don't mean to brag, but I've made more'n that in a few minutes, dealing poker Dodge City style. Are you sure the little I snuck in with the candy will last you to the end of the week?"

"Heavens, yes. But I can't keep it! What would people say if they found out a man was—well, *keeping* me?"

He laughed, but didn't answer as the waitress put coffee and cake on the table between them. When it was polite to talk again, he said, "Nobody has to find out anything. And at the risk of turning your pretty head, keeping a gal in your class would cost more than I'm likely to ever see."

She blushed and stammered, "What do you mean, a girl in my class, Custis?"

"I didn't mean that dirty, Miss Angela. I know you ain't that kind. But what I meant was that if you were, you'd be mighty costly. If you were a wicked woman and I was a dirty old rich man, I'd likely have to shower you with diamonds and pearls instead of groceries. So eat your infernal cake and let's say no more about it."

She laughed weakly and said, "You're incredible. I think I've just been insulted, and yet I feel flattered. Do you really think I'm as pretty as—well, one of those fancy girls one hears about?"

"You're as pretty as Lillian Russell, judging by her pictures in *The Police Gazette,* and you know what they say about her and Diamond Jim Brady, Miss Angela."

Her face got pinker and she said, "You stop that. You're making me feel all fluttery, and I really should be crosser with you than I am."

He just grinned and sipped his coffee. Changing the subject had gotten her off her foolish financial discussion. He asked her about the job she was after, and she said it was at an office on Montgomery Street. She ate some cake and started looking more cheerful as they made small talk. But then she spoiled his lunch by asking, "Have you found out anything about my poor father, Custis?"

He saw no need to upset her stomach too, so he shook his head and didn't mention his suspicion that Dandolo was likely picked clean by the crabs by now. "While we're on the subject, though, Miss Angela, you said your father had a workshop out back. Do you know if he had a battery of electric wet cells?"

She frowned and said, "No. Why would he have played with electricity? He's a machinist."

Longarm noticed she was still using the present tense, as though her father were still alive. He already had her down as sort of innocent, so he didn't correct her. He thought for a moment and said, "He might have been trying to invent something, like that Tom Edison. I hear a man can make money with electricity. But if he didn't have wet cells at his home, he might have known someone who did. Do you mind if I get personal, Miss Angela?"

She dimpled and said, "You seem to make a habit of that."

"This ain't about you, it's about your father. I've reason to believe he had a girlfriend. A petite and dark Eye-talian lady who dressed sort of fancy and rode about in her own carriage.

You'd tell me if you knew anything about that, wouldn't you?"

Angela stared incredulously at him and replied, "My father, with a woman?"

"That's generally the way folks match up, Miss Angela. I know you thought of your father as an old man, but even a fifty-year-old has feelings. He never mentioned her to you?"

"Good heavens, no! Why on earth would he be sneaking off to see a woman I didn't know about . . . Oh, dear!"

She'd lowered her eyes again and was red as a lobster, so he saw no need to explain the facts of life further. He could see she was catching on to them, even if she seemed a slow learner. She swallowed some coffee and pulled herself together enough to say, "You must think I'm awfully naive. But I somehow never thought about my father like that."

He said, "Most kids don't think about their folks like that, even after they find out that the yarn about the stork was a fib. But since you don't know who the gal was, let's just drop it."

She wouldn't. She asked bleakly, "Do you think my father ran away with this other woman?"

"No, Miss Angela. He valued you too high to do a thing like that without telling you. By the way, did you ever get his last paycheck? He had a week and a half's wages coming when he vanished, since the mint pays every two weeks."

She looked surprised and said, "I never thought to ask. I don't see how it could be coming to me, unless they were sure he was . . . you know."

He knew, and he was sorry he'd mentioned the matter. Angela wouldn't get her father's back pay if they found out he was a crook, either. He'd have to study on just how he worded his final report.

They finished their coffee, and when he asked if she wanted a second cup, she said she had to see about that job, and that she'd pay him back one way or the other. He didn't see that she owed him all that much, and even if she did, there was nothing a proper young gal like her could offer that he wouldn't be a no-good skunk to accept. Sooner or later he was going to have to tell her that her father was probably dead. But it might be possible to save the poor fool's reputation and leave her with decent memories.

Chapter 10

The library up the street had books about the wonders of modern science, so Longarm hunkered down in a corner and boned up on his metals for a spell before he went on to Gump's Department Store. The snooty salesgirl said she'd had lunch alone, thank you very much, but she took him to see the manager anyway.

The manager was a frosty-headed old gent who looked like he combed his hair one at a time. But he was friendly and willing to help out Uncle Sam. He said Kilbride was fired, whether he knew it yet or not, for he'd been warned about coming in late, sometimes listing to starboard.

Longarm asked for Kilbride's home address, and the manager wrote it on a card for him, saying, "I don't think you'll find him there, Deputy. I telephoned him when I got in, and he wasn't there."

"Kilbride has a telephone, in a roominghouse?"

"Of course not. They've just begun to install them in the better homes and businesses, and only a small part of town is hooked up as yet. But there's a telephone in the drugstore on Kilbride's corner, and they've relayed messages for us before. The druggist said he'd send his boy over to the roominghouse and call back. But they didn't, and when I called a second time they said Kilbride didn't seem to be at home. Lord knows, I'm not too surprised. He must have tied one on last night."

Longarm hadn't thought Kilbride was drunk when he'd last seen him, late last night. But of course a serious drinker didn't need more than an hour or so to get drunk. He thanked the manager and headed for the street. The stuck-up salesgirl intercepted him and asked if he needed any other information. He said he'd come back if he thought of anything, and she reminded him she got off at six.

He left smiling softly. She still looked like a man would have to climb a ladder to kiss her. But maybe that was her problem. Gals who scared gents off like that tended to lead lonesome social lives.

He hailed a cab and gave the driver the Noe Valley address. It took some hilly time to get there, for the Noe Valley was a sort of sneaky little district tucked in a fold of the hills south of the Slot. The driver pulled to the curb, and, sure enough, there was a drugstore on the corner with a telephone pole out front. Longarm paid for the ride and went up the steps of the roominghouse. A colored gal with a kerchief tied around her head came to the door and said the landlady and everybody else was out. He flashed his badge at her and she let him in. He asked her if she had a key to Kilbride's room, and she said she didn't. But she led him up to it and waited while he knocked on the door. Nobody answered, and when he tried the knob it was locked. The colored girl asked what he thought he was doing when he took out his pocket knife and unfolded a blade that could have gotten him in trouble with the law if he wasn't already working for it.

He said, "I aim to pick the lock, miss. You just go on with your sweeping if you find this too unconstitutional for you."

She wandered off down the hall, muttering that she'd done her best to mind the house, but that they never paid her enough to mess with the law.

It took him a minute to open the door. He wasn't sure what he was looking for, but he went in to see if it was interesting. He stopped and stared down at the two high-button shoes jutting out from the far side of the made-up bed. They had somebody's feet in them. He closed the door and stepped around the bed.

Kilbride had been killed quiet but sort of messy. The man's

146

face looked peaceful, considering that his throat had been cut from ear to ear.

Longarm looked down wistfully at the corpse and said, "You were talking too much about gold coins, old son, even if you did try to throw me off with that bullshit way of making 'em. They didn't need you once you'd showed 'em how to order costume-jewelry stock, and cutting your throat beat cutting you in on the take. You and old Dandolo sure mixed with mean and greedy crooks, didn't you?"

He dropped to one knee and went through Kilbride's pockets. He didn't have any fake double eagles, and he hadn't been packing a gun; the rascal who'd been waiting for him here had likely known that before he went for him with that knife.

Longarm stood up and tugged thoughtfully at his mustache as he judged the time it would take the blood all down the front of Kilbride to dry as much as it had. The timing was wrong for it to have been the killer they'd sent after Longarm. The gang had a posse of executioners. Kilbride had left the Doyle house alone. They wouldn't have followed him all the way from there. Knowing where he lived, they'd had someone waiting. It had been neater than knifing him on the street, but the killer sure had nerves of steel, if he'd sat in this dark room half the night waiting for an unpredictable drunk to get home sooner or later. Longarm put himself in the killer's boots and sat in the dark for a spell. It made him nervous. He wouldn't want to wait in ambush more than an hour or so. The killer had known when Kilbride was due in. Could they have made an appointment?

Longarm started going through the drawers of the dresser across the room. It was mostly filled with shirts and socks and such. But he found a bottle of Holland gin in a brown paper bag. He found a jewelry supply catalogue like one Fong had given him, too. One page was folded like somebody wanted to remember it. He opened it and, sure enough, there was an ad for sheets of red brass stock that looked as good as gold. He put it in his pocket with the others. Tracing mail orders could take time, but there'd be time enough before the trial, if he could maybe cut a few corners and catch up with the gang sooner. He let himself out, leaving the door unlocked.

On the stairs, the cleaning woman asked if it was all right to do Mr. Kilbride's room now. He shook his head and said,

"You don't want to go in there, miss. There'll be some policemen here in a little while, and you just show them the way and stay out in the hall. Do you live here in the house?"

"Nossuh, I just comes to clean. Why?"

"Never mind. If anyone here heard anything, they'd have likely said so. I got another question. What does the landlady look like? She wouldn't be young, pretty, and Eye-talian, would she?"

The colored gal looked surprised and answered, "Miz McKail? She's old and fat and grumpy and she sure ain't Eye-talian. She went over to Fisherman's Wharf to see about Friday's dinner. But she'll be back in a little while."

"Keep her out of Kilbride's room until the police arrive, then. I'll see if I can scout 'em up at that drugstore on the corner."

"Is Mister Kilbride in trouble, suh?"

"Not anymore. He used to be a crook. But somebody killed him."

He left her looking sort of ashen and went to the corner druggist. They said they sure did have a new telephone, for they were up to date in Frisco. He told them about the murder and asked them to call the law. One druggist blanched and went back to the wall telephone while his assistant asked Longarm more details.

Longarm said all he knew was that somebody had cut Kilbride's throat. Then he said, "You might know something I don't. I can see this drugstore serves as a neighborhood message center. Was anybody waiting around for Kilbride, late last night?"

The druggist said, "I couldn't say. We close after dark. Why?"

"I just barked up another wrong tree," Longarm said. "Thought somebody might have gotten a message he was headed home. Reckon they just did it the old-fashioned way."

The druggist using the telephone came back to say the police were on their way. Longarm thanked him and said that as much as he'd like to hang around and watch, he had to attend to other chores.

He went outside and looked up and down the street for a cab to hire. He didn't see any, but he wasn't about to walk all the way. As he stood there undecided, he stared up at the telephone pole in front of the drugstore. Other wires ran along

148

up there, but he saw that only one led down to the roof of the druggist. There didn't seem to be another telephone connection anywhere on this block. Of course, the man at Gump's had said not many people had them in yet. . . .

Longarm suddenly blinked, snapped his fingers, and said, "Hell, of course!"

He went back inside and told the druggist he wanted to talk to the U.S. Treasury Office. The druggist said he didn't know the exchange. Longarm bulled his way behind the counter to the telephone, cranked it alive until he got the operator, and told her what he wanted. She was a smart old gal and it only took him a few minutes to get through to the Treasury Office. Naturally, mere agents like O'Hanlon and Coletti didn't rate their own telephones, but he told whoever was at the other end to have them meet him at Columbus and California at sundown, knowing they'd report in before they knocked off for the day.

When he went out again, he saw a police van coming down the street behind a high-stepping bay. He ignored it as he crossed the street and made himself scarce. He'd legged it about four blocks before he spied a passing cab and hailed it. He said he wanted to go to Gump's. So they went there.

He found the snooty-looking salesgirl standing lonesome in front of a case full of jade play-pretties. "Listen," he said, "I can't make our date at six. But what's your name and where can I look you up later, to sort of celebrate?"

She looked startled and said, "My name is Helen Manson, but I didn't know we had a date, Deputy Long."

"Call me Custis. Don't you want to help me celebrate, Helen?"

"I'll have to think about it. What are we celebrating?"

"I just got smart as hell, and I won't have to go back to Denver for a couple of days. I'm on an expense account and got me some extra dividends to blow, too. Why don't you stop fluttering those long eyelashes and write down some address or another?"

"I can't," she said. "I live in a very respectable boarding house, and we're not allowed to entertain gentlemen callers." She saw that he was fixing to give up and added quickly, "Where are you staying, in case I reconsider?"

He told her the Palace, and she said she'd think about it, but not to get ideas. He said he could see she didn't get out much, and he'd be proud to take her out in style if she could see her way clear to drop him a line stating where and when. She said he was a forward idiot, and they parted amicably.

He went back to his hotel and had a bath and shave before changing to a fresh shirt in case he got lucky, later. When he went down to the lobby, there was a perfumed envelope in his box. Helen Manson said she'd meet him at eight at a discreet tearoom just down the street. He knew she'd sent it over by messenger, and it was nice to see that she was a gal who could make her mind up quickly. But the timing was awesomely close. He wasn't sure he'd be ready to meet her at eight. He wished they had those telephones connected up more. It sure would be something if a man could call a gal up and whisper privately in her ear. But little folk like him and her had to make do the old-fashioned way, and he didn't have time to run all the way back to Gump's and tell her he doubted he'd be free by eight. He knew they had a telephone connection at the hotel desk. He considered trying to reach her on the store manager's telephone. He gave it up as a foolish move. She'd likely be more upset by that than by being stood up at the tearoom. There wasn't an excuse he could give the manager that wouldn't give the show away. Disappointing her wouldn't hurt as much as getting fired for improper behavior.

He checked his watch, found that it was still ticking, and saw that he had plenty of time to meet the other federal men in Chinatown. He headed there on foot, enjoying the stroll, for it was a nice clear late afternoon, and he was feeling pleased with himself.

He found a saloon near Columbus and California, on the eastern edge of Chinatown. He took a seat near the window so he could see when and if the others arrived. Up the slope toward the more Chinese part of town, the sky was getting rosy, but sundown was sort of an indefinite time, and he should have stated an exact time.

He sure wished Helen hadn't been so infernally definite about meeting him at eight in that tearoom. He wasn't going to make it unless things went as smooth as silk, and that was too much to hope for.

A familiar figure was passing the saloon, and as he recognized young Jimbo Corbett, the youth spotted him too, and came in to join him. Jimbo had on a new suit and tie. When Longarm commented on it, Jimbo looked sheepish and said, "Aw, I really have started night school. That's why I'm dressed so sissy. Me mother found out I was knocking about with the Lambs and threw a fit. So I promised her I'd really go to night school once in a while."

"That sounds sensible as well as obedient, Jimbo. What subject are you taking?"

"Accounting. Ain't that a bitch? It's funny, but I do seem to have a head for figures, and it wouldn't be bad to have a grand white-collar job someday. Sure and I'd be ever so dandy working as a bank teller, don't you think?"

Longarm laughed. "It sounds sage and sane, next to knocking heads together for Boss Buckley. You're giving up on the boxing, then?"

"Och, bite your tongue! It's a tournament I'll be entering in a week, staged by the church to raise money for charity, and you may as well know I'm favored to win over that bogtrotter from Our Lady of Mercy. Sure, and guess what name I'll be fighting under. Och, you'll laugh."

"No I won't. What are they aiming to call you, the Barbary Pirate or the Bully of the Bay?"

Jimbo grinned and said, "No. It's Gentleman Jim they're calling me. It started as a joke because of me schoolish ways, next to the other Lambs. But Father Murphy says he likes the sound of it for an Irish lad."

Longarm looked Jimbo up and down, appraisingly. "Gentleman Jim Corbett, eh? It's sort of catchy. I'll be watching for you in *The Police Gazette* in times to come. What weight are you fighting, Gentleman Jim?"

"It's a light heavyweight I am now but I'm still growing."

"I noticed. You'll top out a heavyweight in a few years. How old are you now, Jimbo?"

The youth looked sheepish and said, "Old enough. I'm almost fifteen."

Longarm laughed and said, "Jesus, you'll be a moose when you're full grown! I took you for at least eighteen or nineteen. It's no wonder your mother worries about you at night!"

Jimbo shrugged and asked, "What are you doing here with the sun going down, Longarm?"

"Waiting for some other lawmen," the tall deputy said.

"Och, do you have a line on them scamps you're after?"

"Yeah, but you go on to night school and bone up on your figures, Jimbo. I won't need you this evening."

The boy looked hurt and asked, "Can't I come along? Sure

and I could gather all the Lambs you need with a whistle of me lips."

Longarm shook his head. "It's getting too serious for good-natured brawling, Jimbo. I thank you for the offer, but I want you out of here by the time my backups get here."

The youth started to protest, then shrugged and got up to leave. He'd only been gone a short while when Longarm spotted O'Hanlon and Coletti standing across the street, looking puzzled.

He went out and hailed them as he crossed the street. They asked what was up, and he said, "Thought you boys might like to share the glory when I busted in on the counterfeiters' headquarters. Are you two all there is?"

"You never said you needed a posse," O'Hanlon replied. "You say you know where the gang is?"

"Sure, up the slope on the far side of Chinatown. I got the address from the city directory. It's a pasteboard box works. Or it was, until it went bust in the depression. It's under new ownership, but so far they haven't seen fit to open up as any particular kind of business. It's just a one-story brick building with its windows painted over. I've passed it more than once, not paying it much mind since I didn't know they were using it as a headquarters and private mint. As I recall, there's a main doorway in front and a service entrance on one side, and that's it. Three of us, and two ways out to cover. I was hoping you'd bring along some help, but we can manage."

He started walking up California. They fell in on either side, but O'Hanlon said, "Hold on, damn it. If you're sure you know the place, why don't we get some help? What's the hurry?"

"Sunset and a tearoom. It'd be a bigger boo to raid after dark, and I'm tired of chasing folks through your foggy streets at night. I just went to jaw with a suspect on the other side of the Slot and found him with his throat cut. They're acting wild and desperate, and might be going out of business any day now. With the weekend coming and the banks due to close, they may be planning a last flood of counterfeit double eagles."

He brought the other federal agents up to date as they legged it up the steep slope. They seemed to like his tale, but as they got to Grant Avenue, Coletti nudged Longarm and said, "We're being followed."

Longarm glanced back, muttered, "Aw, shit," and stopped

as Gentleman Jim Corbett and four other Barbary Coast toughs legged it up the slope after them. One of them looked suspiciously like the big bastard who'd knocked him in the bay with a plank.

Corbett smiled broadly and jerked a thumb toward the familiar but ugly figure. "This is No-Nose Brannigan, Longarm. I just ran into him, and he said he wanted to be friends with you, too. These other boyos are Lambs, like me."

No-Nose Brannigan had a nose, albeit a small button in the middle of his big, beefy face. He held out a hand to shake and said, "Sure and we didn't know you was a pal of Gentleman Jim's when we jumped you the other night. But wasn't it a grand fight we was after having?"

Longarm shook the fellow's hand, but said, "I don't know, boys. This ain't a street fight we're walking into. We're after men who play with guns and knives."

O'Hanlon nudged him and asked, "Are you crazy, Longarm? These thugs make us seven, and seven beats three any day of the week!"

Longarm started to say that Jimbo, at any rate, was too young to tag along. But Coletti said, "Even seven might not do it. How many are there in this gang of yours, Longarm?"

"Don't know. They ain't my gang. They'll likely want to fight on the other side." —

O'Hanlon nodded at the young toughs and said, "Welcome aboard. I'm deputizing all five of you. Are any of you packing guns?"

The looked blank. Gentleman Jim said, "Aw, who needs guns?"

Longarm took out his derringer, unsnapped it from its chain, and said, "Stick close to me, Jimbo. You know how to fire that little rascal?"

Jimbo nodded and put the derringer in his pocket. No-Nose Brannigan looked sheepish and pulled out one of those awful nickel-plated things that could serve as a dagger, a knuckle-duster, or a single-shot pistol depending. He said, "I picked this up after our fight the other day."

Longarm said he was glad. The others admitted to a mixed bag of things they shouldn't have been packing.

O'Hanlon said, "I'm starting to feel a lot better about your box factory, Longarm, but I still don't understand how you spotted it as the headquarters. How did they have it listed in the city directory, under 'C' for 'Counterfeiting' or 'Q' for 'Queer'?"

Longarm said, "I'll explain later. There's an outside chance I guessed wrong. So let's not bust anybody up unless they act surly when we bust in on 'em."

He led his little army on. At the next corner, a uniformed copper was eyeing them dubiously as he swung his stick, so Coletti flashed his badge and said, "We need you. This is a federal raid."

The copper looked relieved as he fell in beside them, saying, "Is that all? I thought you buckos was trouble on me beat."

So now there were eight of them, and the copper was not only a trained lawman but packing a serious-looking S&W .38. Longarm began to think he might make his date at the tearoom after all.

The others failed to share his optimism. Coletti sounded sort of sulky as he said he couldn't figure how Longarm knew so much after such a short time in town. O'Hanlon said, "Yeah, we heard you were good. But we're good too, and they killed our man Sloter, and all we've been able to do about it is run around in circles ever since."

Longarm said, "Cheer up, gents. Sloter had cut their trail when they ambushed him. I ain't all that bright. I've had certain advantages over you local agents. They were laying for me when I got to town. So, from the beginning, I've been working closer to them than you have."

"They must have been expecting those agents Washington sent, too," Coletti said. "Somebody working for Uncle Sam must have betrayed them and set you up!"

Longarm shrugged. "I doubt if it was anybody high enough on the totem pole to matter. My boss, Marshal Vail, has an alibi, even if I thought he needed one. Folks were getting shot out here before we heard about the case in Denver, and anyway, Billy Vail hardly ever sends word in advance to the crooks he sends me after."

"You think it's somebody from the mint?" Coletti asked.

"Nobody high up. Aside from risking a good job and a pension, anybody important over there wouldn't have needed to use old Dandolo as a dupe. They could have borrowed a set of dies for the gang, run off a shithouse full of fake double eagles, and smuggled them back with nobody being the wiser."

"Jesus," Coletti gasped, "what a crooked imagination you have! How do you know somebody didn't do just that?"

"Couple of reasons. Like I said, they wouldn't have had to flimflam Dandolo if they had access to real dies. They wouldn't have had to act so ornery, either. Don't you gents know we never catch big crooks working for the government? Hell, given a position like old Coogan at the mint, I wouldn't need any secret factory. I'd just stay after work with a few sheets of red brass and run my own coins off private. Who'd question a supervisor testing the government machinery or whatever? Let's not worry about how they found out about me and the others. We'll sweat the details out of them after we take 'em. That's the place, on the uphill corner across the street."

They paused to study the nondescript brick building across the way as a cable car came up the slope. Longarm said, "Let that car pass before we make our next move. You can see that the front door's just a door. There's a side entrance wide enough for a dray to load. It's wood, with no windows. The side wall's solid brick, so they can't see out on the far side. We'd best split up and cover from both angles. I want Jimbo here with me. A copper's uniform may save some confusion as I walk in the front door."

O'Hanlon nodded and said, "I'll cover the side entrance. Coletti, you stay with Longarm so that Treasury makes an arrest, no matter what. Half you Lambs come with me as soon as the cable car's passed. How do we exchange signals, Longarm?"

Longarm said, "Well, if the front door ain't locked, we won't need many signals, as we'll walk in with the drop on them. If you hear me busting down the front door, wait a spell to see if anybody tears out into your loving arms. If they make a fight of it, just bust in behind 'em as best you can and we'll have 'em in our crossfire. Be careful, though. We'd sure look dumb shooting one another."

O'Hanlon nodded grimly and said, "We'll have them front and flank, and we all know each other's faces. Shall I go first?"

Longarm nodded, and as the cable car passed, the Treasury man and four of Buckley's Lambs crossed over and ducked around the corner of the building.

Longarm led Coletti, the copper, Jimbo, and No-Nose Brannigan across the hard way, facing the front door and a front window that he sincerely hoped was painted over on the inside, as it appeared to be. As they drew their weapons and eased up to the front entrance, he cocked his ear and heard what sounded like a blacksmith shoeing a horse. He glanced up and saw a cloud of steam hanging over the roof, salmon pink in the purple sky of sundown. He took a deep breath and tried the door. "Locked," he muttered.

No-Nose Brannigan said, "Hell, it's only wood," and hit it with his shoulder, splintering the latch as he dove through the entrance and wisely crabbed to one side while Longarm followed, fast, and shouted, "Everybody freeze!" His .44 muzzle was raised to cover any and all that might need covering.

It seemed to work. The dozen-odd men in the cavernous interior stopped what they were doing to stare openmouthed at him. The steam-powered triphammer taking up most of the center of the shop kept stamping the same brass blank over and over, ignored by its frozen operator. Most of the others had just been lounging about on boxes and barrels, doubtless waiting to fill their pockets from the nail keg of brass double eagles near the improvised mint.

Coletti and Jimbo moved inside to back Longarm's play as the gang slowly rose or sort of shifted their weight, undecided.

Longarm said, "You boys are all under arrest. Which beats being dead if anybody tries anything foolish. My youthful assistants will pass the hat, and I want you to keep your hands polite and give over your guns one at a time." Just then, an imperious voice shouted in Longarm's ear, demanding, "What is the meaning of this? I've proclaimed a Peace of God!"

It was the Emperor Norton. The old lunatic had spotted them from his passing cable car and dropped off to pester them. Longarm turned his head for a fraction of a second, and swore as he realized his mistake. The split-second distraction had given some son of a bitch time to throw something at the overhead lamp and knock it out, plunging the interior into semidarkness as all hell busted loose!

"Somebody get him out of here!" Longarm snapped as he moved to one side to avoid being outlined in the doorway. No-Nose Brannigan grabbed the Emperor and tore outside with the old man slung over one shoulder like a kicking and screaming sack of grain. They just made it as a gun went off and sent a slug through the open doorway after them. Longarm fired at the flash, and Coletti's gun went off as somebody else fired from a corner at them. At that moment, the side entrance exploded in daylight and shattered planks as O'Hanlon and his bunch hit it together.

Then things started getting confusing. The open side entrance shed more light than illumination in a room filled with blue gunsmoke. Longarm got his back in a corner and held his fire as O'Hanlon stood outlined in the other doorway and proceeded to throw lead every damned way. Longarm saw a wounded man stagger back and fall screaming into the pounding jaws of the coin machine. As it chewed him up, Longarm shouted, "Take *aim*, you crazy bastard! Some of us are on your side!"

A staring face materialized from the smoke in front of Longarm, and since he didn't recognize it, Longarm blew it away. Another tried to get past Jimbo, who'd apparently forgotten the derringer in his pocket.

When the gang member slashed at him with a bowie, Gentleman Jim said, "Surely you jest," and busted his jaw with a scientific right cross. The copper had another on the cement floor and was methodically pounding his head to a pulp with his billy as the guns fell silent. Everyone's ears rang while they waited for the smoke to clear.

No-Nose Brannigan came back in, looked around blankly, and asked Longarm, "Jasus, is it over? I didn't get to hit anybody!"

Longarm could see better now. He counted seven others on their feet, and the floor was covered with silent or moaning forms.

"Are all your people still with us, O'Hanlon?" he called out.

The Treasury man faded into visibility out of the smoke and said, "Yeah."

Then he stiffened, raised his gun, and fired at a counterfeiter struggling to rise, saying, "That's for Sloter, you son of a bitch!"

"Take it easy," Longarm said. "We got us some loose ends to wrap up, and dead men tell no tales."

Coletti moved over to his partner and took his arm, asking, "Are you all right, O'Hanlon?"

O'Hanlon shuddered, recovered, and said, "Yeah. I had my Irish up, but he's right. Let's see if any of the bastards are still breathing."

Longarm took out a match and struck a light. He found the

fallen lamp and relit it, standing it on a barrel. It smoked with its glass gone, but they could see better now.

Coletti looked around and marveled, "Welcome to the last act of *Hamlet*! I make it twelve, no, thirteen. There's one breathing in the corner, but I don't think he's going to make it."

Longarm glanced at the gutshot, shabby man Colleti meant, and turned to the copper. He said, "You'd best call for an ambulance and report this to your superiors. Use that telephone over there on the far wall."

The copper nodded and stepped over a corpse lying in a big pool of blood at the base of the still-pounding machine. Longarm stepped over to turn the valve and shut it off. Jimbo returned the derringer and said, "That one by the door's still alive, for I only hit him."

Longarm said, "I noticed. But he fell on his own blade. The only one I really wanted to talk to is that jasper with the cinnamon beard." Longarm gestured with a thumb toward a corpse lying face up in a corner. "According to the description from Sacramento, he'd be Clem Taylor. He's supposed to be raising barley up in Weed. But as you see, he'll be lying under it now."

As the copper cranked the wall telephone awake, O'Hanlon asked, "How did you know there was a telephone here, Longarm?"

Longarm said, "That's how I knew where this place was. I looked it up in the city directory. Hardly anybody in Frisco has a telephone yet, but a line of poles runs smack down California Street. It was simple deducting."

"Simple, hell," Coletti snorted. "What made you think the gang had a telephone?"

"They had to. I was ambushed twice on the same damned slope, by somebody who had to know I was coming. Nobody from the gang ever laid for me anywhere else, and I've been all over town. All the other fixes I got into were sort of natural in a rough neighborhood. No offense, No-Nose. I knew nobody was trailing me after I saw that nobody took advantage of me being alone in other parts. Every time they tried to set me up, it was the same way, and that was their big mistake. Both times, I'd left the Doyle house and been intercepted along this stretch of the slope. There's a telephone in the Doyle house and a telephone here. Do I have to draw you a picture? Clem Taylor, there, was supposed to be having a family feud with his sister-in-law. But I know better now. That was meant to throw me off the fact that they were working together. He had a record, and they knew I might have snooped into her family affairs after she started an affair with me to keep an eye on me. It didn't make much sense that a man with a barley farm could be broke, what with beer and other prices rising. Jimbo, would you look around for a carpetbag with some shirts like mine in it? It's likely here someplace, if they didn't just throw it away. They stole it to check and make sure I was really me when their temptress got me in her clutches with a maiden-in-distress act."

He moved the jaws of the stamping machine apart and started to unscrew the top die. It was sort of messy with blood, and he bent to wipe the die on the pants of the man it had chewed to death, before holding it up to the light.

O'Hanlon said, "So they did get Dandolo to steal a set of dies for them."

"No. Officially, since he's got a fine young daughter and was faithful in the end, let's not study too hard on just who made this. It was done electric. He put a real double eagle in the salts and plated it over and over with nickel. I read up on it. You can buy the chemicals for nickel plating easy."

Coletti asked, "Why on earth would you want to plate gold with nickel?"

"Nickel is hard. Almost as hard as alloy steel. He plated the gold coin with layer after layer until it was about an eighth of an inch thick. Then he brazed it to this backing of bar steel and simply dug the softer gold out with something like a dentist's pick. Working under pressure he managed to scratch the nickel some, and that accounts for the scratch in the eight in '1878.' The other mar was already in the coin. Coogan said it was a recalled issue, but they didn't notice, as they used the newest coin they had on hand. As word got about that the coins could be spotted without an acid test, they tried to get their dupe to make them another set. He wouldn't, and they killed him on his birthday. The rest ain't hard to figure out, and I have a date at eight, so let's get this show on the road!"

As he headed for the door, the two Treasury men and Jimbo started to follow. He said, "Jimbo, stay here and help the coppers Boss Buckley will want to know what's going on here, too. You other gents want to come with me as I arrest a couple of widow women?"

O'Hanlon said, "Of course. But I, for one, am still confused as hell. The widow Doyle is a society matron. Why would she be working with these riffraff?"

"For money, like everyone else, of course. Aside from having a private telephone, Gwynn Doyle has been busting a gut trying to get up the wherewithal to buy in on a rising market her fancy friends tipped her off to. She couldn't use the money her husband left her when he died a few years back, because there wasn't all that much. He may have been rich when she wed him, but he died in the depression, likely owing more than he had on deposit in the Bank of California when it crashed."

"Where'd you get that, from her creditors?"

"Didn't have to be all that nosy. The other night she served smoked oysters when oysters are in season and yonder Bay is brimming over with 'em, fresh. She managed to hang on to her fancy house and telephone, but don't it strike you as odd that a Nob Hill mansion should be run without servants? She's been living alone, pinch-penny and proud, whilst waiting for a chance to get rich again. The rest follows as the night the day. Her little widow pal, Calvinia Taylor, was in financial difficulties too. I don't know if she had the idea of making her own money with her crooked brother-in-law, or if he approached her. Judging from his record, he wasn't too bright. But she'll doubtless tell us all about it when we make it to the top of this infernal rise. Nobody back there had a chance to telephone the gals."

Coletti was puffing as he tried to match Longarm's mile-eating stride up Nob Hill. But he was thinking as he trudged, and he gasped, "Hold on. There's a missing lady in your picture, Longarm. Dandolo was lured to temptation and destruction by a dark Italian girl."

Longarm shook his head and said, "Calvinia is dark, but she ain't Eye-talian. She just said she was, in order to make friends with a lonesome fool. I may as well confess, she's good at tempting fools. But, as you boys will be arresting her official, she won't be able to use my rowdy nature in court. That's another reason I invited you both to come along as I wrapped things up."

"Hold on," Coletti objected. "I spoke to people on Telegraph

Hill. Any petite brunette fits the description they gave me of Dandolo's lover. But damn it, they were overheard speaking Italian to each other!"

"So what? You speak English, don't you? You don't have to be Eye-talian to talk the lingo. They told me she had a funny way of talking it. Old Dandolo had a different Eye-talian accent than them Sicilian fisher folk, and they doubtless confused her American accent with some sort of la-di-da Venetian notion. I don't know where she learned the Eye-talian she knew, but she'd been brushing up on it. There was a set of lingo books in Gwynn's study. They were all bound in the same morocco, but the Eye-talian one was missing. We'll likely find it in Calvinia's house when we search it."

"I like it," O'Hanlon puffed. "We're nearly to the top. What's the play? One of us covering the back as you go in the front?"

Longarm said, "Yeah. I doubt they'll be expecting trouble, but they might have a man or two about the house, so it pays to be careful." He grinned sheepishly and added, "They seem to have a lot of men about the house, despite their tale of being lonesome and frustrated. It ain't nice to talk this way about ladies, but this is official business and they ain't ladies. They both screw like rabbits, even though they claimed not to know much about the subject. I allow I was pretty foolish about that until I had time to study on it. Be careful with 'em. They tried to send me on a wild-goose chase north to Weed, and when that didn't work, they tried to have me gunned, even after we'd all acted friendly as hell."

They stopped to catch their breaths as the Doyle house came into view. "Coletti, you take the back this time," O'Hanlon wheezed. "We'll give you a minute's head start."

Coletti nodded and moved on as O'Hanlon shook his head and said, "Jesus, I'm out of shape. Oh-oh, look who's joining us."

Longarm looked back the way they'd come and saw the Emperor Norton coming up the slope, sword drawn. He moved pretty spryly for such an old gent. Aside from being loco, he was used to tear-assing all over the hills of Frisco.

His Majesty joined them and said, "I'm very annoyed with you this evening, Sir Longarm. Why did that young lout carry me across the street and deposit me in an ash barrel?"

"No-Nose meant no disrespect, Your Majesty. I don't either.

But we ain't got time to play with you right now."

"What is transpiring in my realm, Sir Longarm? As your Emperor, I have a right to know! The police are hauling bodies out of that place down the hill, and when I asked them about it, they told me to leave them alone. Has everyone gone mad this evening?"

Longarm glanced anxiously at the lace curtains in the house across the way. The Emperor could get noisy when he was having one of his imperial fits. Longarm said, "We're federal officers about to make an arrest, Your Majesty. You just stay right here and we'll tell you all about it later, all right?"

He nodded at O'Hanlon and said, tersely, "Let's go."

The Emperor Norton tagged along as they crossed the street. Longarm tried to ignore him, since nothing else worked. He told O'Hanlon, "Keep him back and cover me. I'll see if we can get in polite."

He moved up the steps, opening his coat to clear his .44 in case either of the deadly gals wasn't in a loving mood.

He rang the bell, waited, and tried the door. It was locked. Gwynn was either out or not receiving visitors this evening. He looked at his watch, saw that Helen was fixing to be mad as hell, and drew his revolver to bust the glass and reach in to open the latch. He moved in fast and got out of the back lighting. Then he called, "Hey, gals, you here? It's me, Custis."

Nothing. O'Hanlon joined him with the Emperor in tow. Longarm told the old man to put his fool sword away as he led them into the sitting room. It looked empty at first. Then he spotted a human hand lying on the rug like a wilted camellia.

He moved over to the sofa, peered over the back, and muttered, "Oh, shit."

Calvinia Taylor stared up at him, stark naked and spread-eagled on her back. But she didn't look as tempting as he remembered. Her throat had been cut like Kilbride's, and she'd bled some as her life gargled out of her lying mouth.

They heard a noise out in the hall, and Coletti called out to them. O'Hanlon called back, "Move back and keep the back door covered. There's been a murder here, and the killer may still be in the house!"

Then O'Hanlon led the way out as he said, "Let's check upstairs."

Longarm holstered his sixgun and followed him up the stair-well. They got to Gwynn Doyle's bedroom to find the door ajar. O'Hanlon shoved it open and said, "Oh, now what do we do?"

Gwynn lay on the bed with her stockings on and hair pinned up, as though she'd just come home or was about to go out when somebody drove a knife into her, just above the blond pubic hair, and ripped upward, opening her like a watermelon. Judging from the expression on her dead face, it had upset hell out of her. Longarm stared thoughtfully at the blood-splattered sheets and said, "Happened a couple of hours ago. The knife-work looks like the job they did on Kilbride. Looks like somebody was covering some tracks."

O'Hanlon nodded grimly and said, "It could still be a package. The killer must have been one of the gang, and we busted in just as they were gathered to start distributing again!"

Longarm said, "Mighty cool, if one or more of 'em knew about these gals and Kilbride. But whoever it was did it some time back and left us a cold trail."

He consulted his watch and said, "Oh, shit, I'm in trouble. What's the fastest way to get to Market Street from here?"

"Catch the Powell Street line along the ridge, and it'll drop you almost there," O'Hanlon said. "But who the hell are you after? Did you make an appointment to meet the killer, too?"

Longarm said, "No. She's a brown-haired gal with a turned-up nose. But you may be right about her killing me if I stand her up. Or, worse yet, she'll have gone home mad as a wet hen, and I'll likely never forgive myself, either!"

Chapter 11

It was after eight and getting dark when Longarm found the second-story tearoom Helen had told him about. When he got upstairs, it turned out not to be exactly a tearoom. It was laid out in private little cubicles. The Chinese waitress must have had a good description of him, because she led him to the hidey-hole Helen was waiting in, looking pouty as she sat behind a table on an overstuffed banquette of red velvet. She'd let down her long brown hair, and her straw hat, with its artificial cherries, was on the table next to the tea tray. A bottle of bourbon she'd ordered with the tea occupied a place of honor next to the big teapot. Longarm would have ordered Maryland rye, but it was nice to see she thought ahead.

As the waitress left, discreetly shutting the door behind her, Helen said, "I was about to leave. You're almost half an hour late, you mean thing."

He hung his hat and gunbelt up as he said, "I know, and I'm pure sorry. But not as sorry as I would have been, had you not been a good sport about my working late."

He slid in beside her and put an arm around her waist. She sniffed and said, "Just you stop that. What kind of girl do you think I am?"

"Don't know yet. But I'll slow down if you want. I just ran a winning streak, and it'll take me a spell to remember I'm only human."

She started to pour tea as she dimpled and said, "I must say, you're looking very pleased with yourself this evening. What have you been up to?"

He said, "Just put them counterfeiters I talked to you about out of business. Can I spike my tea with some of this bourbon? I feel like this is one night I should be allowed to howl; between sheer luck and sudden brainstorms, I cracked an impossible case so sudden it hasn't quite hit me yet that it's about over."

Naturally she wanted to hear all about it—or said she did. You could never tell with gals. So he leaned back luxuriously with a cup of spiked tea in one hand and Helen in the other as he indulged himself in some modest bragging. By the time he'd gotten to how hard he'd worked to get here on time, she was leaning against him, sharing his spiked tea while she told him how smart he was.

He was getting set to kiss her when Helen sat up with a frown and said, "But, Custis, if the mastermind is still at large, shouldn't you be out looking for him?"

Longarm hauled her in and said, "Later."

Then he kissed her good, with a palm cupped to her soft cheek, and Helen kissed back even better, not resisting when he explored her pearly teeth and little pink tongue. He ran his free hand down to cup one of her breasts, noting that it was being held up a mite by her whalebone corset. He'd suspected that that waistline was impossible.

As they came up for air, she didn't remove his hand, but she said, "Seriously, I'm sort of frightened. Aren't you worried about a killer out there in the night? What if he's looking for you again?"

"Hush, little darling," he said. "He ain't looking for me. If he hasn't left town on the double, he's likely hugging himself for being so slick right about now. When I left those Treasury men on the hill, they were wrapping the case up. They think the killer was one of the gents gunned in the shootout at the coining factory, and there's always a chance they could be right."

"But you said that awful woman's brother-in-law was too stupid to be the mastermind, and the women who might have been smart enough have both been murdered."

"Yeah, with your floorwalker, Kilbride, just as dead, there's not a soul left who could point a finger at anybody. All the likely suspects are dead, save for one lucky queer-passer who might live and says he don't know much."

He started to unbutton her bodice. She said, "Stop that. I still don't understand what led you to poor Mr. Kilbride in the first place? What were you expecting to find at Gump's?"

"Nothing as pretty as you, honey. But cutting Kilbride's trail wasn't as unlikely as it might sound. I was checking all the shops that dealt in such wares, and an ex-jeweler who could order the right red brass would have been working in one or another. Ain't it lucky for us he never took a job somewhere else?"

"Leave my buttons alone! We're in a public place!"

"It don't look that public to me. That waitress would doubtless come back if I fired off my sixgun, but nothing less is likely to attract her attention. Of course, if this place ain't as discreet as you say, we could go to my digs at the Palace."

"Heavens, what kind of girl would go to a hotel with a strange man?"

"A friendly one? I ain't all that strange, honey. I'm just your usual gent."

She sniffed and said, "You mean you're just like all men when you have a girl alone with you. Stop tweaking me like that. You're making my, ah, bust feel funny."

"I noticed. It don't feel funny. It feels good. But we have too many infernal duds on for me to feel you right."

He took off his coat and vest to drop them on the floor before taking her in his arms again to give serious attention to her buttons. She struggled enough to seem proper without really discouraging him as she protested, "I might have known you'd be a Don Juan. Honestly, can't a girl in this town meet a gentleman who doesn't get fresh on the first date?"

He kissed her and said, "Sure they can. They'll be replacing poor old Kilbride with another floorwalker, and if you play your cards right, it'll take him six months to get up the nerve to ask you out."

She laughed and said, "You're just terrible. Besides, I never date men where I work. A girl can get a reputation that way."

"Right, you're safer with a passing ship who can't talk about you later."

She said that wasn't the reason she'd agreed to have tea with him, so he kissed her some more to save a lot of tedious protestations, and while she acted like he was skinning her alive, she didn't have it in her to really stop him. As he got her unbuttoned, she moved her little rump to let him slide the dress up. He shucked her like an ear of corn.

As he got her outer wrappings out of the way, she cried mock tears and said, "Oh, what happened to my dress? You mustn't look at me in my unmentionables!"

Her underwear looked fine to Longarm, but since she said they were not to be mentioned, he didn't comment on the black lace teddy she wore under the tight little corset she was trying to cut herself in two at the waist with.

He rolled her back on the red velvet and kissed her some more as he explored the possibilities. Her silk stockings were on straps attached to her corset, but she hadn't been dumb enough to wear pantaloons, and as he got one hand between her soft naked thighs, he discovered, sure enough, that the lace teddy fastened at the crotch with a snap. She tried to cross her legs as he unsnapped it and ran a teasing finger through her thatch.

She rolled her lips away from his and gasped, "You're touching me, sir! Whatever gave you the idea I'd let you take such liberties?"

That was too dumb to answer, so he got his pants open and rolled aboard while she spread her thighs and demanded that he stop this very instant. As he slid into her, she clamped down hard and sobbed, "Oh, this is terrible! I never meant to let you act so forward!"

But after they'd done it forward a spell, she didn't argue when he rolled her over and started to unlace her corset as he entered her from the rear. She started beating on the red velvet with both fists as she thrust her sweet little naked rump up to meet his thrusts, and as the corset fell open, she sighed and said, "Oh God, that feels marvelous!"

"Yeah, that corset must have been uncomfortable."

"The corset? Oh yes, that feels good too. There certainly is more to you than meets the eye, you brute. Now that I've been ruined, why don't we get out of all these things and do it right?"

He said that was jake with him. So, even though he hadn't climaxed yet, he withdrew and started peeling. She sat up in a state of disarray, blanched at the sight of his naked body, and said, "Oh, I don't know. This is all so wicked."

But she didn't stop him as he got her out of the teddy and rolled down her socks below the knee while he kissed and petted and reassured her.

She giggled and said, "I feel so naked." Which struck him as only reasonable.

She still had on her stockings and high-button shoes. He tried to lay her back on the banquette, but she suddenly leaped up and ran over to hang on the velvet drapes near the door with her bare back to him, saying, "I want to go home. I never should have come here!"

He rose to join her, and turned her to face him.

She plastered her breasts and belly against him, saying, "Don't look at me. I'm so embarrassed I could die!"

He kissed her and bent his spread legs as he ran a hand down to part her nether lips.

As he did so she gasped, "Oh no, we can't do it standing up, can we?" Then, as he thrust into her, she started breathing faster and thrusting back, stiff-legged, and said, "Oh, I see we can!"

He'd dealt with skittish mounts before, so he cupped her buttocks in his hands as he moved in and out.

She sobbed, "What are you doing to me?" Which was another dumb question a man could only answer by doing it faster. She went limp as she came, so he moved her over to the table and spread her on the linen between the tea tray and the bottle, to finish with one of her knees hooked over each of his elbows as he gripped the edge of the table and let himself go.

Her eyes opened wide as she felt him explode in her, and she said, "My God, I'm being served like roast turkey! How did I get in this ridiculous position and for God's sake don't stop! It's happeniiiiing!"

He corkscrewed around inside her to keep her in a friendly mood as she subsided in a series of spasms. Then, since she'd stopped talking silly, he put her back on the velvet to do it right. She locked her high-button shoes on his bounding buttocks and sighed, "Oh, this is the best way. What would you say if I told you I'd never done this before, Custis?"

"Don't," he said. "It ain't polite to laugh at naked ladies.

I may as well confess I ain't a virgin, neither. So let's say no more about it."

She giggled and said, "You're an animal. But in a way I'm glad. I knew you'd be leaving San Francisco soon, and I wasn't sure how I was going to manage to be seduced in time. I've seldom even been *kissed,* on the first date."

"I figured as much," he said. "That's why I didn't see fit to shilly-shally. You shouldn't act so snooty if you really like this, Helen. Most men would take you for a virgin with your duds on. You're sort of intimidating."

"Oh? How did you know I wasn't a good girl?"

"Honey, you *are* a good girl. The best kind there is. But I learned long ago that women do their own seducing. So, when I saw the layout here where you asked me to meet you, I sort of knew you'd planned ahead, too. Are you sure we wouldn't be more comfortable at my hotel? I got me a bed that's a better workbench, and we could take a bath together."

She rolled her head from side to side on the red velvet, partly in negation and partly in passion as she sighed and said, "No, I could never go to a hotel with a man. Only cheap girls do that sort of thing."

He sat beside her, playing with her as he got his second wind. But when he asked if she was ready for another round, she shook her head and said, "I'd love to, but I really have to leave, darling. It's getting late, and my landlady has a suspicious nature. If I'm not home by ten, she looks at me like a dragon, and if I was ever out past midnight, she'd probably ask me to leave."

He didn't argue. He fumbled around on the floor for his things, and found a smoke and some matches. She told him not to leave with her, so he leaned back, naked, to stare wistfully through the smoke at her as she dressed. It was funny how a gal could look as exciting putting on her duds as taking them off. As she snapped the crotch of her teddy closed, he knew he'd seen what she was hiding for the last time. But to be polite, he asked about the coming weekend.

She said, "I'm afraid there's no discreet way to meet over the weekend, darling. Will you be in town Monday?"

He knew he wouldn't be unless they killed and buried him in Frisco. So he told her he figured to catch the Monday-morning train out. She sat on his lap while he laced her corset up the back, and naturally his tool rose to the occasion against the black lace between her thighs. She was leaving just as he'd gotten started. But maybe it was better this way. Helen could talk kind of bitchy when she was cooled off, and he wanted to remember her fondly.

She dressed and pinned up her hair with a skill that bespoke practice he was too polite to ask about. She bent to kiss him and said, "I'm really sorry I had to love and run like this. But you know how landladies can be."

He had to concede a point to Helen's landlady, as the gal flounced out looking like butter wouldn't melt in her mouth. "Jesus," he growled. "She accused *me* of making fast moves. What if I'd moved slower?"

He chuckled and poured himself a cup of bourbon, neat. He supposed he ought to be thinking of paying the tab and getting on home to the hotel, but the evening was young and nobody was waiting for him there. He'd just cool off with some redeye and another smoke or two before he got dressed and went to pay that waitress gal.

Longarm leaned back naked on the red velvet, sipping and smoking like an old contented cat. Some of the mice were still running about, but the local Treasury boys could tidy up after him if he didn't have it all in the box by the time he was ready to leave for Denver. He wouldn't have to tarry to give evidence in court, since most of the gang had been caught red-handed coining money, and the gals he might have had a chore convicting were both dead.

He'd recovered from his all-too-brief orgy and was wondering where his pants were when the door opened and the Chinese waitress came in. She looked startled to see a naked gent sitting there, and gasped, "Oh, I thought I heard you leave, sir. Everyone else has gone home and I came to tidy up."

He saw that most of his important parts were covered by the table between them, and since she didn't seem too embarrassed, he sat up and said, "The lady left early. How much do I owe you?"

"Oh, the lady already paid in advance. She's a regular customer here."

"Do tell? Somehow that don't surprise me as much as it might have. I'll just finish this smoke and get dressed, then. I'm sorry if I, uh, startled you."

The Chinese gal lowered her eyes and blushed as she said, "One grows accustomed to such surprises, working here. You don't have to hurry, sir. I told you everyone else has left and...I'm not going anywhere."

"Yeah, it does look lonesome out. Can I pour you a drink of tea, or maybe bourbon?"

"I'll take bourbon," she sighed. "You've no idea how sick I am of smelling tea. But are you sure you don't mind drinking with a woman of my race?"

He poured her a drink as he asked, "What's the matter with your race? It's human, ain't it? I know some folks here on the Coast tend to be a mite snooty. But I ain't from Frisco and you're a pretty lady, so come and sit by my side and let's say no more about it."

The Chinese girl unfastened her silk sheath dress, took it off, and slid in beside him stark naked, saying, "I am Ming Joy."

"Well, so you are, honey. I hope this ain't a business deal, for, pretty as you are, I ain't in position to pay."

She laughed and picked up the cup in both hands as she said, "You may not be in any position to do anything. You're the nicest-looking man that little tramp from Gump's has ever met here, and I couldn't help noticing other things about you."

"Yeah," he said, "folks do sort of notice one another in their birthday suits."

He ran his eyes over her tawny flesh. The best parts of her were down below the level of the table, too. But she was put together like a China doll, with little teacup breasts stuck to a sleek, smooth torso made out of pale caramel or something else that made a man want to chew on it. She took a sip, made a wry face, and said, "Oh, that's terribly strong. It makes my mouth feel numb, and I don't want to feel numb. I get so lonely working here. No Chinese boys ever come to his part of town, and none of the white men meeting their girlfriends here ever look at me."

He put his arm around her naked waist and said, "They must be blind, then."

He started to draw her closer, but Ming Joy resisted and said, "Confess, you never thought of me as a woman when you saw me outside, did you?"

"Hell, I never took you for no *elephant*. Of course I noticed you were pretty. But let's be sensible. I came here to meet another gal."

She leaned against him as she answered archly, "You certainly did. What has that snooty thing got that I haven't got?"

"Damned if I know. Let's find out."

Chapter 12

A couple of things were waiting for Longarm at his hotel. One of the Lambs had dropped off his stolen carpetbag with a card signed "Gentleman Jim." Young Jimbo seemed to have started liking his new ring name. Nothing important had been in the bag when they stole it, so nothing important was missing. He grimaced as he remembered how dumb he'd been about that. They'd wanted him to save her valise, and later she'd left it for him to go through and read the papers, hoping he'd think she never talked to her criminal in-laws.

There was a note in his box. It was from Angela Dandolo, saying she'd gotten the job and inviting him to sup with her the next evening. That called for another grimace. He didn't mind dining with a pretty gal, but he'd have to tell her she could forget about leaving a lamp in her window for her dear old dad. There was no proof connecting her father to the gang, and he wanted to keep it that way. But how did you tell a young gal that her father was likely providing a meal for the sharks and crabs?

He went up to his room. The matchstick he'd left in the jamb was on the rug again. He sighed and drew his .44 before going in the other door, the way he had done the time when

Gwynn had been waiting in his room.

He was pretty sure Gwynn had shoved that wood splinter in his derringer as they were romping about with his attention on her various patches of blond. One or the other of the two women had busted off the firing pin of his Colt with a pair of pliers the other night, too. They were both dead now, of course. But the gent who'd sliced them up might not be.

He moved into the room low and fast. But there was nobody there.

He holstered the .44 and asked his reflection in the mirror, "All right, old son, what could they have been looking for this time? Those gals knew I didn't leave any papers or valuables up here."

The answer was obvious. His mystery caller had been after *him!* The killer couldn't have known he'd meet such friendly gals in the tea joint down the street. He'd come expecting to find another victim, let himself in with a pick or passkey, and left disappointed.

He stared soberly down at the made-up bed as he considered what might have happened, had he been lying there snoring instead of getting in more joyful trouble with those unexpected dividends.

He pulled out the catalogues he'd gotten from Fong and Kilbride, and proceeded to tear out pages, ball them up, and drop them on the rug. He didn't have to trace the jewelry supplies anymore, and a stranger crunching on paper in the dark made a hell of a racket.

As he moved about, he spotted his shadow moving across the drawn window shade. That reminded him of an old Dodge City trick. He took off his coat and draped it over a chair, then he placed his Stetson on top and moved the rig until the shadow of what could pass for him sitting down was thrown against the shade.

He entered the bath and started a tub. While he was waiting, he went to the bed and moved pillows and covers into as much of a semblance of a sleeping body as he could. Then he went back in the bath, got undressed, and climbed in to wash off Helen and Ming Joy.

He was out of the tub and drying off when a bullet spanged through the glass in the next room. He blew out the light in the bath and came out naked, gun in hand. There was a bullet hole in the shade, smack in the middle of his mock shadow,

174

and the man who'd fired from the street was likely wondering why it was still sitting there so calmly. Longarm blew out the light in that room too, went back in the bath, and cracked the frosted window open for a look-see.

Nothing. His windows faced a side street, and nobody was doing anything interesting down there or on the rooftop across the way. He chuckled and said, "Hit and run, did you? Well, you got a right to be nervous, you son of a bitch. But I'm tired of chasing around in the fog at night. So if you don't come back, I'll deal with you by daylight. That is, if you're dumb enough to still be in town, come morning."

He made sure the doors were locked, then braced chairs under the knobs to keep them that way. He went in the spare room, dragged the mattress and covers off the bed, and carried them to the bath. He used two towels to rub the tub dry, put the bedding in the cast-iron tub, and threw the barrel bolt on the door, locking himself in good before he got in the tub and bedded down for the night.

He was tuckered from all the hill-climbing and screwing, and dropped off right away to sleep the sleep of the just.

Some teamsters having a fight in the street woke him up the next morning, and he saw by his Ingersoll that he'd lain sluga-bed till almost nine. He explored the other rooms, saw that he hadn't been invaded, and put things back in shape for the chambermaid. He shaved and got dressed, and went downstairs and ate breakfast. Then he borrowed the hotel telephone and found, as he'd hoped, that the Federal Building stayed open until noon on Saturdays, like the one in Denver. He told the gent at the other end who he was, and said he wanted to meet O'Hanlon and Coletti in front of the city morgue in an hour. Then he went to the telegraph office and sent some wires. He told Billy Vail what he'd done, and said he'd try and catch a train back to Denver on Monday morning. He wired Sacramento that Clem Taylor was dead and that they could likely have his land back, since there were no surviving heirs to lay claim to it.

Having time to kill, he went back to the Palace and caught hell for the broken glass in his room. He said to put it on his bill, and sat in the lobby to read the morning papers for a spell. Frisco sure was excited about two Nob Hill society matrons being counterfeiters as well as murder victims. Longarm didn't see his own name mentioned among the lawmen given credit for solving the case. A couple of police captains he'd never met in his life had horned in next to O'Hanlon and Coletti as the heroic raiders of the coining plant. The Emperor Norton had done more than they had up there, but they didn't mention him, either.

Longarm was used to others stealing credit. He didn't mind. Billy Vail knew how good he was, and it saved a lot of jawing with fool reporters. The paper speculated that O'Hanlon and Coletti might be due for promotions.

He shrugged, left the paper for others to read, and moseyed out and up the Slot toward the Civic Center, window-shopping along the way. They sold all sorts of odd notions in Frisco, and it made him feel sort of rich as he saw all the things he could afford but didn't want.

He finally got to the morgue, but didn't go in. He knew a whole mess of folks inside, but he didn't want to look at them again. He leaned against a lamp post and lit a cheroot to wait for the Treasury men.

His watch said it was still early, and the dry taste in his mouth said it was late, when he spied a familiar figure coming up the walk. He cursed under his breath. The Emperor Norton was afoot and leading a mongrel on a rope leash. His admiral's uniform looked shabby, but the nice old lunatic swaggered along with one hand on the pommel of his costume sword as he surveyed his realm.

He saw Longarm and stopped, saying, "Good morrow, Sir Longarm. Have you seen my pony? I have a pony, you know, but I seem to have misplaced it."

Longarm shook his head. "Sorry, Your Majesty. I ain't seen your steed, but that's a fine-looking animal you got there. Why don't you take him for a walk in the park?"

"We're on our way to inspect the police. I've commended the department for the way they rounded up those people counterfeiting my money. Why aren't you wearing the medal I decorated you with, Sir Longarm?"

"I'm working undercover, Your Majesty. So, if it's all the same to you, we shouldn't be seen talking together like this."

Old Norton nodded and said, "Ah, mum's the word, eh? I didn't know you were one of my secret agents, but carry on, Sir Longarm."

Longarm heaved a sigh of relief as the old man and his mutt

moved on. The timing had been close, for Treasury Agent Coletti was coming across the avenue, alone.

Coletti joined Longarm and asked, "What's up? Why did you ask us to meet you here at the morgue?"

Longarm said, "Thought it might be convenient if folks got excited. Where's O'Hanlon?"

"He sent me alone. Said he had to follow up on something important, and that I could find out what you wanted."

Longarm took a drag on his cheroot and said, "O'Hanlon was what I wanted. I was aiming to arrest him, but he must have figured that out. Let's see now. He wouldn't be dumb enough to make for the railroad depot or a ferry."

Coletti stared at Longarm, thunderstruck, and demanded, "What the hell are you talking about? Why would anybody want to arrest Agent O'Hanlon?"

"Oh," Longarm replied nonchalantly, "he's the missing link betwixt Treasury and the gang we cleaned up. He cleaned some of it up himself, knowing I was closing in. Night before last he killed Kilbride, and then, yesterday afternoon, when I called your office, he must have figured I was getting warm and, knowing I knew both gals and that they knew him, he went up there before we met, and finished 'em off."

"Come on, Longarm, O'Hanlon was with us on the raid!"

"Sure he was. Shot a wounded man who might have known who he was, too. Jesus Christ, Coletti, you ain't dumb. Do I have to draw you a picture?"

Coletti frowned and said, "O'Hanlon's my partner!"

"No he ain't. No offense, but he's the senior member of the team, and you've just been tagging along as he chased made-up false leads. Didn't it ever strike you as odd that the two of you were tear-assing all over the city as the officers assigned to the case, and that nobody ever took a shot at you?"

"Hell, we obviously weren't getting warm."

"That gang never waited for folks to get warm, Coletti. They gunned your agent, Sloter, a couple of days after he was on the job. They knocked off a couple of agents Washington sent the day they got here. They were laying for me when my riverboat docked, and they started shooting at me before I'd even checked in at the mint."

"Hmm," Coletti said, "that does seem odd, now that you mention how often my back's been exposed to the streets of Frisco. But it's still mighty circumstantial, Longarm!"

"Oh, it gets better. Those gals and the gang were deadly, but they didn't work for Uncle Sam, and neither did Kilbride. The only way they could have known who Agent Sloter was, and that the rest of us were coming, was if some double-dealer working for Treasury told them. O'Hanlon had to know, because you two approached me on the street, not the other way around. They needed someone working around the mint to introduce old Dandolo to that made up Eye-talian gal, too. Calvinia never could have sashayed in where Dandolo worked and asked him if he wanted to go out with her. O'Hanlon was in a position to know which of the many mint workers made a likely sucker, too. Calvinia was good, but she could have blown the whole deal by approaching a man who was a mite more loyal to his employers."

Coletti looked sort of sick as he nodded and said, "Jesus, it's starting to make sense. I wondered why he acted so odd when they told us you wanted to meet us here. He hadn't said anything earlier about another case. It's unsettling as hell to think I've been investigating the case with the mastermind who was behind it at my side every step of the way!"

"Well, he made most of his serious moves when the two of you weren't together. The way I put it together, one of the gals met him social. They both screwed social more than they let on. In the course of conversation, it came out that the widow women were living in genteel poverty, despite their addresses, and that other social friends who still had money had put them on to some mighty heady stock market moves. They knew the jeweler, Kilbride, and knew he was a crook. They had Calvinia's dumb and dangerous brother-in-law and his rough pals for heavy work. O'Hanlon knew he'd be kept abreast of any investigating Uncle Sam did, to make it unlikely they'd get caught. So all they needed was a good diemaker, and we know about Dandolo's part in the plot. By the way, I want him left out when we report this case official."

"I've met his daughter," Coletti agreed. "Us Italians stick together, and it's not like Dandolo hasn't been punished for his errors. But while we're standing here, O'Hanlon is getting away! We'd better get to my office and put out the word on the son of bitch!"

Longarm consulted his watch, saw that he had plenty of time, and said, "Right. Let's hail us a cab."

They moved toward the curb, and Longarm was looking

down the street as a voice behind him snapped, "Oh, no you don't, my good fellow!"

Longarm and Coletti turned to see Agent O'Hanlon staggering toward them like a drunk, eyes glazed and gun in hand, with the Emperor Norton right behind him! Coletti crabbed one way and Longarm went the other as they both reached for their guns. But the old man was in their line of fire, and O'Hanlon had his muzzle trained on the ground now, so they held their fire as the double-dealer took another step, pitched headfirst off the walk, and died a dusty, rusty death with the Emperor's sword standing upright between his shoulder blades!

"He was pointing that gun at you, Sir Longarm," the Emperor cackled.

Longarm said, "So I see, and I feel mighty dumb about it. I thank you, Your Majesty. But what happened to your little doggy?"

Norton looked about, confused, and ran off yelling, forgetting all about his sword. Longarm thought it was just as well. The tinny weapon was dull-bladed, but the tip had been sharper than anyone thought. He pulled it out and told Coletti, "I'll stay here while you go in and get the morgue attendents. I see no need to pester them about the old man, do you?"

"Hell, why confuse an already confusing case? But will you confess to something, off the record?"

"Sure, what is it, pard?"

"Asking to meet you here, right in front of the morgue. You were hoping it wouldn't have to go to trial, weren't you?"

Longarm shrugged and said, "Yeah. I knew I'd never be able to prove it with all the possible witnesses dead. But, lucky for us, O'Hanlon was afraid to risk that and, lucky for me, his luck run out."

Chapter 13

Longarm waited until after supper to tell Angela Dandolo that her father was dead. He hadn't wanted to spoil her celebration of the new job and the check the mint had sent her once they knew for sure he wouldn't be coming back to work.

They'd gone into her parlor and were sitting on a sofa in the twilight when he got around to it. He left out the dirty parts and just said there was reason to believe that her father had been waylaid on the way home on his birthday. He said, "You're father might have been a hero, Miss Angela. We think those counterfeiters were after him to help them coin queer, and when he wouldn't do it, they had to make sure he never told on them."

She might not have heard that last part, for, when she heard that her father was dead, she started to blubber up and fell faint against him. So he held her gently and patted her shoulder, keeping it brotherly.

It wasn't hard. Longarm was aware of her perfume and the clean smell of her golden hair as he held her sobbing young body against his in the bittersweet evening light. There was no getting around the fact that she was a lovely woman, but she felt as much like a hurt, lost child, and he knew romance was

180

the last thing she had on her mind right now. She was crying all down the front of his shirt, so he took out a kerchief and wiped her closed eyelids gently, as he searched for some comforting words.

But what good were words when you'd just twisted a dagger in a pretty gal's heart, like he'd had to? He started to say that the men and women who'd hurt her father had paid for it with their own lives, but he knew she wasn't spiteful-natured enough for it to matter much.

"Miss Angela," he said, "at times like this there ain't much a friend can say. But if there's a thing I can *do,* don't hesitate to ask."

She sniffed and said, "Will you let me give you back the money you lent me? I don't need it now, and it made me feel so poor to need it!"

He said she could pay him back when he left, and she settled deeper in his arms with a little sigh. He held her quietly, knowing that was what she needed. She was likely making up for the fact her real father would never cuddle her again. It made him feel awkward.

The whole damned house smelled like a woman lived there, and it got more discomforting as it got darker. A lamplighter lit the street light outside, throwing a soft square of yellow light against the far wall as they sat there quietly in each other's arms. She'd stopped crying and just cuddled there, as though she meant to stay forever.

He said, "It's getting late, Miss Angela. I'd best be getting on down the road."

"Don't go," she said. "I can't face the dark alone, yet."

"You want me to light the lamp, Miss Angela?"

"No, that's not what I mean, Custis. I just don't want to be alone. It's not that late. Just stay with me and . . . keep me company."

He didn't answer as he held her some more. A few minutes later she gave a little giggle and said, "Oh, my stars! I just realized I'm sitting in the dark in a man's arms. I've never done that before, and I think I should be shocked."

"Are you shocked, Miss Angela?"

"No. I've never felt so safe and protected since I was little and my mother held me like this. I'd be afraid if you were another man, but I know I don't have to feel afraid with you here."

Longarm grimaced in the dark. First the fool gal thought he was her father, and now she wanted him to be her mother! He said, "Hell, get your hat and let's see if we can wear you out enough to sleep."

"What are you talking about? Where are we going, Custis?"

"Out to paint the town. It's safe for a gal to ride in my company now, and I've been too busy ducking to really enjoy old Frisco."

"You want to take me out on the town, with my poor father just dead?"

"Enough's enough, Miss Angela. Your father ain't just dead. He's been dead a spell, and you've done enough worrying. What you need now is distracting, and I need some too, to keep me acting decent. Get your hat and let's get out of these infernal shadows!"

So she did, and they went out to spend what was left of his expense allowance. They rode the cable car and had chop suey in Chinatown and saw a bawdy show at the Parthenon by accident. He'd thought it was just a big fancy restaurant where you could sit at a table and drink steam beer and eat oysters while you watched a variety show on the stage up there. How was a stranger in town to know that a gal in pink mesh tights covered with big black rubber spiders was about to come out and do a sassy dance like that? The spider dancer looked scandalous enough when she first appeared amid catcalls and whistles, but then, as the band played on, she commenced to peel her spiders off and throw them out to the audience. One landed on their table and Angela laughed. But Longarm blushed, for the spider had been placed strategically and the pink mesh was thin enough to see that the spider gal shaved regular, everywhere.

A couple of baggy-pants comics came out and told dirty jokes he hoped Angela was too young to get. Then another girl came out in a floradora skirt and either danced or tried to kick the hanging ceiling light out, and no matter how young anyone was, they could damn well see that the high-kicking strutter wasn't wearing any underpants. So Longarm suggested they go to Fisherman's Wharf. But Angela said she was having fun, so they stayed. It might not be a good night for Angela to look out across the dark waters of the Bay, but for a proper girl, she sure was seeing more of Frisco nightlife than Longarm thought he ought to show her. He didn't buy her anything stronger than steam beer, but by midnight she was staring sort of owlishly and talking silly. So he took her for some coffee and then he took her home. As they got out of the cab, she stumbled and would have fallen, had he not had her by the arm. She was drunk as a lord, or make that a lady, since he'd behaved himself in the cab, even when she wound up with her head in his lap.

He unlocked the door and Angela said, "Whee, I just found out I could fly!" But he grabbed her before she could land on her snoot. He picked her up and her head fell back limply as she muttered, "Oh, I feel so funny."

And then she was out like a light.

He carried her inside and kicked open doors until he found her bedroom. He laid her down and put her hat on the dresser. Then he took her shoes off and put them on the rug, where she'd find them in the morning. He stared morosely down at her in the dim light. She looked desirable in the lamplight through the lace curtains, and she was sure as hell available.

He muttered, "Might have known beer would hit her hard in the state she was in," as he gently unbuttoned her dress and slid it off her.

She wasn't wearing a corset, just a white silk shimmy shirt, and matching knickers bloused about her upper thighs. Her dark stockings were held by laced garters above the knee, exposing enough creamy thigh to make a man's mouth water. He knew if he took anything else off her she was going to wake up unsettled. So he made sure all the windows were locked, and fixed the door so it would latch behind him as he left.

Rincon Hill wasn't far from his hotel, and he needed cooling off, so he walked it, puffing furious on a cheroot and feeling disgusted with himself. He'd known when he took her out that Angela was innocent, and the platonic evening had been intended to do just what it had. He'd pleasured her enough to get a night's sleep without pleasuring her the way no man had a right to treat an orphaned virgin. It had been a fine, innocent evening, save for some of the entertainment. But it had been some time since he'd spent so much time and money on a gal and said good night without even a handshake. That didn't bother him as much as the fact that he had half an erection. His fool tool just didn't have a lick of sense around a pretty gal, innocent or not.

He got to the hotel, and as it was too late to do a thing about the natural cravings Angela's perfume and big brown eyes had

183

left him with, he went up to his room. As he approached the door, he suddenly stopped dead in his tracks and muttered, "Aw, shit, this is getting tedious as hell!"

His match trick had worked again. There was somebody in his room, for he heard movement on the other side of the panels.

He repeated his ploy of entering through the other room of the suite, gun drawn, and popped in to throw down on the two gals in his bed. He didn't pull the trigger, for they were both naked under the covers, if he was any judge of such matters, and they were both smiling at him as friendly as hell.

He holstered his gun as he nodded and said, "Howdy, Helen. I see you changed your mind about hotels. Who's your sidekick?"

The saucy-eyed Helen Manson introduced the redhead giggling beside her as her roommate, a Miss Georgie Barnes, and added, "Georgie is going to Cheyenne on Monday morning, and when I told her you'd probably be aboard the same train, she said she was dying to meet you. So here we are. I paid the bellhop to let us in to wait for you. It wouldn't have been discreet for two young ladies to lurk about a hotel lobby late at night."

Georgie said, "I don't usually act so forward on a first meeting, but Helen told me you were a man of the world, and I wanted to get over the first awkwardness before we boarded the train."

He said that sounded reasonable and trimmed the lamp. But as he started to undress, he was laughing like hell, and Helen asked him what was so funny.

"I ain't laughing at you," he assured her. "I'm laughing at me. I come home feeling a mite broody at my folks for raising me to do right by ladies. But I see virtue really can be its own reward, and I find this situation complimenting as hell!"

He climbed in between them, and as he nestled between their nude curves, somebody took him in hand. He naturally thought it was Helen, and since she seemed to want to be the leader, he grabbed for her first.

She sniffed and said, "That's not my perfume you're wearing. I might have known you were with another woman all this time!"

But Georgie gave his erection a playful yank and said, "If he's been with another woman, he's even wilder than you

184

promised, Helen. Dear Lord, he most certainly is raised to do right by ladies!"

So they all started going crazy for a spell, and it was a real chore trying to decide which of them was best as they played follow-the-leader. Snooty, bawdy Helen was the wildest, while the redhead seemed to have the more interesting insides. He knew he'd never have been able to manage them as a team if he'd yielded to temptation back at Angela's house, and he knew Angela would be grateful, too. But he couldn't help wondering, as he rolled off Helen to take care of Georgie again, what Angela would have been like.

Watch for

LONGARM AND THE MOONSHINERS

forty-second novel in the bold Longarm series
from Jove

coming in March!

LONGARM